Souls Undone

Souls Undone

Rick Marshall

Copyright © 2020 Rick Marshall All rights reserved

The characters and events portrayed in this book are fictitious. Any similarity to real persons, living or dead, is coincidental and not intended by the author.

No part of this book may be reproduced, or stored in a retrieval system, or transmitted in any form or by any means, electronic, mechanical, photocopying, recording, or otherwise, without express written permission of the publisher.

ISBN-13: 9798646704734

Cover design: Andrew Marshall
Library of Congress Control Number: 2018675309
Printed in the United States of America

Dedication

To all of my family members and friends who endured the multiple mistakes I had made as they read the early drafts of my manuscript.

Acknowledgements

Cover Design: Andrew Marshall

Chapter 1

Magee pushed softly on the brake as the road seemed to disappear and become a short driveway. "I guess this is the proverbial end of the road," he said aloud. Ahead was a steel-slatted gate at least ten feet tall. He eased the car toward it and stopped about five feet away. He glanced at the sides and saw a heavy metal fence running out into the forest. He noted the razor wire on top.

The caller hadn't mentioned there would be a gate. He wasn't sure what to do next until his eyes caught movement near the top of its left side. There was a camera rotating. It stopped with the lens pointed directly at the driver's side of the car. He waited, assuming the gate would open. Instead, his cell phone rang.

"Mr. Magee?" a man's voice asked.

"Yes," he replied cautiously. He didn't recognize the voice, but caller ID let him know the number. It was the same one that had reached him a few days before. That conversation had brought him to this gate. Then, the caller had been female.

"Can I assume it is your car now facing the entrance to our clinic?" the man responded. Magee thought it was an odd question. He could offer a safe 'yes' as an answer but decided not to.

"If your clinic is behind a rather forbidding looking steel gate, I'd say that's a good bet." He waited for a reaction. After a short pause, the man responded.

"Would you mind rolling down your window, sticking your arm out, and waving at the camera?" the man asked calmly. The tone was professional, suggesting Magee's comment was taken simply as an affirmative response. He responded in kind by doing specifically what he was asked to do. A few seconds later, the gate began to slide to his right. The man's voice continued, "The drive to our main entrance is roughly another mile. I'll be waiting at that gate to take you to your meeting."

Magee watched the gate complete its slide and then moved the car forward along the road. He glanced at his odometer so he could check the distance when he arrived at the next gate. Details had always been important to him. In his mirror, he saw the gate close. He drove along the road as it curved through the hills. The forest was thick on both sides. Each curve prevented him from seeing more than a hundred yards ahead. Magee didn't see any other cameras as he drove but couldn't shake a feeling that he was being watched.

The drive from the city had been pleasant, much of it easy in the flat valleys that run between the coastal ranges north of San Francisco. The hills beyond that were rolling until he left 101, taking 162 toward Covelo, and driving toward the mountains to the east. Now the road snaked through a forest without revealing any view of what lay behind it.

It wasn't long before another fence ran beside the road on his left. Finally, around one of the curves, he came to a second gate. It was smaller and simpler than the previous one. He saw it sliding open as he pulled toward it. A man standing behind it stepped through when the opening was wide enough. He pointed for Magee to pull off to one side. The gate behind the man closed again. He was still standing just outside it when Magee got out of his car and faced him. The man looked serious and appeared to be studying Magee intently. Magee was doing the same to him.

Magee stood six feet and one inch. The other man was taller by at least five inches, which would give him an advantage in most confrontations. Magee kept himself in shape and could tell that the other man did too. He had a fit build and look, but Magee recognized his stance as more military than athletic. His hands were folded together neatly in front of him. He wore a tailored black business suit, with a bright red necktie. The shoes were neatly polished.

He was an impressive figure. The only flaw Magee could see was a thin scar that ran up the man's left cheek. For a moment, Magee wondered if he should have worn a suit and tie instead of an old corduroy blazer, open-collar shirt, and blue jeans. The thought passed quickly.

The study ended and the man walked toward Magee, extending his hand in anticipation of a handshake. His facial expression had changed from serious to friendly.

"I'm Paul Rosner, Mr. Magee. It's a pleasure to meet you," he said, grinning as he pushed his hand forward to grasp Magee's. His mannerisms seemed open and friendly, completely different from what Magee expected based on the professional demeanor he displayed earlier.

"Ditto," was Magee's response. As their handshake ended, Paul gestured with his left hand toward the gate and the two men began walking. Paul withdrew a device from his pocket and with a click, the gate began to slide open again. They walked through into a courtyard that was surrounded by buildings. Paul pointed toward the front door of a small one just beyond the gate.

"My office is in here," Paul said as he pulled the door open and held it for Magee to enter. "There are a few formalities to talk about before you meet with Doctor Klein. But mostly, I want to give you more information about me so that you are completely comfortable with accepting the job that was discussed by the Doctor." He motioned to the entrance of a small office.

It was plain. There were no windows. Nothing hung on the walls. In the center was a large desk, the surface of which was bare. Magee entered and took a chair in front of it. Behind it, a credenza held several binders between two heavy-looking bookends shaped into large black falcons. Paul went to the other side of the desk and sat down in the only other chair. "First order of business," he said, "do you prefer to be called Mr. Magee, or just Magee, or perhaps a first name?"

"Magee keeps it simple. No need to use the Mister," Magee replied. "Of course, I've been called a lot of things in my life based on what I do." His comment brought a smile to Paul.

"I can imagine that," he said back. "You can call me Paul if you don't mind. Somehow it makes me feel a little more relaxed when people are comfortable using my first name." He smiled as he opened a top drawer of the desk and removed a thick manila folder. When he flipped the cover, Magee could see the top item was a form that had a photograph of Magee stapled to it. Paul picked it up and held it in front of him as if seeing it for the first time. Then he set it aside, picked up the remaining pages, and thumbed the edges as if counting them. He returned them to the folder and closed it, leaving only the page with the photograph on the desk. He looked up at Magee again.

"First, I hope you weren't too put off by my security process on the way in. It's necessary for the work we do here." Paul paused for a moment as if waiting for a sign of confirmation. When Magee simply shook his head slightly, he went on. "We have the outer ring of fencing, and the gate, to protect the patients here from the outside world. We have the inner gate to prevent the patients from leaving before they should." Again, Paul paused and looked at Magee, then continued.

"The simplest way to start would be to tell you all about the clinic and what it provides. But instead, I'm going to talk a little about myself first because I want to create a level of trust between us. Maybe a small level at first, but hopefully it will grow larger over time. I think that trust might be incredibly helpful to us, sometime down the road."

Paul opened a lower drawer in the desk, and removed two glasses, and then followed those with a fifth of Jack Daniel's Tennessee Whiskey. "The file I just reviewed tells me this is your drink of choice. Yes?" He glanced up at Magee as he poured an inch into each glass. Magee noticed the bottle was already half-empty before he poured.

"I take it you didn't buy that just for me," he said as Paul slid the glass over to him. Paul laughed as he reached for his glass.

"No," he said, "but it didn't hurt to find out that you and I both share a taste for some of the finer things in life. Sorry I don't have ice in the office to go with it." He raised his glass and waited for Magee to do the same. Magee followed the lead, touching Paul's glass with his. Paul took a swallow after the touch. Magee lowered the glass without drinking. Paul frowned slightly. "I hope you won't make me drink alone, Magee. It isn't polite to your host."

Magee looked down into the glass and swirled the whiskey around a bit before he said, "I have no intention of letting this go to waste. But first, I thought I might find out a bit more about why I'm here. You said this is part of some 'formalities,' but I can't believe that every guest that arrives gets this treatment." He paused briefly, then continued, "and when did you become my 'host', not my prospective client?" The frown on Paul's face turned back to a smile.

"Fair enough," he said. "But I'd like to hold you to that statement about not letting it go to waste before I'm done." With that, Paul downed the rest of his drink. He pushed the paper with the photo and the manila folder to the side. He leaned forward with his elbows on the desk, clasped his hands together and began to speak. "Let's get a little more into the details. You're right. Not every 'guest' who comes here meets first with me in private. But I believe when Dr. Klein spoke with you about doing an investigation, she told you we are concerned about what might become a threat to our clinic. There was an incident, so I have tightened our security up a bit. Part of the *formalities*, as you put it, is for me to get to know you a little before you meet with Dr. Klein.

"The file I pulled out told me about the whiskey, but it also told me you are very good at what you do. You didn't seem surprised at all about the size of it, or even that we had someone collect information about you before we called for your help. Another person may have wondered why we would go to that trouble, but you accepted it as if it was a normal part of hiring you. That tells me something about you. Either you knew about us doing it before you got here, or maybe you're a good actor, or maybe everyone has you investigated before they give you a job.

"If it's the acting thing, that's probably good. I can imagine it would make it a lot easier to dig out information from people. As far as everyone completing a full investigation before hiring you, I can't believe that would be necessary," Paul said, making a skeptical face and shaking his head back and forth as he said it. Then he stopped and looked again as if he was sizing Magee up. "Or," he continued, "it could be that you knew about it before you arrived." Magee sat quietly and waited for him to continue.

"I hope it isn't that one," Paul said, "cause, I could draw more than one conclusion about why *you're* here." Paul didn't wait for a reaction from Magee but just went on speaking. "So, let me tell you a little more about me. I suspect there are things you have already guessed. You probably know I'm ex-military. You might even know that I did three tours in Afghanistan a few years back, that it was a hellhole there, and most people who serve come home broken in some way. At least, the ones who were normal when they went do.

"I was no exception. I was in a bad way when I got back. I didn't have much luck getting work, and when I did, I couldn't keep it. I was in and out of a few jails for breaking some faces, usually because I said the wrong things at the wrong time in all the wrong places and to the wrong people, even if they deserved it." Magee pointed to the scar that ran up the side of Paul's face.

"Looks like someone might have tried to break yours," he said. Paul laughed.

"Yeah," he said, "but that came when I was on tour. I fought pretty darn well before I joined up, but the military made me even better at it. Took out a lot of bad guys over there. But when I got back, I wasn't the 'me' that went over. I started spending a lot more time fighting, and sometimes too much time looking closely at the wrong end of a gun. Finally, after one of the fighting jams, I was ordered into a hospital for psychiatric evaluation." He stopped again for a moment. He looked down at his empty glass as if he was considering a refill and then moved on. "It was there I met Doctor Klein.

"She was assigned for my evaluation. I had been kept in a locked room at the hospital for a few hours before she came in to do the initial interview. When I first saw her, I thought, 'Hell, she isn't much older than me.' And I also thought she was beautiful. Tiny, with long, black hair falling onto her shoulders. Great figure. Dark eyes that seemed to drill right through me. And a smile. I hadn't been seeing too many of those for a while. But she was smiling. Here she was, coming in to see a guy who had been ordered by a court to see a shrink. She wasn't scared or nervous. She was just smiling as if she was really happy to be doing what she was doing. She was patient. She talked with me for five hours that day, even after I spent the first hour trying to intimidate her with my attitude. She just kept asking questions with a smile and listening. Mostly listening. Even when I wasn't talking, it seemed like she was listening to me breathe." Paul stopped again and this time seemed to gaze far away, remembering that time. Then he turned back to Magee.

"Sometime during those hours, I began to open up. Little by little she pulled things out until it seemed like I was just talking about everything I had bottled up inside." Paul pulled out the bottle again and poured a little more into his glass before looking up to Magee. "I think you probably get the picture. There was more treatment after that, but for the most part, I knew that day how I was going to get back to being normal again. She taught me how. That was ten years ago, and I've been with her ever since, helping her in any way I can." He stopped talking and looked expectantly at Magee as if he was waiting for him to respond.

"Yes," Magee said. "I think I have the picture." He raised his glass and finally took a sip. Paul smiled like the act was a small victory.

"Okay, then," Paul replied. "There's just one more thing to make clear," he added. "For ten years, I've been dedicated to that purpose, helping her, so to speak. And part of that job is to protect her with my life. If anything, or anyone, was a threat to her or to what she was trying to accomplish, I would eliminate it. She has my complete, unwavering, and unending loyalty." He stopped and cleared his throat. "I tell you this so you understand, and then anticipate my actions if the situation depends on it. You won't have to guess. It goes back to my military training. Best to know how your fellows are going to act before you get into a situation that demands quick decisions. According to your file, you didn't serve, so I take it you haven't been exposed to that." He smiled again. But this time it was the kind of smile that was just a punctuation point. Something you add to put finality on a point made and understood by both parties. "Now, let's get you to your meeting with Dr. Klein, and I'll tell you a little about the facility on the way."

Paul pushed his chair back from the desk and stood up. Magee did the same. He left the whiskey glass and contents on the desk and followed Paul out. They walked into the courtyard where Paul waved his arm at several connected buildings, describing their purpose as they walked. The buildings were architecturally plain, but each was well maintained and landscaped on the outside. There were two larger buildings each with three floors. Paul explained that one of them contained the residences of the staff at the clinic. The other housed patients and some treatment facilities. Paul pointed to a smaller connected building. He told Magee it was where medical procedures would be done, if necessary.

"Is that the one where you do lobotomies, if necessary, of course?" Magee asked. Paul ignored the question.

On the opposite side of the courtyard was a similar-looking building, connected to a Victorian-styled house. The building held administrative services. Paul raised his arm and directed Magee toward the house.

"This is Dr. Klein's residence, and also her primary office," Paul said. "You'll be meeting with her here." He walked up the staircase leading to a wide and covered front porch. Directly in front was a double door leading into the home, with two simple wooden screens. Behind those, the interior doors were open, allowing the breeze to blow in. Paul opened one of the screens and motioned for Magee to enter.

"This is where I'll leave you for the time being," he said. "Go through the parlor. You'll find her office on your left. She should be waiting, although probably she'll be working through a stack of folders on her desk. It's her daily ritual to review each patient's file for any notes that were made the day before. After the review, she may amend the patient's treatment plan and let the staff know. I've got other matters to attend to, but I'll catch up with you when you are done." Paul extended his hand again. Magee shook it and walked through the open door. As it shut, he turned to watch Paul bound down the stairs and hurry back toward his office.

Magee stood a moment longer and looked out the screen at the buildings they had passed. He could see the hills beyond their roofs. There was little noise except for chirping birds and the rustle of trees. At one end of the courtyard was the gate that he and Paul came through after he parked. At the other end was a building that looked like a large garage. Magee guessed it was a maintenance building. Beyond it, he could see cars parked in an open area. Everything seemed to be well thought out and well managed. There was a sense of peace he didn't feel in the city. Still, he had been called here to investigate something. So far, he had no idea what it was.

Chapter 2

Magee walked through the parlor into a hallway. He saw the open door on his left. He peeked around the corner as he tapped gently on the frame.

No one sat behind the desk he saw straight ahead. On it was a large pile of manila folders, as Rosner had predicted. One of the folders was lying open, a pen laying across a half-written sheet of paper on the top of its contents. The empty chair behind the desk was pushed back and turned slightly toward one side as if someone had been sitting there and left it recently. He looked that way and saw a closed door. After a second, he heard water running and determined it must be a bathroom. He stood in the center of the doorway and waited. The water stopped and the door opened. A woman stepped out.

She was not what Magee had expected to see. Paul had described her as he had seen her when they first met. But that was some years back. Her figure was still complementary, but her hair was cut short and swept back from her face. It was completely gray. Her face was pretty, with fine features, but years of smiling were showing in the crow's feet around her still dark eyes. Those eyes widened as they made contact with his. She smiled and Magee understood why Paul had been so impressed with it.

"You must be Mr. Magee!" She said enthusiastically. He was still standing in the doorway. She walked toward him with her hand extended, never losing eye contact. "I'm so happy to meet you," she continued as she grabbed his hand with both hands and shook it. Magee recognized the voice as belonging to the woman he had talked to on the phone. "Please come in and sit down." She motioned to a sofa to his right. He hadn't noticed it before and took the opportunity to look around the rest of the room as he walked toward it.

The decor was pleasant. The wallpaper had large, bright flowers. An oak cabinet behind her desk held several significant looking hardcover books. Most of the walls were covered with prints of Monet gatherings. On one wall was a rectangular frame made of mahogany which seemed out of place from the oak in the rest of the room. It had two hinged doors that could swing open. Magee concluded it must be newer than the other things, and guessed it held a presentation screen behind it.

Dr. Klein lifted a teacup from her desk and walked toward an overstuffed chair near the sofa. It seemed to engulf her small frame as she sank into it, making her look even tinier. Magee chose the end of the sofa closest to her chair. He had never needed to see a psychiatrist in the past, but he imagined it would be a similar sort of setting if he had. He settled in on the sofa and waited for her to begin.

"Did Mr. Rosner take any time with you or did he bring you directly here?" she asked.

"He and I had a bit of conversation in his office, and then he explained the use of some of the buildings as we walked over here," Magee answered. He paused briefly and added, "He asked me to call him Paul. Do you normally call him Mr. Rosner?"

"Well, yes," she replied, "We're both professionals. He calls me Dr. Klein. It's important for the tone we set here at the clinic." She paused for a moment to smooth her skirt. She was wearing a tailored women's business suit, grey in color, and very much in keeping with her comment. "Did he give you the details of the incident we want you to investigate?" She gave him a quizzical look, tilting her head slightly.

"Not really," Magee replied. "He did mention that something happened, but he spent most of the time talking about himself. How he came to know you. His role at the clinic. His background in the Military and when he came home." He stopped, realizing that Rosner never did explain what Magee was supposed to investigate. He felt a flush of embarrassment that he hadn't pressed the issue. "I think mostly he wanted me to understand how seriously he took his job of protecting you." Klein smiled again. Not her broad, beaming smile she had given him earlier, but a subtler one, as if acknowledging the truth of Magee's assumption.

"Well, he does do that!" she exclaimed. Magee wasn't sure whether she was referring to being protective or serious. Then she added, "He's been helping me a long time. Long before I started the clinic. He was one of my earliest patients, not long after I finished my internship." She looked down for a moment, then continued. "Frankly, I appreciate his dedication. I couldn't have accomplished what I have without it."

"Do you mean the Clinic?" Magee asked.

"Mostly, but even before that. The clinic, though, was his idea. It came not long after his treatment was completed. We remained close once he was able to get back to normal, and one day he just came to me with the idea. Did he tell you anything about what its purpose is?" she asked. Magee shook his head.

"Not really, Doctor Klein. He mostly just described the function of the buildings we passed on the way here," Magee replied. Klein put her teacup down on the table next to her and emphatically placed her hands palm down on her legs. She leaned forward.

"Well, then," she said, "I suppose I should describe it to you!" She seemed excited as if she'd been asked to do something very important. "Assuming Mr. Rosner didn't tell you anything about me either, I'll start by describing my background. I graduated from medical school as a physician and then began my training in the broad field of Psychiatry. I wanted to do something in mental health, and specifically the mental health of individuals, but I didn't have a specific interest beyond that. By the time I opened the clinic, though, I had decided to focus in one area.

"We have a unique practice here. Our core purpose, of course, is to practice Psychiatric medicine. But we limit that to one type of problem, and one problem only, Dissociative Identity Disorder." She stopped as if waiting for a reaction from Magee. When he gave none, she continued. "Do you know what that is?" she asked. She stopped to get Magee's response. He only shook his head. She continued. "Split personalities, at least two," she paused for effect before continuing.

"I was exposed to it soon after graduation from medical school. I had developed my interest in mental health and decided to specialize further. It started with my residency at a VA hospital. I'm sure you can understand why mental health is necessary at those locations." The look on her face turned from excitement to sympathy. Her eyes softened for a moment, then began to grow wide again. "It was there I first worked with a patient who had been diagnosed with it.

"I'll admit that I was skeptical. Oh, I thought for sure it was a real disorder, but it wasn't honestly two or more personalities. It was just one that figured out a way to look like two and then convince others." She shook her head slightly from side to side as if she was now disagreeing with that idea. "I worked with that patient for over a year, fully expecting to have some breakthrough that would support my belief. And then after that, of course, some sort of treatment plan to get him back to health." She paused and shook her head again. "But no matter what I did. No matter how deep I dug. No matter how many consultations I had with other physicians; I walked away becoming a believer." She took a breath and went on. "Oh, I had a couple of other patients during that time that had the same diagnosis. But I was able to solve their disorders. In some ways, they kept me thinking I was on the right track. All I needed to do was to keep working with the other one. But in time I just came to believe that he truly had two separate people inside him.

"Imagine that, Mr. Magee. Most of us go through life as only one person. Everything we know is categorized that way. We're all individuals. All we ever have inside our brains are ourselves, only one individual each. But some people seem to have more than that inside. Some have many. In most cases, only one individual is present at a time. Sometimes, though, these individuals can communicate with each other. At least in a way that one or more might remember something another did or said." Klein had edged up a little on her seat again, leaning forward closer to Magee. He could feel her belief fueling her passion for the subject. She drew another breath before continuing.

"Over time I worked with others who reinforced the belief. The disorder is still very rare. Less than three percent of patients who need mental health treatment have it, in varying degrees. And the majority are males!" she exclaimed as if she was surprised by the statement. She suddenly turned her head toward her desk as if looking for something. Then she stood up. She turned her head back to Magee.

"Forgive me, Mr. Magee. I should have offered you something. Would you like some coffee, or perhaps tea?"

Magee nodded. "Coffee would be nice. Regular, just black, no sugar." Klein turned toward her desk.

"Computer," she said, "Ask Anne to bring us one cup of caffeinated black coffee and my regular tea." A small round disk on her desk lit up around its edge.

"Of course, Dr. Klein," a male voice answered politely. "Would you like any snacks with that? Cookies, crackers, or anything else?" Klein looked over at Magee, who held up a hand and shook his head no.

"No, thank you. That will be it," Klein answered back. Then she turned back toward Magee and sat down in the chair again. "I hope you'll indulge the keyword I have for my little helper. I was a big fan of the Star Trek series when I was younger. Do you remember that, Mr. Magee?" He nodded. "The captain was always addressing the computer as 'computer'," she continued. "Of course, back then, a computer would have taken up the whole studio. So, they could only pretend it was something in a remote location." She smiled slightly again. "It will take a few minutes for the coffee to arrive."

She sat down and leaned back into her chair again as if beginning to calm down from her excitement. She smoothed her skirt again and seemed to be collecting her thoughts.

"I guess I tend to get a little carried away when I talk about this. I don't usually have the opportunity to sit 'one on one' and describe it." Her tone was quiet. "Getting back to the clinic, it's unique. Every patient we have is here because they've been diagnosed as having DID. It is the only clinic of its type in the country. I mean it is the only place that treats multiple patients with precisely the same disorder. Others also include normal disorders." Magee laughed. Dr. Klein suddenly realized what she said and laughed too before starting again.

"Basically, I found what I believe to be a very effective treatment for the disorder. My success is not one-hundred percent, but most of my patients will be cured completely, and the others are capable of controlling the disorder with the help of continued treatment and a small combination of medications."

"Do you mean you can reduce the number of patients you are treating by eliminating some of their personalities?" he asked with a smile. He regretted it almost immediately when he saw her frown.

"Pardon me?" she asked.

"I'm sorry, Dr. Klein," he quickly apologized. "Sometimes I joke around a bit too much. It can result in impolite behavior. Forgive me." He added another smile. Klein's eyebrows furrowed a bit and then relaxed.

"Well, as I said, I can't cure one-hundred percent," she began again. "But our rate of success is much better than what you will see in other facilities treating similar patients. Also, we limit the number of patients we treat at any given time. The maximum we have ever had at one time was I think twenty. I'd have to look in our records to say exactly. I tend not to remember the total because it isn't important. I have too many other things to remember.

"Besides," she continued, "I suppose I *would* have to count each personality to get to the total." Now it was her turn to smile at the joke. Magee responded in kind. He took it as a signal she was not offended. "In any event," she continued, "we are also a very private place. We must be. We owe it to our patients. The people who come here are usually suffering in more ways than one. Part of the treatment must help them feel they are in a safe place, away from unwanted scrutiny and judgment. When you arrived, you would have experienced some of the steps we've taken to prevent unwelcome guests." Magee signaled yes with a nod.

"And we've been generally successful for many years, at least until the incident that caused me to call you for help," she added. Magee thought back to last week when he received her call.

Their call was brief, only about twenty minutes in total. At that time, she told Magee that she needed an investigation into an incident and had received his number from a friend. She said the matter needed the utmost discretion and the referral spoke highly of his ability to provide that. He had assured her then that her friend had been right. She went on to describe that she managed a medical facility out of the city and asked if he could start as soon as possible.

Normally, there would be far more conversation before Magee agreed to meet with a client. He would talk about his fee, fitting the job into his schedule, and other business matters to avoid misunderstandings and an unnecessary trip on his part. This time, though, something in her voice appealed to him. At first, he couldn't put his finger on it. But as she explained that her friend had told him all about his qualifications and the cost, he realized that the thing in her voice was fear. Magee didn't need to think about agreeing to an initial meeting. He was always sympathetic to a woman who was afraid, even if it meant a three-hour drive just to find out the details.

Her voice didn't have the same tone now that he arrived, but his curiosity was piqued. Since he had put other possibilities on hold, he had nothing to lose by continuing to listen.

"Would you like to give me a description of what happened?" he said to her.

"Yes," she replied, "that would be appropriate." She cleared her throat before going on. "We had received a call from someone who claimed to be a relative of one of our male patients, but his name was not on our list of people associated with him. Let me explain. When a patient 'checks in,' or 'is checked in' by a guardian, we create a list of names of all the people who may know he or she is here. Generally, it's a very small list. We keep it that way to maintain their privacy. The caller wasn't on our list, but he knew the patient's registration number, the date he had been admitted, and the history of why he was here." She paused for a moment and changed her tone as if making a side comment.

"They all have a history, you know. Something that occurred that finally made them seek help; or made someone who loves them seek help." Then she resumed her normal voice. "The caller let us know he would be coming for a visit and expecting to talk with the patient privately. Still, we didn't just agree and schedule the appointment. The person handling the call told him we would not be able to allow entry unless he came with someone who was already identified on the list. Then that individual could have us add other names if there would be other visits. The caller pleasantly replied that he understood and would be bringing the brother of the patient. I mean, he said the brother's name directly. The brother is on the list. So, our staff member made the appointment for the day before I made the call to you.

"We never expected anything other than a routine visit and made only the normal preparations. Our security hadn't been changed yet. Mr. Rosner only did that after their visit. At that time, it was normal for them to call us from the main gate and proceed to the second gate after we opened it. At the second gate, they would park their car and ring the buzzer. The gate would open, and they would proceed to the office of the administration building." She stopped for a moment and drew a breath. "Things started that way, but then went strangely rather quickly.

"We had expected two people, the brother and the person who called. But three people showed up. When they walked through the second gate, two of them headed to the administration office as expected. The third, however, hung back. After the gate closed, he started walking directly toward the patients' living quarters. When the other two reached the office and entered, the receptionist alerted Anne, my assistant, and she came out to greet them. She realized immediately that neither one was the brother. She asked them to wait for a moment and picked up the phone to alert Mr. Rosner. I think that's the only thing that kept things from getting completely out of hand." Before Dr. Klein could proceed, there was quiet tapping on the door of her office. She turned toward it.

"Come in, Anne," she said. The door swung open and a pretty woman came in carrying a tray. She looked briefly at Magee and then continued directly to the desk. Magee watched her as she put the tray down and turned back to the doctor. Magee estimated her to be in her mid-thirties. She was tall and thin. She wore a simple yellow dress and an open sweater, not a suit like Dr. Klein was wearing. Her blond hair fell to just above her shoulders in a cut that framed her face. Her skin was clear, and her blue eyes seemed to give her a natural beauty that required little makeup. Magee guessed her to be Scandinavian by descent.

"Thank you, so much, Anne," Klein said. Then she gestured toward Magee. "I want you to meet Mr. Magee. He is the investigator I spoke to on the phone," she added. She turned back to him. "Mr. Magee, this is my assistant, Anne Farrow." As she spoke the other woman walked toward Magee and extended her hand.

"It's a pleasure to meet you, Mr. Magee," she said. "Welcome to our clinic." Magee rose off the couch enough to make the gesture of standing, shook her hand and sat back down.

"Thank you," he said. Anne stepped back to the desk. She lifted a teapot from the tray and poured tea into Klein's cup. Then she picked up the coffee cup and brought it to Magee. She turned back to Klein.

"Will there be anything else, for now, Dr. Klein?" She asked. Klein shook her head.

"No," she said, "not as far as the coffee goes, but your timing is perfect. At the moment I was just describing to Mr. Magee the incident in the office with the visitors. I had just reached the moment that you had realized the brother of the patient wasn't with them." Anne nodded and looked back at Magee.

"It was all very strange," she said. "I could see immediately that neither of the two was the brother. I had a lengthy meeting with him when he brought his brother to us. I interviewed him for all of the details we needed. It was six months ago, but I still remember what he looked like." Magee looked over at Klein and back to Anne.

"I take it the man that was still outside wasn't the brother either," he said.

"At that moment," Anne said, "I didn't even know there was another man. I just knew that we were supposed to have two people, and the ones who showed up didn't include the brother. So I called Paul to have him come over and sort things out. Then I called Dr. Klein to let her know of the situation." She turned to Dr. Klein and spoke, "Dr. Klein, I have to get back to my office. I have a call scheduled with one of our service providers. I hope you'll excuse me."

"Of course, Anne," Klein replied.

Anne reached into the pocket of her sweater and brought out a card. She turned to Magee and handed it to him. "This is my card, Mr. Magee. When your meeting with Dr. Klein is finished, I'll be back so that we can complete the administrative details surrounding your work with us."

"Anne is my right hand around here," Klein added. "She's very capable and I expect will be very helpful in providing you with administrative assistance, or providing information about the clinic, or making contacts with the rest of the staff, if necessary." Anne nodded. "I'd truly be lost without her."

"Thank you, Ms. Farrow," Magee said.

"Please," Anne replied with a smile, "Call me Anne." Magee returned her smile and watched as she turned and left the office, closing the door behind her.

Chapter 3

Magee appreciated the coffee. The whiskey he had sampled earlier was good, but it had left his mouth slightly dry. Now, he filled his mouth with some coffee and swished it around before swallowing. He thought about what he knew so far, which wasn't much. He still hadn't heard what, exactly he would be investigating, but he could be patient a little longer.

Everything he had heard was interesting and already he had a list of questions on his mental note pad. That pad, existing entirely in his mind, was one of the reasons he was so good at what he did, as Rosner had quoted from his file. He could listen to detailed descriptions for a long time and still retain them in his head. Along the way, he could make notations of specific questions that needed to be answered and bring them up when the person finally ran out of things to say.

So far, the details hadn't needed to be questioned. He did have other questions about Rosner, Klein and the clinic that he would ask in due time. For now, he just needed to listen. Klein finished a sip of her tea and started again.

"Now," she said, "where were we?"

"I believe you were saying things could have gotten out of hand," Magee answered.

"Oh, yes," Klein replied. "I remember. So, after Mr. Rosner received the call from Anne, he came immediately from his office and out into the yard in front of the Administration building. The first thing he saw was the third man moving toward the patient's building. He shouted to the man to stop, which, fortunately, he did.

"The man walked back to where Mr. Rosner was standing and asked if there was a problem. Mr. Rosner explained that he was not allowed to walk around the grounds unaccompanied. The man insisted he meant no harm. He was only taking a look around while he was waiting for the others to return from the office. Mr. Rosner suggested, politely I'm sure, that they both go to the office so they could discuss the visit. The man agreed, and Mr. Rosner showed him the way and walked along with him. When they arrived, Mr. Rosner asked the men to wait in one of our conference rooms until they could receive approval from me." Klein's tone changed slightly. "I usually provide approval for all visits to protect the patient's progress. It depends on my current assessment of the patient's frame of mind." Magee nodded that he understood and Klein continued.

"Anne had already alerted me to the situation, so I came to the office as soon as I finished the notes I had been making. She and Mr. Rosner were waiting for me." Klein stopped to sip some more tea and then began again.

"We discussed how we should proceed. Occasionally, we do have people who show up without appointments and hope to get in to see one of the patients. Usually, those would be people who have discovered somehow that a patient is here and expected they will be allowed to see them. They call us from the main gate and, in the past, we've let them come in as a courtesy and determined their circumstances. As you know, we're a bit of a drive from anywhere so people can sometimes get upset if they've driven all the way here and can't speak to the person they want to see. Sometimes we contact the patient's registered advocate to determine if we should allow the visit. If we reach the advocate, sometimes they allow it, but other times they suggest it is not a good idea."

"Did you attempt to call to confirm in this situation?" he asked.

"No, not immediately at that point," Dr. Klein replied. "The circumstances were already too weird. We had scheduled an appointment expecting the brother to be there, but he wasn't. Three people showed up instead of only two. And one of them started walking around unescorted among the buildings," she added. "We were still trying to sort things out when one of the men came out of the conference room. He asked if there was a problem.

"Paul told him no," she added, "but we had expected the brother to come. And then the man's answer made things even weirder." She paused. Magee assumed she wanted him to ask why. He indulged her.

"Even weirder how?" he asked. Klein shook her head and squeezed her lips together. Her eyes grew wide.

"He said he *was* the brother," she said as if she still couldn't believe it. Magee laughed.

"I suppose there could have been more than one, right?" he asked. Klein shook her head no.

"According to all the records we had," Klein replied, "there had been an older brother of the patient, but he died years before. And both parents were gone. The brother that checked him in was the only living relative." Magee followed up.

"Could the records have been wrong?" he asked. Klein shrugged her shoulders.

"I suppose that could have been possible, but highly unlikely in this case," she said. "The family involved is a very prominent one, and one with a public persona." Then she paused as if thinking about it. "Of course, even prominent families have secrets. I suppose they could have had secrets to keep. Everyone has some secrets. But I still think it's unlikely."

"What happened next?" Magee asked.

"Well," Klein continued, "Mr. Rosner simply asked the man to provide his identification. The man looked surprised, almost as if he hadn't expected that. He fumbled with his pockets as if searching for it. Then he announced that he must have left his wallet at home by accident. But he insisted that since he had signed the admission papers, he could sign again so it could be matched to the signature on record. He even stated the registration number of the patient. His voice had grown louder as he spoke, and he appeared to be frustrated.

"I think Mr. Rosner had heard enough at this point. It doesn't take much for him to get suspicious of people. He looked over at Anne who was frowning. She shook her head no, and Mr. Rosner turned back to the man and told him he would have to come back when he had proper identification. By this time, the other men had also come out of the conference room and overheard his statement.

"At that point, the men all looked at each other for a moment without speaking. Then one of the men, but not the one who said he was the brother, calmly said that they understood. He added that it was unfortunate, but they would make arrangements to visit at another time with the appropriate documentation. He then apologized for any inconvenience they had caused and said they would be leaving. Mr. Rosner thanked them and offered to show them out. He asked me to wait there at the office until he returned because he had a few items he needed to discuss with me. He made the visitors wait a moment while he moved around the counter and appeared to be searching for something behind it. Then he looked up and told me he thought he left a folder with the items there, but he must have left it in his office. He would pick it up when he was on the way back.

"Then he left together with the men. I watched them all from the window as they made their way to the gate. Mr. Rosner opened it, shook their hands, and watched as they went through before turning back toward his office." She stopped and smiled before beginning again. "Then things got even stranger!" she added. The smile became more devilish.

"Suddenly, those of us in the office could hear the men talking. I still saw them through the window. They were huddled just beyond the gate. But we could hear them loud and clear inside. Their voices were being picked up on the intercom next to the gate! We could hear every word." She looked at Magee and waited for him to react. He smiled as well, anticipating that whatever they had been talking about was very interesting.

"I'm sure there is a reason that you could suddenly hear them, and why do I suspect it has something to do with Mr. Rosner?" Magee asked. Klein laughed.

"You're right. When Mr. Rosner checked behind the counter and talked about a misplaced folder, he was just using that to flip the intercom switch. We don't use the intercom much because most people are expected and are instructed to just ring the buzzer. But it still functions. Part of the original design when we built the place." She seemed pleased with the way it had taken place. It was a bit of subterfuge that was probably uncommon for the clinic.

Magee surmised that the clinic was normally an unexciting place. Certainly, people came and went. But there was mostly no drama in their day to day interactions. He knew Dr. Klein was excited by her work, especially when she was successful with a patient, but the general everyday business was likely pretty serene. Klein's smile disappeared, and she began speaking again.

"It was then that I heard what caused me to be concerned. I had been watching the men as they stood outside the gate. I could hear one of them saying to the men with him that the others would not be pleased. I don't know what he meant by that, but the one who had claimed to be the brother said something like 'we shouldn't just leave' and 'It's not too late'. Just then, I noticed Mr. Rosner leaving his office and heading back over to Administration. When he saw them huddled at the gate, he turned and asked them if they needed any more help. Of course, they smiled and waved at him, and one of them replied no, that they were just leaving. Then the one who spoke in the office turned to the others and, more or less, herded them to the car. Mr. Rosner waited there, watching until the car pulled away, and then continued over to the office."

Magee understood why she and Rosner concluded there might be a threat, and why there was fear in her voice when she called. These men had come for a purpose. The way events unfolded they weren't successful. But, at this point, he was far from understanding what that purpose was.

"Did you report this incident to the police?" he asked before she could continue.

"Oh, no," Klein replied. She paused. "For two reasons," she added. "One, no one was harmed at the time. There wasn't any physical confrontation or any damage to anything. They left fairly quickly once they understood our policy. And even if we had reported it to the local police, you probably know they couldn't do any serious investigation. We're under the county Sheriff's jurisdiction. Frankly, it's a big county. They don't have many resources." She stopped.

"And the second reason?" Magee asked. Klein cleared her throat again and narrowed her eyes.

"I probably should have mentioned this earlier, Mr. Magee. We have a very special group of patients here. Yes, they all have one thing in common as we discussed. But also, a majority of our patients are members of wealthy families who pay a substantial fee for us to treat their loved ones. For that, they expect a high degree of discretion from us. Any publicity at all about our facility or the patients we keep would be very upsetting to them. We must maintain a very low profile." She paused again as if waiting for a reaction. When Magee gave none, she went on. "That may sound like we are more concerned about money we might lose instead of the safety of the patients. But it's more complicated than that.

"I said 'a majority' of our patients are wealthy. The rest of our patients are here because they have no families to speak of, except broken ones, and often no means of support, for that matter. We've sought out those who had been institutionalized in facilities that were rarely able to help them. We bring them here and treat them the same way we treat our wealthy patients, and we've had success with them as well. We can do that because our wealthy patients pay enough to cover those costs. That's why we are careful about the concerns of their families."

"I understand, Dr. Klein. I've had my share of wealthy clients. It pays the bills and lets me take on interesting cases when I want to." Klein smiled.

"Then you understand why we thought it best to hire someone like you," she said. Magee returned her smile.

"Yes," he added, "but you should know that based on what I know now, I'd put your clinic into the same category as my other wealthy clients. You haven't heard my pricing yet," he chuckled. She laughed too.

"And you, Mr. Magee," she said, "haven't heard the most interesting part yet. I haven't played the recording of the other things those men said as they were standing by the gate." Magee raised his eyebrows.

"Please go on then," he said.

"Well," she started, "I guess I'll get to the recording first. One of the reasons Mr. Rosner turned on the gate intercom was that it is connected directly into our computer system and we keep a recording of the conversation every time it is used. We do this for multiple things. It's more practical than trying to write everything down. It's invaluable to me when I'm working with a patient because I can go back and get every detail I need for treatment. And I can give instructions to the staff as easily as I ordered coffee earlier.

"We didn't have all that technology when the clinic was built, but we did have rudimentary systems. So, over time as we upgraded, we hooked most of the older systems in too. That includes the intercom." She stopped and turned toward her desk. "Computer, please play the recording of three blind mice for me now." The device lit up again.

"Of course, Dr. Klein," the device said. "Starting now." The recording began with Rosner's voice.

"I'm sorry you had to drive way out here and didn't get to have your visit," Rosner said. Magee could envision him shaking the hands of the men as he spoke. "I hope you understand that we have certain procedures we must follow."

"Of course," one of the men said. The voice was calm and showed no sign of disappointment or anger. "Perhaps we'll be more successful when we return."

"Till then," Rosner said. For the next few seconds, Magee heard the noise of feet shuffling, and a metal gate sliding. He presumed that Rosner was heading back toward his office during that time. One of the other men spoke.

"The others will not be happy about this," the man said. A different voice followed.

"We shouldn't just leave," the voice said. "It isn't too late," he added. At that point, Dr. Klein reached over and lightly put her hand onto Magee's arm but didn't interrupt the recording. The man's tone sounded urgent. "I need to speak to him!" he added. Then the third man spoke.

"I understand your concerns," he said. "But think for a moment. There are many staff members and even patients in there. Nothing would be served by creating a scene now. We have an obligation to the others as well. And though you think that they won't be happy, you're wrong. They will reach the same conclusion as I already have." There was silence for a moment.

"You're right, of course," one man answered.

"Yes," the other one added impassively. There were a few more seconds of silence and then Magee heard Rosner again.

"You guys need help with something else?" he asked from a distance.

"No," the third man replied. "We were just leaving." At that point, the computer voice came back.

"Was that satisfactory, Dr. Klein," the voice asked. "Will there be anything else?" Klein turned toward the desk.

"Yes, and no. Thank you, computer," she answered. Then she turned back to Magee. "The man speaking when I touched you is the one who claimed to be the brother. He seemed nervous the whole time he was with us." Magee understood that she was talking about the very voice who had said they shouldn't leave.

"Okay," he said. "That did make it interesting." He crossed his arms and then cupped one hand on his chin. "What was it you called them?" Dr. Klein smiled.

"The Three Blind Mice," she said. "It's was just our way to have some name to refer to when we talk about them."

"Cute," Magee said. "They did seem a little weird, didn't they?" Dr. Klein leaned forward.

"Yes but, wait. I still haven't gotten to the most interesting part yet," she said. Magee uncrossed his arms, put his hands together and leaned forward also. Klein continued. "Remember that when this appointment had been set up, a person had called our office and cited the registration number of the patient they wanted to see. They also gave the name of the patient. And they said they would bring the brother of the patient with them. And they gave the brother's name. That was why we agreed to make the appointment in the first place.

"Then, when these men came, one of them pretended to be the brother. They told us they would be back. So, after the men left, Mr. Rosner and I spoke about what to do. He said the first thing he was going to do was call the contact number for the brother, and see who would answer." Magee interrupted.

"That was a good suggestion," Magee confirmed. "Did the brother answer?"

"Mr. Rosner didn't reach him," Klein continued. "At least not directly. Someone else answered his phone. He asked who was calling and we gave him our coded answer." She paused. "I should explain. It's part of our privacy protection. When we initiate a call to the registered advocate, we never know the circumstances of who will answer. If it isn't the advocate directly, we have a special response that will alert the advocate as to who is calling. We identify ourselves as Mr. or Ms. Stevenson and say we are calling about the book he or she ordered. The call either gets passed to the advocate or they take a message for them, and we'll get a call back when it's possible.

"In this case, the person that answered the phone wasn't the brother, but he recognized the coded answer. He identified himself as the brother's attorney, and he understood who we were. He told us that our patient's brother had died, unexpectantly. Of course, we asked how. He said of an aneurysm. He added that he was very glad we called. Our clinic was on a list of names he had received to be contacted under certain circumstances. He had been working his way down the list." A look of sadness overtook her. She looked down again and moved slightly in her chair. "It's funny. I understand it's all part of life. People die unexpectantly all the time. As a doctor, I'm trained to be compassionate but detached from these types of events. Still, I knew I would have to tell our patient the news. And I dreaded it. It wasn't that I knew it may impact his treatment. It's just hard to remain unemotional when you have to give someone that news." Magee considered this an appropriate time to ask another question, perhaps to take her mind off that part.

"The timing seems a little suspect," he offered. "Were they visiting around the actual time of death?"

"No," she continued. "their visit was a week after. I called you the day after that. And based on what the attorney said, the brother had died at the end of the week before." Magee raised his hand at that point and scratched his head. Klein was right. This was even *more* interesting than what the men had said. There were now a lot of details and his mental note pad was getting full. He knew that sooner or later he would have to start writing it all out to make sense of it.

"I have to ask," Magee said. "Is it possible for someone to cause an aneurysm? I mean, is it possible that the brother was murdered?"

"I don't think so," Klein replied. "At least, not that I know of. That ability didn't exist when I went through med school. And I don't see how it could now." She looked pensive for a moment and then added, "I can certainly find out." She started to turn her head toward her desk. Magee raised his hand and she stopped.

"Homework assignment," he said with a smile. "No need to bother the computer with that just now." Klein laughed. "Besides, we have enough other things to start with. I've seen cameras in different places since I arrived. I hope those are part of the enhanced security features you've added since the visit."

"Oh, no," Klein said. "They've been here a long time. And they did take pictures of the men. They don't provide video recording, but they take turns taking a series of snapshots on a rotation basis. It's more efficient than having so much data to store." She turned again toward her desk. "Computer," she said, "Show me the photos of three blind mice." Magee briefly wondered how the computer was going to do that, but the doors on the mahogany frame that hung on the wall swung open revealing a TV screen. Three photos appeared showing a clear view of each face.

"We had the computer select the best facial views of each man and enlarge them to give you a pretty good view. These, as well as other ones, are all in the file we printed out to give you. Mr. Rosner insisted we consolidate everything we could into one place so you would have it. That is if you agreed to do the investigation." Magee was looking at the screen and studying the faces. They were just average. They could have been anyone from anyplace. After a moment, he turned back to her.

"Oh, I think you've made things interesting enough for me. I may be able to help," he said.

"I'm so glad!" Klein exclaimed. "I want you to know that I've been very worried about everything that happened. I don't normally have anything to worry about but my patients. Mr. Rosner and the rest of the clinic staff are extremely competent. They take care of all the details but keep me informed as necessary. Even in this case, they handled things quite well. But obviously, getting to the bottom of this is outside of what they normally do."

"I don't know about that," Magee said. "I think Mr. Rosner could handle some things you wouldn't expect him to."

"Yes, I suppose you're right. I do know his whole background," she said. "But he doesn't do investigating for a living. So, I'm happy you're here," she added. "And I'm sure he will be of great assistance. He *is* intensely protective of me. If he thought these men were going to harm this clinic or me in any way, I wouldn't like to think about what he might do." Magee nodded.

"Well, I guess I'll just have to make sure he won't have to," he said.

Moments later, Anne Farrow returned to Klein's office based on instructions from Klein to the computer. She brought with her a three-ring notebook containing the file that Klein had mentioned. After Anne provided him with the file, Klein asked that she provide him with any other information he might ask for.

"I hope you will excuse me now, Mr. Magee," she said, "We've been talking for a long time, and I do have to get back to my work. Anne can handle everything you need. And she won't hesitate to contact me if you need me for something else." She offered her hand to shake.

"Of course, Dr. Klein," Magee answered, accepting her hand. Then he turned to Anne and they walked together toward the door. Suddenly, he stopped and turned back to her. "Oh, just one more quick question," he said. "Is there anything special about the patient they came to visit?" Klein didn't hesitate.

"Nothing," she said, shaking her head. "He suffers from the same thing the rest of the patients do. He exhibits all the same symptoms and has been responding to the same treatment." Magee nodded.

"Thank you, Doctor," he said and followed Anne through the open door. Klein shut it behind them.

"That was a long meeting, Mr. Magee," Anne said as they walked down the hall. "Is there anything you need right now? Another coffee or to use the restroom?" she offered.

"There is one thing," he answered back. "Please just call me 'Magee'," he added. Anne laughed.

"Just Magee?" She asked. "No first name?" She smiled. Magee took a moment to appreciate her beauty before he answered.

"I'm not comfortable with my first name," he said. "Magee works best. Although I've been called worse and answered too. I could use a restroom stop if it's no trouble."

"Of course. There is one on the way. But regarding your name, you have aroused my curiosity. Maybe, sometime, you'll explain why you're uncomfortable with it," she said, coyly.

Chapter 4

Magee splashed cold water on his face and gazed into the restroom mirror. Klein was right. Things had certainly gotten interesting. His mind had already turned to a review of what he knew so far. The incident had been unnerving to Rosner and Klein. Enough so that it caused Rosner to say he was prepared to protect her at all costs. But from Magee's perspective, it seemed an unnecessary worry at this point. The visitors may have posed a threat to her, but there was no indication from what he had reviewed. They seemed more concerned about the patient they were trying to reach. And when they were denied, they left without further problems.

He felt uneasy as if he had missed something. Was there something else that occurred, or was there something unrelated they were worried about? Magee began to run down the facts he had gathered on his mental notepad. First, Rosner had ensured Magee was aware that his selection didn't happen from a quick leaf through the Yellow Pages under Private Investigators. The photograph Rosner had matched him to in his office was recent, taken as he left a meeting with a client. He recognized the building in the background. Magee knew exactly the time and place of that meeting. It was also the day he received the telephone call from Klein.

He thought about the possibilities of what that meant. One possibility was that Rosner had somehow gathered an entire file of material on Magee, including a recent photograph and a description of his favorite whiskey, between the time of the incident and Klein's call. Even if true, he couldn't draw any conclusions about what that meant. He didn't know enough about Rosner's sources for the file, or who might have provided the recommendation. The entire file could have been provided to him from one of Magee's previous clients, along with an updated picture just to make sure Rosner was talking to the right person.

A second possibility was that Rosner may have had him investigated before the incident, perhaps to have a reliable investigator if needed on short notice. That was certainly within the realm of possibility. Rosner struck him as extremely capable of thinking ahead. His military training served him well. But why hire an investigator to investigate an investigator. Why not just hire the one who put together the file? Was there something unique about Magee that made him specifically qualified for this job?

As he dried his face and hands, it also dawned on Magee that the greater portion of the file may not have contained any information about him at all. Rosner made sure he saw the picture, and page it had been stapled to, but he didn't look at the rest of the pages. Perhaps Rosner merely wanted to see his reaction. He decided he could explore this later. Anne was waiting for him to return.

He thought about seeing her come into Klein's office. She had moved so gracefully. She wasn't too much younger than him. He had noticed she wasn't wearing a ring but also knew that doesn't mean much anymore. He looked in the mirror again and ran a comb through his hair. He still had plenty, although there were a few strands of gray appearing on each side.

He figured it was natural. Some of the work he had done over the years was difficult and stressful. More lines had appeared on his face over the years, too, particularly around his smile. He couldn't tell what she thought of him at this point, but he decided he wanted to get to know her better. He left the restroom and made his way back down the hall to where he had left her.

"All set?" She said as he strolled up. She was smiling again. He found himself smiling too.

"Yep," he said, "and ready to get your perspective on things." He thought he saw a faint blush move across her face quickly and then fade.

"I'm sure that Paul and Dr. Klein have told you everything important," she said. "I'm don't know what I can add to the details, but I do have some other things to discuss." She pointed to a hallway. "This connects to the business offices. My office is there." She began walking and Magee followed. "I have responsibility for the administrative departments of both Dr. Klein's practice and the clinic."

"Ah, finally," Magee said. "I get to talk to the person that's really in charge of this place." Anne laughed.

"Well, I'm glad you recognize that. Someone has to pay attention to making things work around here. I have to work out the details for exactly how and what we will pay you, your access to and from the premises, and where you'll stay when you need to. You did bring a suitcase, as instructed. Correct?" Magee nodded. "Good," she added. She continued down the hall and turned into an office with her name by the door. Magee noticed the title as he entered, "Vice President, Administrative Services."

"It sounds like a lot of responsibility," Magee said, waving his hand toward the sign. She nodded.

"Some days, more than others." She paused for a moment as if considering which one today was, and then continued. "But I wouldn't trade this job for yours!" she said, emphatically as she sat down behind her desk. She reached in a drawer and pulled out a thick manila folder, very similar to the one Rosner had. Magee was curious about her job comment but decided to hold that question for another time. Instead, his eyes focused on the folder before he spoke.

"I see that you also have a file on me. I've gotten quite popular, it seems," he said. Anne saw a puzzled expression from him as he looked at the folder.

"Oh, this," she said, holding the folder. "This is just a copy of the file that Paul has." She said. "I assume he discussed what is in it when he talked with you. Didn't he?"

"Not really, other than to offer me a glass of Jack Daniels," he replied. His expression changed to a smile.

"Oh, yes," she said. "There is that. He was funny when he found that information in there." She pursed her lips together and lowered her voice into a mock, male tone. "He said 'This is our guy! This is a man's man. This is who we need!'" Then she laughed. Magee laughed, too.

"What else is in there?" he asked. She stopped laughing, reached down and opened the file. Magee could see that the top page was the same one that Rosner had, with a picture stapled to it. She picked it up.

"Well, I scanned it before, but let me have a look, now. There's a whole lot of detail about you, but it's all identified with just the name of your firm. No mention of your first name." Anne flipped past the first page and onto the second. "It's quite well organized. There's a table of contents," she added. She scanned the list. "It starts with a biographical list by year. Okay, you were born. That's good. Oh, my," she looked up, "I would have thought you were younger. You don't look Forty-Two," she said. Magee winced. He was glad she said he didn't look that old, but he would have preferred she didn't know how old he was. She went on. "Your father was a Staff Sargent in the Army, so you moved around a lot as a kid: Different states, a few different countries, base schools, and..." Magee raised his hand and interrupted.

"Can we skip the actual individual details and just read the categories covered?" he asked. Anne seemed embarrassed.

"Of course," she said. "I'm sorry. I didn't mean to get into the personal side." She cleared her throat before continuing. Magee sensed that she felt bad and instantly regretted that he had stopped her.

"Look," he said. "I only meant that I kind of know all that stuff. I'm just more interested in the general idea of what's in there." He smiled, hoping that she would reciprocate.

"I understand," she said. "I was just hoping I could find out in here why you hated your first name." Then she smiled. Magee relaxed. It was a perfect response. They both laughed. Anne looked at the contents again. "Well, beyond the personal information, it seems to have a list of several clients you have worked with over time." She flipped to that section of the file and scanned the first group. Then she looked up. "Just looking at the first company, they've listed a lot of data about the work you did for them, the outcome of the investigation, the amount you were paid broken into categories, including expenses and your time, and a general description of the level of satisfaction with your work." She thumbed through a few more entities. "It's a very thorough report, and all of the satisfaction levels seem quite high. Very impressive." Magee frowned.

"I guess from your perspective, it supports your organization's choice of me for a job," he said, "But from my perspective, it makes me wonder why it has all that information. A lot of should be kept confidential based on my agreements with the companies or people who use my services. How in the world does someone lay their hands on all that information in one place so that it can be passed on to a prospective client? And in a relatively short time frame at that." Anne furrowed her eyebrows.

"I suppose you are right," she said. "It's an impressive piece of work, for sure. On the one hand, it does kind of put you at a disadvantage from a negotiation standpoint," she added. "But, on the other hand, let's suppose that the record of satisfaction speaks for itself. You start with a strong position from that standpoint alone. And for someone in need of quick results, you have them over a barrel."

Magee sensed that by directing the conversation away from the personal items, he caused Anne to focus on her administrative responsibilities. Part of her tasks concerning the clinic included negotiating with service providers. She was evaluating the current situation from how it might affect his arrangement with their organization. He recognized that she now had control of the conversation. It was an odd situation for him. Usually, when he engaged with others in the course of his work, he was either in control or at least on equal footing. He felt that way with Rosner earlier, and with Klein in her office. He was not used to being in a situation where he had less control. It was an uncomfortable feeling. In some ways, it was like the unease that he had felt earlier in the restroom. He leaned back in his chair and sat silent for a moment. Anne looked at him.

"Is there something wrong, Magee? You look a little concerned," she said. Her words were a spark. His ego kicked in and he immediately shook his head.

"Nope," he said and then grinned. "I guess I got carried away thinking about how I was going to investigate that information, after I'm done with this investigation, that is."

"I suppose that's appropriate," Anne said. "Although, I doubt very highly that Paul will tell you where the information came from. It will present a challenge. But, judging from your record, you'll probably be successful." She smiled and then added, "I'd be happy to give you a copy of this report, of course. After all, it isn't anything you don't already know."

"I appreciate that, Anne," he replied. It was the first time he had used her name since their introduction in Klein's office. There was a brief glimmer of recognition in her eyes accompanied by a smile. She shuffled the papers of the report back into a single unit and placed it in the folder, pushing it to the side of the desk. Then she turned to the credenza behind her and retrieved another three-ring binder. She placed it in front of Magee.

"Open it," she said and waited for Magee to turn the cover. He found several sections separated by tabbed filler pages. It began with a contents section, and then followed with descriptions on each of the following tabs. The first was titled "Non-Disclosure Agreement". The second held "Protecting Patient Confidentiality". As he glanced at the others, he noticed that all but one contained a lengthy subject description with a signature line recognizing he had read and agreed to the terms. The exception was a duplicate of his client agreement he had used for a previous investigation, but the name of the clinic had been substituted for the original client. Anne had signed that form and included her title at the clinic. The final section was titled "Compensation".

Anne continued, "The binder is for you to take, to read and to sign where appropriate. I've taken the liberty to populate a number into the daily rate portion of the compensation form." She paused and added, "Yes, I did take into account the compensation numbers I found in Rosner's file.

But you'll notice I've bumped the number from the most recent client by ten percent.

"I hope that alleviates any concerns you have about what was contained in the file. I don't really know what the investigation will reveal. It may yield nothing of substance and the whole thing may just go away. On the other hand, it is too important to treat this lightly. All of us here were a bit concerned about what happened and exactly what else might happen. We're hopeful that it does turn out to be just an odd occurrence and we can return to normal." She stopped and waited for Magee to respond.

Magee sensed something in her voice. It was similar to what he sensed as he had first talked to Klein. There was an implication. He could tell she was concerned. There wasn't fear in the usual sense, but there was something of a request. She was asking for his help.

He didn't speak right away. He adjusted himself in his chair, letting his left elbow rest on the arm, and drawing his hand up to hold his chin, as if in thought. He looked directly at her, and directly into her eyes as if searching for something. At first, she moved her head as if she was going to turn away. But then she fixed her gaze on his eyes and kept them there. It may have been for five or ten seconds, or it may have been more. Magee wasn't sure but when he did decide to speak, he knew she was telling the truth.

"I appreciate your candor, and I sense your concern," he said. "So far, this has been a very interesting day. And I guess I have my homework to do tonight," he added. She laughed.

"Don't worry. I used to be a Graduate Assistant while working on my master's degree. I graded a lot of papers and I'm a pretty easy grader," she said, still laughing. "And speaking of tonight, you said you have your suitcase. So, we need to get you into your room for tonight. You can refresh yourself before dinner."

"Will I be using a room reserved for patients?" Magee asked. "There's only one of me." Anne laughed again.

"Of course not," she said. "We have a complete facility set up like a hotel arrangement. We often have families of the patients staying with us for extended periods. I'm sure you'll be quite comfortable. Tomorrow we'll discuss the next steps, and I'll get you set up into the security system so you can come and go as you need. I assume that you'll want to have some follow up discussions here, and then head back to the city to continue. Paul did request that you join him for dinner. I hope that's okay with you."

"Will you be joining as well?" Magee asked. Ann started to respond but then paused as if mulling over the question in her mind.

"Oh, I'm not sure you want me there," she said. "I know Paul wanted to have some time to strategize with you on the next steps. I've already discussed with you the next steps I'm interested in. If I come to dinner, I'm likely to just keep trying to find out why you hate your first name." Magee laughed.

"Well I might prefer to spend my time trying to dodge that question from you rather than strategizing with Paul," he answered. "In fact, I know I would prefer it. I'd really like it if you were there." Magee added. He saw Anne blush slightly. He did too. Anne finished collecting the papers in the folder on her desk and then placed it back in the drawer.

"I hadn't planned on dinner tonight," she said, "but I will check with Paul. If he has no objections, I'll tag along. I guess I do have to eat, right?" Magee nodded.

He had surprised himself. Just like earlier when he discovered he was not in control of the conversation, he found himself acting completely out of character. His approach was usually one of patience. When working, he was a quiet receptor, listening to the signals that were being sent. He might steer a conversation by asking specific questions that took someone down the path of giving him what he wanted to know. But he had always found letting others speak about what they wanted to speak about led to more information than him seeking to extract it.

This was the second time he suggested something that was more in line with his personal feelings than with his investigation instincts. He had asked her not to review his personal history. Partly because he already knew it, but also because there might be something in it that he didn't want her to know. There may be a time and place, he thought, but it wasn't today. At least it did confirm, though, that the whole file was genuinely about him.

After tidying her desk, Anne rose and indicated it was time to go. She waited as he went out first, then shut and locked the office door behind her. She pointed down the hallway toward an exit. When they stepped outside into the courtyard, Magee realized he had lost track of time. The sun was low in the sky and it would be dark soon. He remembered that he had skipped lunch as he drove out to the clinic and realized that he was hungry now. Anne opened the gate and waited as Magee collected his suitcase from his car, then led him down a path to a building set away from the others.

"This is the hotel," Anne said as they approached a large square building with three floors. "It's more of a combination Apartment-Hotel facility. Those of us who live on the clinic campus have apartments on the bottom two floors. The guests stay on the third. The other facilities are all on the ground floor, including a very nice restaurant for the guests that the staff can also use if they like." She motioned toward the entrance. "The lobby is just inside that door," she said. "Follow the instructions on the kiosk inside and it will provide your key. Paul made reservations for six o'clock. You'll have some time to yourself before then, but there is a full bar at the restaurant if you want to head down earlier." She kept walking straight along the path on the side of the building.

"Aren't you coming in this way as well?" Magee asked.

"No," Anne said, turning slightly back toward him as she continued walking. "Residents have another entrance on the other side. But I'll be down later if Paul doesn't object," she added. He watched her until she turned the corner and disappeared. Then he turned and entered the lobby.

Chapter 5

Navigating the lobby and the kiosk was simple, and moments later he unpacked the necessities from his suitcase. His room was a small apartment, having a separate living area and kitchen in addition to the bedroom and bathroom. There was a desk in the bedroom, but he decided to sit at the kitchen table. He placed the binder on the table and started leafing through the sections.

Half an hour had passed by the time he read through all the sections and added his signature to most of the documents. The two that were left unsigned were the Compensation document and the copy of his standard agreement that Anne had signed. He had read through it and determined nothing had been altered except the names. Still, he had not yet decided to take this case.

He thought back to earlier in the day when he had been contemplating what he had been told. The threat still did not seem to be dire as Rosner had suggested it was. Even Klein seemed more relaxed than she had been on the phone. Then again, the circumstances surrounding the incident were not normal. There must have been some motivation for these people to spend the time to drive to the clinic to visit with the patient. Magee started thinking through the possibilities.

He had been doing investigation for as long as he could remember. As an Army brat, he moved often. The first thing he would have to do on arrival in a new camp was to size up the situation. It was a matter of survival, since wherever he went, he had to make new friends, or sometimes enemies. The key was analyzing how people were acting, figuring out the different motivations they might have, and deciding on the most likely one given the circumstances.

So far, from what he knew about the three blind mice, is they wanted to talk to someone. Klein had already said many of the patients came from rich families. Willie Sutton said it best. He robbed banks because that's where the money was. People who are going to steal money are always going to steal it from someone who has it. The mice could simply be working a scam of some sort.

Magee thought back to the recording Klein had played. What was it that one of the mice said? They had an 'obligation' to the others. Somehow that statement didn't line up with his experience with scammers. It didn't rule out money as a motivation, but usually, scammers want quick results. And the "others" in this situation would reach the same conclusion as the leader and be perfectly happy with leaving the scene at this point. It implied something more elaborate.

Magee understood he could think about some other motives, but before going further he decided he'd have to find out more about the patient. He didn't even know if the patient had money or not. Klein had only told him the family was 'prominent.' She also said there was nothing different about this patient's illness from the others at the clinic. He had already signed the forms related to protecting patient confidentiality, but he wasn't sure if that alone would allow him to talk to the patient. He decided that would be a question at dinner.

He checked the time and chose to go down and have a drink at the bar as Anne had suggested. He hoped she might show up too. He had felt something the moment she came into Klein's office. Of course, she was attractive. But there was something more. There were moments when she carried herself with confidence. But there were also other moments, particularly when they were alone but not speaking. At times she seemed slightly less sure of herself as if not certain how he would react. It was a small bit of vulnerability. She would probe a little, but not go too far until she could sense where it would lead. Then she'd follow up with a smile.

That's all it took for him. He had known many women and had his share of short relationships. The ones that lasted longer always had that trait. They started with a little flirting, like picking up something about him that was interesting, and then circling back around to it later in the conversation. Ultimately, there would be a hint of uncertainty about something identified with a concern. This time, it was hope that he could help them get back to normal operations.

Klein had seemed that way during their initial conversation but seemed more at ease now that he was here. Anne was still unsure about where it all would lead. Suddenly, he also wanted to know. He opened the binder and flipped to the two unsigned sections and quickly added his signature. Then he cleaned himself up a little and headed downstairs to find the bar.

The restaurant had a nice atmosphere. It was simple, not fancy. There were booths along each of the sidewalls and tables organized in between. The bar was located on the far side of the room, away from the entrance. Magee was surprised to see what looked like a dance floor under a part of the tables which could be uncovered by rearranging them, and there was a small stage not far from the bar.

It wasn't crowded but had a fair amount of people in booths and at some tables. Magee couldn't tell which might be visitors and which might be staff. They all looked just like normal people out enjoying a dinner at a normal restaurant. He walked through the area toward the bar and more than a few people stopped talking and watched him cautiously. Others continued with their conversations without even noticing. He assumed that the ones watching were part of the staff that knew who he was and why he came. The others might be visiting some of the patients.

Magee was a creature of habit at a bar. He liked to have a seat at the end. Hopefully, it would back up to a wall and allow him to see the entrance, giving him the ability to see as much of the rest of the room as possible without turning his head. He considered the options and chose one that best fit. No one was behind the bar, and he was the only one sitting at it. Within a few, seconds a young man came out of a door at the opposite end carrying plates of food. The man spotted him.

"Be right with you," he said smiling. Magee nodded and the man turned back and delivered the plates to a couple sitting at one of the booths. After a brief conversation with the couple, he made his way back to the bar and down to Magee.

"How are you, Mr. Magee?" he asked. Magee showed no surprise on his face but glanced at the name tag pinned to the man's vest.

"I'm fine, Stan," he said. "How are the wife and kids?" The man did look surprised but allowed the smile to return quickly.

"I'm not married, and I was never told about kids if there are any," he laughed and continued. "Can I get you what you usually drink?" This time Magee laughed.

"I guess my reputation proceeds me," he said. "Again," he added. "Sure, why not." Stan turned and walked down the bar a few steps, reaching down under and bringing up an open bottle of Jack Daniels. He dipped a glass into an ice drawer until it was half full and then poured in the whiskey to the top. He was grinning broadly when he set it in front of Magee.

"Anything else for right now?" he asked expectantly. Magee didn't answer immediately. Instead, he looked down and picked up the glass, swirled the contents a few times, and then took a healthy swallow. Then he looked back at Stan.

"I suppose you read my file, too," he said. Stan gave a quizzical look.

"File?" he asked. "No one gave me a file to read," he added. "It's just that Mr. Rosner was in last night and kept talking about you. He said you'd be coming in tonight, and I should serve up your usual, and then he described it. Did he tell me the wrong thing?" Magee laughed slightly.

"No, Stan. You did fine." He swirled the glass again. "Talked a lot, though, huh? What else did Mr. Rosner say?" He watched for a reaction, but Stan just grinned.

"He told me you were a private investigator. I've never met one before. Must be exciting work. He said you'd be working on the three blind mice issue." Stan was young. Magee knew that Stan may have had a romantic picture of private detectives. He had probably grown up seeing TV shows or movies that showed how the P.I. always figured out the crime, and somehow got the dame, and told the police everything they needed to put someone in prison.

"Well, it's not actually what you think it might be, Stan. How old are you, by the way?" he asked.

"I'm twenty-five," Stan answered, looking as if he still expected confirmation on his profession. Magee took another drink.

"I'm guessing you watched a lot of TV shows when you were younger. You know, the ones where a P.I. would be solving a crime, maybe need to fight a bit, but by the end of the show figured out what happened and was there when the police took the bad guy away." Magee paused to check his reaction and went on. "It's not really like that, you know. It's tedious and a lot of time downright boring. And usually, it's just gathering a lot of information about something and writing a report that gets sent to someone else so they can make their own judgment. And it's mostly not dangerous at all." Magee stopped and waited for a response. Stan had listened but not shown any reaction.

"Oh, I did watch a few of those shows," he said, "and I know that's mostly fantasy. But I am a bartender. I'm supposed to be the one people talk to about their troubles and get advice. So, I ask everyone about their occupation. Now I know a little more about P.I.'s." Magee laughed and took another swallow. Stan excused himself so he could attend to some of the others in the room.

A moment later Magee saw Anne enter the room. Gone was the simple dress and sweater. The new dress was black and came just up to her shoulders. It accented her shape far more than her work outfit had. Her heels were higher, and with a gold chain around her neck, Magee thought she looked quite elegant. When she saw him, she smiled and came toward him. He watched her approach and wished the room was larger so it would take longer. He stood from the stool before she arrived.

"Hello, Magee," she said, still smiling as she eased herself onto the stool next to him. He smiled back. "You seem to be right at home here."

"I usually am at a bar," Magee answered. "But now I feel like I'm underdressed. You look stunning." Anne blushed and looked down, smoothing her dress with her hand.

"I like to dress a little nicer after work if I'm coming down here. Particularly when I'm going to be having dinner with visitors." She turned for a moment and waved at Stan, who was returning to the kitchen with some empty plates. She watched as he set them down at the end of the bar and came toward them. Stan smiled broadly.

"Good evening, Anne," he said, as he instinctively reached under the bar for a wet towel and wiped the space in front of her. "It's good to see you. Will you be joining Mr. Rosner and Mr. Magee for dinner?" Anne nodded. "Very good," Stan said, still smiling. "Would you like something to drink right now?" he added. Anne looked over at Magee's glass.

"I'll have what he's having," she answered.

"Of course," Stan replied, then with precision fetched another glass and returned with what he had served to Magee. Anne turned to Magee as Stan placed the glass in front of her.

"I guess I need to try this to see why it's so popular," she said, lifting the glass to smell the contents before taking a small sip. She scrunched her nose in a way Magee hadn't seen before and he let out a laugh. She laughed too and then raised the glass in front of her. "Here's to a successful investigation." Magee did the same, touching his glass to hers before taking a healthy swallow.

"I haven't met too many women who enjoy a good glass of whiskey," he said, "but as far as the investigation goes, you'll get your money's worth." He paused, then added "By the way, speaking of money, I've signed all the paperwork you gave me. You were right. The compensation is more than adequate." Anne smiled but then became more serious.

"This is important to Dr. Klein, and to me, actually," she said. "Paul is concerned, but not as much as we are. He originally wanted to pursue it himself, but we convinced him that his job was to stay focused on security at the clinic. We didn't want him away, chasing this down, if something more serious happened back here." Magee looked at her face and saw the concern in her eyes. It was precisely the kind of look that brought out his protective side.

"That's the right choice," Magee said. "I'm not sure where this will lead, but we know these guys showed up from somewhere, and we'll have to find them to figure out what they really wanted." He looked down at his glass, took another swallow and added, "Even I will feel a lot better knowing Paul is back here. This place is pretty isolated!" He watched for her reaction. She seemed relieved. She looked at him again and smiled. He did too. "So, how does someone like you choose a place like this to work?" he asked.

The minute the words left his mouth he regretted it. It was the third time he said something to her that was completely out of character from what he would normally do. The phrase "someone like you" implied he had made a judgment about her. In his business, that was not something you wanted anyone else to know. He prided himself on not revealing what he thought about clients or even the people he was investigating. It was part of not giving them an edge. He had learned early that when someone thinks you have an opinion about them, it becomes something they can use to their advantage. It doesn't matter whether the opinion is good or bad, it just gives them a bit of knowledge which may change the way they interact. He watched to see her reaction.

Anne didn't answer quickly. She looked at her glass as if contemplating how to answer just long enough to make him wonder how guarded her answer would be. Finally, she spoke.

"I could answer that a lot of different ways, Magee. But like I said earlier, I'm an easy grader. So, tell me first. What kind of 'someone' do you think I am?" She was smiling in her usual way. Magee took it to mean she wasn't upset. He cleared his throat. His face was a bit flushed.

"Well," he started, "You're obviously a beautiful young woman who is not wearing a wedding ring. That might mean you are either single or currently unattached in that way. It just seems that you might want to be somewhere that has more social opportunities. Unless there is someone here that you might have a relationship with. But you're having a work-related dinner which didn't require that you look even more beautiful." He cleared his throat again. Anne chuckled but didn't offer anything that might let him off the hook. She sat silent and waited for him to continue. Finally, he added, "I suppose you could have just wanted to impress Stan." Ann laughed out loud.

"Well, Mr. Magee. I hope that your last statement isn't a sample of your brilliant detective work," she said. "Let me just say it's complicated and leave it at that." She smiled and finished her whiskey in one swallow, then motioned for Stan to come over. When he arrived she asked for a Diet Coke. He looked at Magee who signaled he was still good. As he was bringing Anne's drink, he pointed toward the other side of the restaurant, where Paul Rosner was just coming through the door.

Magee stood when Paul approached them and extended his hand. The two men exchanged a strong handshake, perhaps a little stronger than it would have been if Anne wasn't there. Then Paul turned to Anne and spoke.

"Anne, you look even more beautiful than usual." He smiled and kissed her lightly on the cheek. She smiled in return and stood partially to receive it. Stan pointed to a booth that was set for three along the far side of the room. Anne led the way, and once she was seated, Paul sat next to her. Magee slid in across from them as Stan placed menus in front of each. Anne spoke first.

"What do you recommend tonight, Stan?" she asked.

"For you, Anne, I recommend the Flounder. It arrived this morning from the coast. Freshly caught last night. I'll also bring you a glass of Chardonnay, chilled to just the temperature you like."

"Perfect," Anne replied. Stan turned to Magee.

"I don't suppose you have a recommendation for me since you didn't read my file," he said. Stan smiled.

"On the contrary, Mr. Magee," Stan replied. "I'm a professional. I take everything I can surmise from a person and then make a recommendation based on what I have available. In your case, I recommend a Kansas City steak, rare, with a hint of basil leaf. The flavor will mix exquisitely with your drink." Magee frowned slightly.

"I thought you were a bartender, Stan. I've never met one who can describe food that way," he said. Stan laughed.

"Well, I consider myself a professional in many different disciplines," Stan replied. Magee nodded his acceptance. Stan turned to Rosner but simply waited. Paul had picked up the menu and appeared to be reading it from front to back. Stan continued waiting. Magee and Anne simply watched. Finally, Rosner spoke.

"I'll have a cheeseburger. No fries. Caesar salad. And my usual to drink," he said. Stan appeared satisfied and collected the menus, then headed back toward the kitchen. Anne chuckled. Magee just continued looking at Paul, as if waiting for some explanation. Paul had unrolled the napkin in front of him and removed the silverware. He placed the knife to his right and the fork to his left. Then he arranged the napkin neatly on his lap. He looked up.

"I'm starved," he said.

Chapter 6

For a time, the conversation remained casual. Paul asked Magee about his accommodations. Magee explained that they were more than satisfactory and better than most of the places he had stayed for previous investigations. Anne suggested that the weather for his drive out from the city must have been good and asked if he'd had any trouble on the road. Magee said no and then asked them both if they ever left to visit the city much. They shook their heads. Stan returned with fresh drinks and the small talk continued.

Finally, Magee pressed Paul on the exchange with Stan, who had been so meticulous with Anne and himself but completely detached from Paul's order. Paul started to explain that it was just a little game he played with Stan, but Anne interrupted him.

"Oh, come on, Paul," she said smiling. "It's more about being a control freak." She turned to Magee. "Paul doesn't like anyone making his decisions for him, and he spent the first week Stan was here making sure he knew that." Paul's face turned red, but he was smiling.

"Guilty," he acknowledged, then added, "but in my defense, I just prefer to make my own decisions about what I eat. Don't you, Magee?" There was a nod from Magee. He saw Anne glance at him with a raised eyebrow.

"But you let him order for you," she said.

"Yes," Magee answered, "but not without comment. I was impressed by his professionalism," he added. In his head was what he didn't say. As usual, he didn't like to reveal his true feelings about things until he had a sense of what others may have revealed what they thought he felt. He liked to maintain the ability to surprise people. It was also a lesson he learned as he moved from base to base when he was young. Anne frowned her disapproval but quickly smiled again.

"Well, he is quite knowledgeable," she said. "He's changed a lot of things in the short time since he came on board. The previous manager had been here since we opened. He was well qualified, and the food was good, but pretty much standard stuff. The atmosphere had gotten a little stale. Not as many people were coming in anymore." Paul chimed in next.

"It's true. The people who work here must have a social outlet. If they get too isolated and just stay home all the time, they tend to leave quicker. Anne is pretty good about trying to keep them actively involved, sort of like a family environment." Anne blushed a little from Paul's compliment.

"How do you do that?" Magee asked.

"Well, it's mostly just organizing things that can keep them busy when they aren't working. Sometimes it's exercise classes or even educational things. Other times its movies or entertainment. It's part of keeping things running smoothly," she said. Magee glanced around the room and saw that there was still a good amount of people. He raised his glass toward her in a mock toast.

"As I said earlier, the person really in charge," he said. Anne laughed and raised her glass to his and was followed by Paul. It was then that Stan approached carrying plates of food. For a moment, their conversation stalled as Stan carefully placed their orders in front of them.

"How does everything look?" he asked. Each one nodded their approval in response. Stan looked at Anne first. "Anything else I can get for you?" he asked.

"No, Stan," she answered. Everything looks perfect." The same question went to Magee who also approved. Stan then turned to Paul.

"I know you like your burgers very basic," Stan said, "but I ground the beef for this one from the same cut of meat I served to Mr. Magee. Then I added a secret ingredient to the mix along with a splash of cayenne pepper and minced garlic. I hope it makes it a little more interesting." Paul stared at his burger for a moment, then turned to Stan and made a polite smile.

"I'm sure it will be very nice," he said. Stan smiled, then excused himself and headed back toward the kitchen. Paul watched as Stan passed through the kitchen door and then looked down at his burger again. "I hate it when he does that," he grumbled. Anne laughed.

"That's just his way of reminding you that you aren't always in control," she said.

"Yeah, I know," Paul said. "Last night I ordered plain spaghetti and he brought out a plate with meatballs on top arranged to look like a smiley face: two eyes, a nose, and a broad smile." Everyone laughed.

"It seems like one, big happy family here," Magee said. "I guess you guys have been working together for a pretty long time, huh?" Anne had been sampling her fish but stopped to answer.

"Not really," Anne said. "I mean, Paul and I have been with Dr. Klein for a long time. So, I guess we are a little like family. But Stan just joined us a few weeks ago. He just seems to fit in very well."

"He knew about the visit of the three men when I talked to him earlier. Was he here when that happened?" Magee asked. Anne nodded.

"Yes," she said, "he started about a week before." Magee looked down at his dinner and pushed at his steak with his fork as if in thought.

"What are you thinking," Paul asked.

"Did the other manager quit or did you decide to make a change?" Magee asked Anne.

"He quit suddenly," she answered. "He had a family emergency, so I told him to take a couple of days to take care of it. He left right away. Then the day after that, he called me and said his brother needed long-term care, so he wouldn't be coming back." Magee frowned.

"How did you deal with that. Seems like it would have taken you a long time to find a replacement," Magee said. "It isn't likely you would have too many candidates nearby. Especially as good as Stan."

"I didn't have to search for one," Anne replied. "The manager told me he had a replacement in mind and had already spoken to him about the job. He said he had known him before and knew he could step in immediately and do a good job. He gave me his number and I called. It was Stan. Then he visited so I could interview him. He liked the place. I liked him, and so I offered him the job right away. He did need two days to make arrangements before moving out here, but since then it has worked out fine." Magee looked down and poked at his steak again.

"I can see that you are thinking there may be a connection to the mice in some way," Paul said. "How so?" Magee looked up again.

"I don't know yet," he said. "It may just be a coincidence, but experience has taught me that sometimes coincidences turn out not to be so coincidental." Everyone was silent for a moment. "Did you run a background check on him?" Magee asked Paul.

"No," he said shaking his head. "It was an unusual circumstance. He came highly recommended, and Anne had interviewed him, and we needed someone right away," he added. Then he frowned. "I hadn't updated security procedures at that point. But I did spend a lot of time with him the first week to get to know him. Then, the mice came, and everything changed. I guess I'm going to have to look a little more closely at Stan now. Maybe find out more about him." Paul leaned over and looked toward the kitchen door, then back at Magee and Anne.

"Well, it seems we've started getting into the business part of our conversation," he said. "We'll have a little while until Stan returns." Then he looked at Anne. "First, did Magee sign the non-disclosure?" he added. She nodded. "Good," he said turning back to Magee. "So why don't you share your thoughts about everything so far?" he asked. Magee had taken a bite of his steak and wasn't ready to comment. He finished chewing and then used his napkin to wipe his mouth before speaking.

"I think that Stan knows his stuff. This is really, really good," he said. Paul laughed.

"Yeah, I know, we've already talked about that," he answered. "But what do you think about the job so far, and the whole situation? The last time I talked to you in my office, I didn't give you any of the details. Now you know what kind of situation we are dealing with." Magee smiled and put down the napkin.

"It is weird," he said, "but not the weirdest I've seen, at least for the moment. It might get weirder, though. There is the whole thing about the mice and how they acted while they were here. Then there is the thing about the brother of the patient dying before they scheduled the appointment. Finally, there is the attorney for the brother. How long had the brother been dead without the attorney calling? He said that the clinic was on the list to contact and he was working his way down the list. It strikes me that if the brother was the guardian for a patient at the clinic, that means he is likely to make contacting the clinic a high priority if something happens to him. And it follows that his attorney would know that. For some reason, the attorney didn't get around to calling at all until a week had passed. Doesn't add up." Magee paused. Anne and Paul looked surprised.

"I guess I hadn't thought about that," Paul said. "But perhaps the attorney was busy with a bunch of other things and figured that the contact could wait." Anne scrunched her nose at Paul.

"Hmmph," she snorted, then added, "I wouldn't hire an attorney that did something like that. His responsibility should have been to notify next of kin as soon as he could." Magee smiled and nodded. Paul shrugged.

"Okay," he said, "then how do you think we should proceed?"

"I think we have plenty of things to look at," Magee said. "We're going to have to find the mice. Dr. Klein said two of them signed in at the office. We'll need to verify the names they used. Also, did you get the attorney's name?" Paul nodded. "I'll need to go see him when I return to the city. But I think before I leave, I'd like to start by talking with the patient," he added. He wasn't prepared for the reaction from Anne and Paul. They looked at each other first, then back at Magee. He realized they both looked as if his idea was a bad one. Paul cleared his throat as if he was ready to speak, but Anne held her hand up to signal him not too. Then she turned back to Magee and spoke.

"I understand why you might think it may be helpful," she said, "but…" she paused for a moment, as if gathering her thoughts, then continued. "You might find it difficult to get a straight answer." Magee had begun to take another bite of his meal but stopped. He put down his fork and just listened. Anne went on. "Dr. Klein had met with the patient just after Paul found out about the brother's death, and before she made her call to you. She determined that he needed to know his brother had died." Anne stopped and seemed to search for how to continue. "It was a tough call. The patient had been responding well to treatment, and she couldn't be sure how he might be affected by the news. But in the end, she decided it was the right thing to do.

"It didn't go well," Anne continued. "The patient got angry and began shouting, first at her and then just in general. It was highly unusual." Paul had been fidgeting as she was talking as if he had something to add.

"Unusual isn't what I'd call it," Paul interrupted her. "It was unsafe!" he said with a frown. "She should have asked me to join her."

"Alright, Paul," Anne acknowledged. "It shouldn't have been unsafe. It was, but nothing bad happened after all." Paul still fidgeted. Anne continued. "We do have certain protocols for interacting with patients. This time, Dr. Klein didn't wait for anyone else to arrive. She thought the patient would be more sorrowful. The anger took her by surprise, and she responded with her alert button. Those of us who interact directly with patients always carry one. Rarely are they used, but if they are, it takes a few moments for someone to respond. She was alone for a short time with an angry patient who could have harmed her. He could have taken his shouting to the next level. Instead, he stopped shouting at her and then just kept shaking his fist and screaming up at the ceiling. The response team had to restrain him physically and then medicate him." She paused to see Magee's reaction.

"What was he saying?" Magee asked. Anne hesitated and looked down at the table when she responded.

"He said 'I warned him,'" Anne said softly. Then she looked back up at Magee. His eyes were focused on her. His face was stern. It was as if he was sensing a danger. Till this point, he had assumed the situation was curious, but not necessarily dangerous. No one was threatened by the mice. And Dr. Klein had indicated the brother was not likely murdered. Even if the situation was a scam being planned for money, it wasn't necessarily going to involve someone getting hurt. Now it was different. Someone who had been warned ended up dead. Magee understood it could have been a coincidence, but his experience told him otherwise. He turned to Paul.

"Were you part of the 'response team' that arrived?" he asked. Paul grimaced.

"No," he said with attitude. Then he softened, "I got there as soon as I could, and the team had already applied the medication and had the situation under control. Dr. Klein was a little shaken, but she was still more concerned about the patient than herself." Magee could hear the regret in his voice.

"We all talked about it after the fact," Anne said. "Dr. Klein admitted she should have waited and promised to do it next time. But you probably should ask her about it yourself. She swears it was the first time the patient has shown any strange behavior." Magee flashed an awkward, sideways smile. Anne read it and realized the irony of what she said. She laughed. So did Magee. Paul frowned.

"Still, could have been worse," he said. "We should all be glad it ended alright."

"Yes, but something tells me it may not next time," Magee said.

"What do you mean?" Anne asked. Magee sighed.

"In my experience," he started, "if someone is warned that something is going to happen, and then something does happen, it usually means whoever gave the warning knew something that the other person didn't. The inference, in this case, is that the patient knew that something bad could happen to his brother. He warned him about it, and then something bad did happen. Let me ask, do you monitor or record conversations between patients and family members?"

"No," Paul responded. "Sometimes Dr. Klein records her sessions with patients, but not always. It depends on a lot of factors." Magee followed up with another question.

"So, if the brother was here for a visit, the patient could have issued a warning and you wouldn't have known," Magee stated. This time Anne responded.

"No, not in this case," she said.

"How can you be so sure," Magee asked. Anne looked directly into his eyes and replied.

"This patient has been with us for just over six months," she answered and then added without moving her eyes from his, "The brother has never been here to visit since he checked the patient in." Magee glanced at Paul as if looking for confirmation. Paul agreed. Magee turned back to Anne. She was still searching in his eyes as if looking for something. Magee realized she was seeking understanding. Did he realize her concern? It was what he felt earlier in her office. She wasn't showing fear exactly, just that she knew something was wrong somehow. Something bigger was happening. She knew it meant things were going to change somehow. For the clinic maybe. Perhaps for her personally. She was still requesting his help to guide her through it. It was the kind of unspoken request that he found so attractive in a woman. He wanted to tell her things would be okay. He was there and ready to help. But that would wait for another time. For now, he would focus on the task at hand.

"I guess it means we have a lot to unravel then," he said. "I'll need to talk to Dr. Klein again, to get her view of the patient." Then he turned back to Anne. "So, why can't I talk to him if everything is under control now?" Magee asked her.

"You can," she said. "I said earlier you just may not get a straight answer. We've talked with him more than once since that time, and he always responds in the same way. He calmly keeps repeating the same phrase over and over."

"You mean that he warned him?" Magee asked. Anne shook her head.

"No," she said. "He says, 'Now he'll understand.'"

They didn't talk for a long time. They simply ate until each had finished their dinners. Stan had returned with another round of drinks and stated that they were being so quiet they must be 'really' enjoying the food. No one acknowledged it. Finally, Paul spoke.

"Tomorrow should be interesting," he said. "I suppose it is a good idea for you to at least try talking to the patient after we get Dr. Klein's permission of course." Magee nodded.

"I'll let her know first thing in the morning," Anne offered.

"What happens after that?" Paul asked.

"I'd like to reach out to the attorney to see if I can come to talk to him," Magee said. "Beyond that, I'll try to get a lead on the identities of the mice. They likely drove here from the city. I have some sources I can check with."

"Ok, I'll give you the attorney's info in the morning," Paul responded. "It sounds like we have a plan. I'm ready to call it a night," he added. "What about you two?" He looked first at Anne and then at Magee. They both gave a glance toward the other, then turned back toward Paul. Magee spoke first.

"I'm going to stay and have one more drink while I think about how all of these pieces fall together," he said. Anne chimed in.

"Can I stay for a bit with you," she said to Magee. "I still have some follow up questions for your agreement." Magee simply nodded. Paul made a slight frown.

"Okay. But don't stay up too late kids," he said. "I have a feeling tomorrow is going to be an interesting day."

Chapter 7

Magee waited until Paul had left the restaurant and then turned to Anne.

"Why do I have a distinct impression that he wasn't happy that we were staying behind?" he asked. She gave a small smile.

"Maybe he's jealous," she said. Magee arched an eyebrow.

"Is there something between the two of you?" he asked, hoping that there wasn't. Anne looked down at her empty glass. Then she glanced around the room looking for Stan. Magee looked around too and saw him cleaning off one of the other tables. He signaled and happened to catch Stan looking his way. Magee turned back to Anne. "I've got him," he said. "He's headed our way." He took another look around the room and noticed it had cleared out quite a bit. He glanced at his watch and saw it was 10:30. "I guess tomorrow is a working day for most of the crowd in here." He said to Anne. She looked up from her glass.

"Yes," she said, "but some will have a day off. Normally, we offer a lot for flexibility in how we create schedules.

"What about you?" Magee asked. "What kind of a schedule are you on? Anne hesitated for a moment.

"Well…" she began, "right now I'm on whatever schedule I need to be on to make sure we get this investigation off to a good start." She looked down at her glass again and then added, "I can have another drink if that's what you are wondering about." She smiled. Magee did too. Stan arrived at the table.

"I see Mr. Rosner has left. Can I get anything else for the two of you?" Stan asked.

"Let's see, Stan," Magee started, "what would you recommend as a good after-dinner drink. You know what you served us. What would be good with what we've eaten." Stan looked thoughtful for a moment.

"We have some very fine Fernet Branca. It's my personal favorite for after dinner. It's an Amara, and that will complement both your dinners. And, the best part is that tomorrow you will be absolutely fine when you awake, regardless of how much alcohol you consumed the night before," he said. He smiled. Magee glanced at Anne who nodded approval.

"Sounds great, Stan," Magee said. "Where did you learn your craft?" he added. Stan smiled again.

"I started young. My parents owned a restaurant in the city. I pretty much worked there my whole life."

"What's the name of it?" Magee asked. "I'm heading back to the city tomorrow. I'd like to see if the food there is as good as it is here." Stan paused briefly, then shook his head.

"I'm afraid you won't be able to," he said. "It's closed now. I'll be right back with the Fernet," he added as he turned and headed back toward the bar. Magee turned back to Anne.

"I guess that explains why he's so good at what he does. Been around it forever," he said. Then he added, "You said earlier that you hired him on the recommendation of the previous manager." Anne nodded. "Did he give you a resume or a list of references other than the manager's?"

"Not a resume, but he did fill out our regular application," Anne replied. "There is a section on references, and he listed at least one."

"I'd like to see the name of the reference tomorrow before I go back. Like I said earlier, the timing of his hiring may be a coincidence, but I still need to look into it." Anne smiled again.

"And like I said earlier," she offered, "based on your references I'm sure *you* will do a very thorough job." Magee laughed. He looked back toward the bar and saw that Stan was returning.

When he arrived at the table, he set down the bottle with two small glasses. He carefully filled each, handed them to Anne and Magee, then stood to wait for them to taste it. As he watched, Magee raised the glass to his mouth and poured the whole amount down in one quick drink. Then he grimaced and let out a small cough as if trying to hold in a much larger one. Stan's mouth fell open and a horrified look came over him.

"Mr. Ma...Maa...gee," he stammered. "You were supposed to sip it! It isn't whiskey!" he exclaimed. Magee sat looking down at the table. He held his hand palm up toward Stan as if shielding himself from the criticism. Small coughs continued every couple of seconds. Anne was still holding her glass in one hand but had covered her mouth with the other and was watching Magee with wide eyes. It was obvious the hand over her mouth was stifling a laugh. Multiple seconds passed with each of them holding their poses. Finally, the coughs stopped, and Magee summoned the strength to speak.

"Habit," he said weakly. The tone was hoarse. Anne dropped her hand and laughed out loud. Stan finally gained his composure and smiled. Magee brought his hand down and shook his head back and forth quickly for a moment.

"I'm so sorry, Mr. Magee," Stan said. "I should have warned you." Magee shook his head back and forth again, more slowly.

"No, Stan," he started, still a little hoarse. "Not your fault. I'm not used to sipping things I'm supposed to enjoy." He held his fist to his chest. Stan finally relaxed a bit and smiled and turned toward Anne.

"Anne, I know I don't have to warn you," he said

"No, Stan. You've served it to me before. I can handle it," she confirmed. Then she made a worried face and looked at Magee. "You okay?" she asked. He nodded but still had a pained look on his face. "Why don't we head back to my place. I have something that will take the sting off," she said. The pained look turned to relief. He nodded again. Anne stood up. "Thanks, Stan," she said in a pleasant tone. "Dinner was excellent, as usual."

"Thank you, Anne," Stan replied. "Mr. Magee, I'm so sorry I didn't tell you that the Fernet is better when sipped." Magee stood up, still holding his fist to his chest. He smiled at Stan and cleared his throat.

"Don't worry about it, Stan," he said. "I'll have to try that stuff again sometime now that I know that. Did your parents serve that in their restaurant?"

"Yes, theirs was a very upscale place. But you can find it at any good restaurant in the city."

"I'll have to remember that," Magee said. "But what you consider to be a good restaurant, and what I might think is a good one is probably different. Do you have any recommendations?" he asked.

"Oh, yes," Stan said with a smile. "I would recommend the 'The Blue Lady'". It's the best restaurant in the city." As Stan was talking, Anne had come over to his side and taken hold of Magee's arm as if he was going to need help walking. He let her help lead him toward the exit, moving slowly away from the table as Stan began to clear the dishes. When they passed through the doors to the restaurant, Anne felt Magee straighten and begin to walk normally. She eased her grip on his arm.

"Are you better?" she asked? Magee let out a slight laugh.

"I'm fine," he said. "I didn't have a problem with the drink, although I wasn't crazy about the taste." Anne started to pull her hand away from his arm. Magee reached over with his other hand and held it there. "You can leave it there," he said. "I like it." Anne smiled and moved her hand completely through the crook of his arm as they kept walking.

"So, what was that in there?" she asked.

"Did you notice his reaction when I asked him for the name of his parent's restaurant?" he said. Anne thought for a moment.

"If I remember, it took him a second to respond," Anne said.

"Exactly," Magee answered. "He never did give the name. It was almost as if he was uncomfortable telling it to me. I don't think it was natural. If my parents owned a restaurant, and I basically grew up there and am still doing what I learned there, I'd be happy to talk about the place."

"I don't know about that," Anne interjected. "I can't even get you to tell me your first name!" Magee laughed.

"No, seriously," he said. "It just wasn't the type of reaction I would expect. Yes, he could have told me that it was closed, but he probably would have talked a bit more about it." He stopped walking for a moment and turned to face her. "When I asked him about another restaurant, he gave a glowing review. He said it was the best restaurant in the city. He could have added that it's only because his Parent's restaurant closed. Either way, restaurant owners often have close ties to other restaurants of the same type. So, it will be a starting point for finding out more about him when I go back to the city." He paused as if thinking and then asked, "Did he fill out paperwork like an application for employment when you hired him?"

"Yes," she answered. "He had to fill out some of the same things you did. He listed at least one reference place of employment. Remember, he isn't that old. And besides, I had the recommendation of the previous manager."

"Did you call the reference?" he asked. Anne's shoulders slumped a little and she looked like she had realized something she didn't want to admit.

"Well, as I said, I had the recommendation of the previous manager. But I did call the place he listed and the person who answered said it was temporarily closed because it was changing owners. I guess I know now that it must have been his parents' place."

"Did you ask if you could reach the previous owners?" Magee asked. Anne's shoulders slumped a little more.

"Yes, but the person said the reason for an owner change was the death of the previous owner," Anne replied with a sigh. "I guess that means one of his parents must have died. He never mentioned that during the interview. I didn't even realize it when he said it earlier. Poor kid." Magee agreed. He knew how tough it is to lose parents. His own father had been killed in action during the Afghan war.

"I guess that could explain his reaction," Magee said. He looked around and saw they hadn't walked far away from the restaurant entrance. He turned back to Anne.

"Ok, which way now," he asked. "Are we still headed back to your place?" Anne let her jaw drop slightly.

"Ahem," she started with a stern voice, "now that I know you are not injured and needing immediate medical care, you still think I should take you back to my place?" She put her hands on her hips. Magee felt a flush.

"Sorry," he said. "I guess I just wasn't ready to call it a night. I was having too good of a time, even if we were doing more shop talk than not shop talk. I was kind of hoping I could find out a little more about you. Sort of the conversation we were having before Paul came in tonight." Anne took her hands from her hips and put her arm back through Magee's and gently pulled him in the direction they had been walking.

"And I was hoping to find out a little more about you. It's this way," she said with a smile. He smiled too.

They came to a door with a sign above it with the words 'Staff Quarters." There was a keypad to the side. Anne entered a number and the door swung open. They walked down a long hallway of doors with names on the front of each. They stopped in front of one with 'Farrow" on it and a similar keypad.

"Not very subtle, is it?" Anne said as she punched the numbers on the pad. The door opened and they stepped inside. The inside was much roomier than Magee had expected. Several lights around the room came on automatically.

There was a large and open living area with contemporary furniture. The wall beyond it was mostly glass, with a door in the middle looking out over a large patio. To his immediate left was an entrance to what appeared to be a kitchen. The left side of the open area had a well-polished oak table with four chairs. Beyond that on the left but closer to the glass wall was an entrance to another room. To the right were entrances to two other rooms. Magee let out a low whistle.

"Very nice," Magee said. "Much nicer than my room." Anne laughed.

"It's one of the perks of working here. Dr, Klein insists that the staff have very nice homes. It's all part of keeping us happy to work so far away from the city," Anne said as she walked toward the kitchen. "Why don't you take a seat over on the sofa," she said. "I'm going to have some wine. Can I get you something to drink?" Magee walked to the sofa and sat down.

"I'll just have some water, please. Unless you think I still need something to counteract the effect of the Fernet." He answered. He heard her laugh in the kitchen.

"No," she said. "I get it. You can hold your liquor."

When she returned, she brought a tall glass of water with ice and a smaller glass of red wine for herself. She handed him the water then retrieved two coasters for them from an end table drawer and placed her wine down on one.

"I know that this will sound trite, but I'm going to ask you to excuse me for one second while I slip into something more comfortable," she said. Magee smiled.

"You seem to be completely comfortable in the dress," he said. "Or maybe it just looks completely comfortable on you. Did I tell you how stunning you look?" Anne blushed.

"Yes," she said smiling, "and now it's time for you to see the real me." She walked toward the bedroom. Magee stared out the glass wall at the patio. It had been dark for a few hours now. There was a light shining down on it. Beyond it, he could see the dim outline of pine trees. It gave him an uneasy feeling. The set up didn't seem very secure. The trees provided a lot of coverage but were about eighty feet from the windows. The distance was fine, Magee thought, but it wasn't lit. If someone wanted to, they could easily hide in them and see the comings and goings of the staff members on this side of the building. They could also cross the distance in darkness and not have to worry about being seen.

He made a mental note to ask Paul about security regarding it in the morning but then decided not to. If he did, Paul would know that he had come back to Anne's place from the restaurant. He still wasn't sure if there was or had been something between Anne and Paul. He wouldn't want to ruffle Paul's feathers without good reason. Anne hadn't answered his questions earlier about her involvement with anyone else.

While he was still thinking about it, Anne came back from the bedroom. Gone were the high heels and dressy dress. Instead, she wore a loose tee top and what he considered to be a short skirt. The gold chain was still around her neck. She definitely looked more comfortable but still looked beautiful to Magee. There was an easy chair next to the sofa near the end where Magee was sitting. She plopped into it and drew up her legs on the cushion. She rested her elbow on the arm of the chair and chin on her fist and looked at Magee expectantly. He was a little caught off guard. For a moment, neither spoke. Then Magee cocked his head.

"Sooooo....," he drew out, not sure what she expected him to say, "you said it was complicated." Anne looked surprised, then smiled.

"Oh, you remembered that," she said.

"Well, hard not to remember. It wasn't an unequivocal 'no'. Anything but that leaves a man to wonder," he said, "So how 'complicated' is complicated?" Anne smiled and then frowned. She readjusted herself in the chair.

"I am thirty-five, Magee." She seemed a little irritated. "You can imagine I've had some relationships in the past. Some good. Some bad. In fact, I was married once. It didn't end well. But to give you a direct answer, I am not in any relationship right now. Not anyone here, or anyone anywhere else." Magee felt uncomfortable.

"I'm sorry," he said, "I guess it was the wrong thing to bring up." Anne smiled again.

"No, don't be sorry," she said. "I guess I overreacted. The problem is, I don't like to talk about past relationships, even the good ones. Obviously, they weren't good enough to last. So, I've learned to accept what happened in the past and go with the flow." Magee nodded.

"I think I get it," he said. "I've had a few relationships, too." Anne smiled.

"Well, I already knew that," Anne said. Magee raised an eyebrow. "I mean, I did read your file. You wouldn't let me talk about any of the personal stuff. Remember?" Magee laughed.

"I suppose it's my own fault. I should have asked you about everything that was in the thing. I'm going to have to spend some serious time reading it, and some more serious time tracking down the people who put it together." They both laughed.

"And you may want to spend some time working on your detective skills, also," Anne said as she slid off the chair and moved next to him on the sofa. "You should have been able to figure out I wasn't involved with anyone else at the moment. You said yourself that I didn't have to dress up for a business meeting. That should have told you I was dressing up for you." She reached up and put her hand around his neck and drew his head down to kiss him on the lips. It was a long and satisfying kiss.

Chapter 8

The alarm was buzzing but Magee couldn't hear it. He was already awake and in the shower. As he finished and stepped out, he quickly found it and turned it off. He checked the time. He would be meeting with Anne, Paul and Dr. Klein in another half hour. He thought back to the kiss from Anne and wished he had stayed with her longer. But that would come in time. He knew not to move too fast. Both of them had been in those kinds of relationships before. He hoped that they could find out more about each other first.

He was happy to find the attraction he felt to her from the moment she walked into Klein's office was reciprocal. He had told her so last night after their first kiss. They kissed more afterword. But as much as he enjoyed it, he eventually suggested they take it a bit slowly, considering the work ahead of them. She agreed the investigation should come first and said that she hoped it would give him the incentive to solve the mystery faster.

Before he left her, they had agreed to meet with Paul and Dr. Klein to discuss the plan for Magee to interview the patient. There would be ground rules, of course. Dr. Klein would insist. Her obligation was always to protect both a patient and any people interacting with a patient. After her last session with this patient, she wouldn't take any chances.

He started to check his mental notepad for clues about what to ask the patient but found it crowded with thoughts of Anne. He remembered the way she laughed and the way she scrunched her nose at his reference to the attorney delay. There was also the way she took his arm when she thought he needed help leaving the restaurant. And of course, he thought of her smile whenever she asked him about his first name. He realized the investigation was now going to be a little tougher.

He decided he could wing the interview. He knew that he would be reminded of things on his notepad as soon as he got back together with Anne and Paul. After dressing, he walked down to the restaurant to get some coffee.

There was a table set up near the door with coffee, tea, and different juices. Next to it were bowls of fruit and cereals, small containers of yogurt, and a variety of bread and rolls. It was the kind of set up he had seen before at business conferences he attended. He took only coffee, just as he had done at those times too. Lids were available for the cups, so he took one and began walking over to the business office.

The morning was cool but sunny, and all was quiet at the clinic. He had never lived in the country. Some of the bases he lived on as a kid were far from major cities, but the base itself was a kind of small city. Usually, trees had been removed to make way for things the military needed, and kids were never allowed to go too far from the clusters of housing. Here, birds were chirping in the forest around them with none of the noises he was used to in the city. The air smelled clean with the scent of pine. He took his time to enjoy it. Out of the corner of his eye, he saw Paul walking from his building toward the business office. When Paul saw him, he waved and changed directions to intercept Magee.

"Morning, Magee," Paul said as he extended a hand to shake. Magee took it and their handshake was as vigorous as it was yesterday when they had met. He handed Magee an index card. "This is the phone number and the name of the attorney…at least the one he gave me. By the way, how'd you sleep?" Paul asked.

"Like a baby," Magee responded.

"Alone?" Paul added. It caught Magee off guard. He thought back to the conversation at dinner. He was pretty sure he didn't tip his hand when Paul was there. It could be the way they looked when Paul came into the restaurant, but they were only having a drink at the bar. He decided he would play it straight.

"Yes," he answered. "Why do you ask?"

"She really looked good last night. I haven't seen her dress up so much in a long time," Paul replied. "She's a beautiful woman. Don't you think?" Magee nodded. *More than you know, Paul*, he thought to himself.

"Well, I will admit that," Magee said. Paul smiled.

"I had a crush on her for a long time after she came to work here," he said. He looked down at the pavement. "But I don't think I'm her type," he added. "I mean, we tried once, but it just didn't work out. It's ok, though.

I'm a big boy and I understand these things." He looked up again at Magee and added, "But just so we're clear, don't hurt her." Magee nodded. It wasn't an outright threat, but he understood that Paul wanted to protect her. He did too. He realized Paul and he had more than Jack Daniel's in common.

"You can be assured of that," Magee said. Paul smiled and they turned and walked toward the office. When they entered, Anne and Dr. Klein were standing in a conference room already talking. Paul gave a rap on the door before entering.

"Are you talking about us?" he said when they looked up.

"Of course, Mr. Rosner," Dr. Klein said. "Anne was just bringing me up to speed on the conversation you shared at dinner." She looked over to Magee. "Mr. Magee, Anne tells me that you have signed all of the necessary paperwork. I'm pleased that you are going to help us figure this out. Apparently, you've come up with some interesting thoughts already and now would like to talk to the patient those men wanted to see." Magee looked in Anne's direction but didn't make eye contact. Then looked back at Dr. Klein.

"Yes, Dr. Klein," he answered, "it seems that he tried to warn his brother about something, and I think we should find out what that was." Klein pursed her lips. She looked back at Anne and then at Paul.

"You do understand that this patient is suffering from a mental illness and anything he tells you may be completely made up to satisfy the interest of one of his personalities?" she said. "It could be even worse than it would have been a few weeks ago. He has had a significant relapse since I told him about his brother's death." She searched Magee's eyes and waited for a reaction. There was none. She sighed. "I'm just not sure," she added. Paul chimed in.

"Why don't we all sit down and talk it through," he suggested.

"Yes," Anne agreed. "Let me get some coffee, and some tea for you Dr. Klein." She left the room while the rest chose seats and sat down. Magee was the first to speak.

"If I may, Dr. Klein, is there a specific reason you don't want me to talk to the patient?" he asked. Klein cleared her throat.

"Mostly I am concerned about how it will affect him," she said. "He's already in worse shape than he was."

"Believe me, Dr. Klein," Magee started, "I also do not want to make it worse for him. So why don't you tell me his history and maybe we can figure out if it's really necessary." This seemed to set Klein at ease. It meant they may still decide not to involve the patient which would prevent further damage.

"Alright," Mr. Magee, "that seems like a good approach. I suppose I should begin with the patient's details and then fill in the history along the way." Magee nodded. "Computer," she said, "bring up the file for Robert Devereaux." On the wall was the same type of mahogany frame as the one in Klein's office. The doors swung open to reveal the screen behind them. The screen lit up with a picture of a young man. Magee estimated he must be in his early twenties. He looked fit and trim, with a rugged face and outdoor complexion. He was wearing a football uniform and holding the helmet with his hand. He was smiling widely. His eyes were bright and focused directly on the camera. The picture faded and was replaced by a page listing personal data.

Name: Robert Francis Devereaux
Born: December 5, 1995
Height: 6'2"
Weight: 180 lbs.
Race: Caucasian
Nationality: U.S. Citizen
Father: Frederic Devereaux (Deceased)
Mother: Barbara Devereaux (Deceased)
Brother: Edward Devereaux (Deceased)
Brother: Jason Devereaux (born 1985)
Education: B.A., Stanford University
Occupation: none

"Computer, pause, please," Klein said, "Note, change 'born nineteen-eighty-five' to 'deceased'." As she talked, Anne returned with coffee and tea. Klein turned to her, "Thank you, Anne. We're going over the patient's file to see if Mr. Magee still will need to interview him." Anne nodded and sat down. Magee looked over to her and finally made eye contact. She smiled. "Computer, proceed," Klein said.

"Wait," Magee interrupted. "Is the Devereaux, in this case, the same as Devereaux Holdings, the conglomerate?" Klein nodded. Magee let out a low whistle. "They have a piece of a lot of industries, but it's still a privately owned, family company."

"Yes," she said. "I told you, Mr. Magee. Some of our clients are very wealthy," she added.

"I know you did, but I wasn't thinking at that level. If I remember, they are at roughly the $50 billion level." The screen faded again to another page and more statistics. The admission date was roughly six months earlier. There was a space labeled 'Initial Diagnosis'. It contained the words 'Dissociative Identity Disorder'. There were other medical references and text typed into other spaces.

Klein interrupted the computer again.

"Computer," she said, "Show police photo at booking." The text faded away and was replaced by a new photograph. He had not changed much since the last photo. But even Magee noticed a difference in his eyes. They no longer looked directly at the camera but instead looked somewhere off in the distance. His mouth was slightly open, similar to how a very old man would sometimes look. Something inside him had changed.

"He had already been diagnosed before coming to us," Klein continued. "He had spent a month at Stanford Medical Center in Palo Alto before his brother brought him here. He had been committed by order of the court based on a charge of disorderly conduct in Palo Alto. His brother had to petition the court for guardianship first and then was able to have him transferred to our facility. Up until the charge, he had no history of problems." She paused. "I think I told you yesterday that there was nothing unusual about him. Now that we are reviewing his case, I realize that may not be the case.

"Usually, there are hints of problems as a child is growing up. But in his case, he just suddenly started acting strangely. He had just finished final exams in his senior year, which meant he had completed all of the required coursework and was qualified to graduate. The university granted his diploma while he was in their medical facility.

"At that time, he suffered from only two personalities. But by the time he came to us he had developed another. Since he's been here, he's developed a fourth. It's a bit of an unusual case. I haven't seen precisely the same thing in my work so far, but it's not inconsistent with how these disorders sometimes go." Klein paused and then spoke again to the computer. "Computer, show photo when he was transferred to us." The screen faded and a new picture appeared.

The man in the picture looked completely different from the one in the first photo, and even significantly different from the one in the second. He was no longer trim but instead had gained a significant amount of weight. He looked much older as if something had aged him prematurely. His hair had receded dramatically, and large bags had formed underneath his eyes. Klein spoke again, "Computer, pause." Then she turned to Magee. "That photo was taken when he was transferred to us. As you can see, his illness had taken a great toll on him."

"What were they feeding him that caused him to gain so much weight?" Magee asked. Klein laughed.

"I don't know," she said. "I guess they just let him eat whatever he wanted."

"It looks like he wanted a lot of things," Magee said. "What can you tell me about the other personalities he has now?" Magee asked. Klein paused for a moment as if thinking of which way to start.

"It's complicated," she said. Magee glanced at Anne and saw her smile. "From one perspective, he has a base personality. We have the details on it from what they gleaned at Stanford. They were able to bring in his brother, of course, but also people who knew him from school. The second personality seemed to come over him suddenly. One day he was normal and the next day he was doing some crazy things. When the police became involved, he was collecting things in a shopping cart and wandering around Palo Alto."

"What kinds of things did he collect?"

"Well, all sorts of odd things. He had a pillow and blanket with some dirty clothes he picked up from somewhere. There was a broken lamp, some cardboard and an empty gallon jug for water. Also, a carving knife. Those were the primary things listed in the police report." She shook her head. "His mannerisms changed, too. He had been a happy and outgoing kid, not shy about talking to anyone. But suddenly, he was acting surlier. From that point, he started yelling obscenities at anyone who happened to get too close to him. The reason the police came in the first place was that he was fighting with a store owner who asked him to move from the front of his store. When he wouldn't budge, the owner grabbed the handle of his cart and started to push it away. He jumped on the owner's back and pulled him away from the cart. When the police arrived, they had to cuff him because he resisted going with them in the car. He kept holding on to the cart and screaming. Finally, they wrestled him to the ground and got the cuffs on. Even then he was spitting at them when they forced him into the car.

"At first when they put him in the holding tank he still wasn't cooperating. They asked him his name and he said he wouldn't tell them. Then after a couple of hours, he calmed down. They finally started to get some answers. They got his name, and his brother's name and number.

"Once his brother got there, he told them who he was and convinced them to get Robert to Stanford for evaluation. It didn't take them long to diagnose him, but they admitted that this case was unusual. The standards for diagnosis didn't apply exactly. Over the first few days, they found he seemed to be switching back and forth between his original personality and the second one. They dubbed it 'the old man'. Both personalities seemed to know the other was there. Sometimes they seemed to be engaging out loud in a fight between the two of them as if no one else was even in the room. The doctors were debating between themselves as to whether this was a new type of disorder when the next personality developed. It was very much more like his original personality. It took immediate control over both the original one and the other new one. He called himself Frederick, which is, of course, the name of his father. And he acted like a father would when he discussed his normal personality. So that made the Stanford guys a whole lot more comfortable with their decision. After the medical report, the police dropped the charges.

"As I already said, they only had him for a month. They thought his case was so unusual they weren't sure they could develop an approach for treatment. One of the staff there was a resident with me years ago before I built this clinic. He suggested to the brother that, if anyone could help, it would be our place. The brother came for a visit and was sold. So, he had him transferred here. But he hasn't been back to talk to him since. He's kept in touch, though, with semi-monthly phone calls to get reports. That is, at least, until his passing." Klein paused.

Magee was still listening intently. He turned to Anne.

"Can you get me the names of all of the doctors who were involved at Stanford?" he asked. Then he turned back to Klein. "Will you provide me with a letter of reference letting them know that I am investigating his situation and need their guidance?"

"Yes, Anne can draw that up for my signature," she said, "but it may not be enough for them to chance violating the privacy policy."

"Well, I'll at least check with them first before figuring out the next step," Magee replied. "Now, what about the fourth personality?" Klein drew a breath.

"That one is three months old and represents a response to his treatment as opposed to an entirely different personality," she said. "Sometimes, a person never really regains their original personality. It simply is pushed down too far inside by the other ones that develop. One of the newer ones becomes dominant and then pretty much stifles the others. In some of the cases, I've had they never reappear. In other cases, they're always there but just kept in check by the dominant one.

"A part of my therapy requires that I keep trying to bring out new ones until I find the one personality I think can function well with others. This last one seemed to have that kind of potential. He calls himself Mark Richard. In some ways, it is close to his original personality, but it seems far more mature than how that original one was described. It's almost like it is an older, more stoic version of what he had been. You know, as you age you find yourself more accepting of things, more tolerant and patient with others. I know we all reach that stage at different times in our lives, so maybe you haven't experienced it yet." Magee laughed.

"I think I know what you mean, Dr. Klein. There are plenty of days I wake up and feel really old," he said. She laughed too.

"Anyway," she continued, "the new personality asserted itself and seems to have retained control since then. We were having good therapy sessions, and he began to heal himself physically, as well. He had been an athlete, so he began to work out in the patient gym. He had a complete routine that he performed regularly, starting slowly with just three days a week. But over time he has built up to six days a week. He also started to read voraciously. We keep several books on hand, for patients who are capable of reading. If they are having good results with the therapy, they also tend to enjoy the reading. In his case, though, he asked if he could order books and have them delivered. When he wasn't exercising or in therapy sessions, he was reading."

"What kind of books was he having delivered?" Magee asked.

"A wide range, really," She said. "Many were books by philosophers, but he also had some on medicine and physiology, and ones on religion, too.

"Things were improving so well that I actually thought we would reach a release point soon," she said, shaking her head. "But of course, that's changed since his brother's death." She shook her head again. "He's not the same since I gave him the news. I mean, this new personality is still in complete control, but it seems more despondent like he's lost hope. I'm not sure what he was hoping for and so far, I haven't been able to get him to open up again."

Magee found that he had been leaning forward while listening. He sat back in his seat.

"Well, I think, Dr. Klein, that is an *excellent* reason for me to talk to him," he said. "He knows that he warned his brother. And he'll know I am investigating circumstances that involve his brother's death. Maybe solving this mystery is something for him to hope for."

Chapter 9

Once everyone agreed that it made sense to proceed, they spent the next two hours planning how it would be conducted. They determined the interview should take place late in the afternoon. Klein had been treating the patient for a while now and explained that was the time when the fourth personality was most cooperative. She hadn't had a formal session with him since she told him about his brother's death, but she had been observing him every day as he interacted with others in therapy sessions.

Mornings were typically rough as there seemed to be some battling between the two other personalities, Frederick and the old man. She said Robert seems to be always dormant now. But in the afternoon, Mark Richard tends to take control and wants to work on getting better.

For Magee, it meant that he would likely stay one more night before heading back to the city. That made him happy because he could spend a little more time with Anne. He thought he saw her smile just slightly when Klein suggested it.

Klein would spend the first few minutes of the interview alone, probing to gauge if there was any reason not to proceed. The others would be watching from the observation room.

If she concluded it was safe, she would do a brief introduction of Magee, why he was there and why she felt it might be helpful if the patient could answer a few of his questions. She said she would be comfortable with a session as long as one hour but did not want to go on beyond that point because she felt it would be counterproductive. Paul spoke up at this point.

"But what if we don't have answers to all the questions Magee has to ask?" he asked her. She frowned, but the frown quickly softened.

"Mr. Rosner," she said gently, "I understand it's important to get as much information as possible, but I've found it's best to limit this type of session to less than an hour." She stopped momentarily to see Paul's reaction, then added, "What I mean is that a session with a lot of questions is taxing on a patient's mind. It's one thing if the patient is asking questions or controlling the conversation, but when someone else is doing it the patient tends to tire.

"It's understandable if you think about it. We are creatures of communication. Usually, personalities are fighting to express themselves. That's why different ones become dominant at different points. We still don't know much about the triggers. In any event, the dominant one finds it difficult to maintain control if they are bearing the brunt of answering a lot of questions. And if Mark Richard loses control, we could be talking to the old man or Frederick, and we couldn't really trust what they might tell us. In fact, they may try to counter everything that Mark Richard tells us because they want to be the ones who dictate what will happen." She paused and looked at the others. Everyone nodded. Magee spoke next.

"I think in an hour I can get everything I need for now," he said. "Once I track down information from the others back in the city, I may have more questions."

"You're probably right, Magee," Paul said. "There are a lot of other things to look at that this guy doesn't even know about."

"Okay, that's settled then," Dr. Klein said. She turned to Magee. "As for the context of the questions, Mr. Magee," she said, "I'd like it if you can avoid giving him the impression that there was foul play involved in his brother's death. As we talked before, based on the identified cause, it can't really be murder." Magee seemed to think for a moment before responding.

"I can agree not to make that impression, Dr. Klein," he replied, "but I have to say at this point we actually can't be certain that it was the cause that was identified." Klein looked surprised.

"But that was what we were told by the Attorney," she said.

"Yes," Magee answered, "but that was in a phone conversation with someone. He may or may not have been who he said he was. For all we know, someone may have a lot of reasons to make it seem like the death was from natural causes. We can't even be sure where he died at this point. I need to get the actual death certificate and see for myself what cause was listed. If he died in the hospital and a doctor signed the death certificate with that explanation, money could have influenced the conclusion. And if he died elsewhere without being transferred to a hospital a coroner would have been called to the scene." Again, Klein looked surprised.

"Surely, you're not suggesting that a doctor, and other members of staff present when he died, or even a coroner would put a false reason in?" she asked. Magee nodded.

"It's exactly what I am suggesting. I've seen it happen. Now that I know who we are dealing with here I'm concerned this case has become a lot more involved," he paused slightly, "and a lot more dangerous," he added. He saw Paul nod. He glanced at Anne and saw the worried look on her face. He wanted to tell her not to worry because he would be there, but he knew that would have to wait until later. Klein appeared to still be surprised by his statement. She was a doctor. Magee understood that it would be hard for her to believe a doctor would agree to compromise medical ethics for a sum of money. Finally, she spoke.

"Okay, Mr. Magee," she said with uncertainty in her voice, "but I still would request that you not explain any of that to the patient." Magee smiled and nodded that he agreed. "So, it sounds like we have a plan," she added, "let's agree to meet in the Treatment Center at 4:00 P.M. In the meantime, I have some other patients I need to attend to." She excused herself and left the rest of them still sitting in the conference room. Anne spoke first.

"Do you really think the brother was killed?" she asked Magee. He nodded and looked at Paul.

"I agree, Anne," Paul said. "The amount of money involved is insane. It just means that a lot more people are going to think it's worth it to run some sort of scam. Even if they don't score big. Sometimes it's easier in the end for someone with a lot of money to just pay small amounts rather than fight about it."

"Right now, it's the most likely reason for the whole incident that occurred," Magee added. "Somehow the mice figure to cash in from the brother's death. They just didn't realize that it would be so tough to get in here to do it. I'm not sure what the angle is, though. But at least we understand why they would be motivated." Anne looked anxious.

"So that makes it more dangerous," she said with a grimace.

"I'm afraid so," Magee said with a nod. "But I wouldn't worry too much about it. Paul will be here at the clinic and will probably tighten security even more. I'll be doing the investigation in the city and nailing down who we truly need to be concerned about." He stopped to see if she had relaxed. He saw she hadn't.

"Look, these guys have to run a scam to score anything. They know there isn't any money here. Whatever they're up to requires a plan which convinces someone to give them part of the family's money. Short of kidnapping the kid for ransom, that involves a complicated sequence of events," he told her. Then he added, "and if they did kidnap the kid, they would try to do it quietly, so no police had to be called. They wouldn't hurt anyone here. Even then, getting paid off would be difficult. The brother that would control the money for the payoff just died. The estate now is going to be tied up for a while so they wouldn't even know who to negotiate with." Finally, he saw her relax a bit. She started to speak but then glanced at Paul and stopped. There were a few moments of silence. Finally, Paul spoke.

"Alright, we have some time before the interview," he said. "I'm going to go back and review my security options. I think I may have to bring in some extra help, just in case."

"Do you need any recommendations from me?" Magee asked. Paul shook his head.

"No," he said, "I've got some friends that I can count on. Guys I served with. I'll bring in two or three to start, and we'll make sure we're protected here. Will you be okay while you're asking questions in the city?" Magee nodded.

"Yeah, I've got friends, too," he said with a smile. "Mostly the kind with badges who help me out from time to time. They'll be there if I need them."

"You going to tell them about all this?" Paul asked.

"No, only what I need to. They trust me. They understand that I will call them in when I need legal enforcement, and they don't have to worry about me being stupid before that." Paul laughed. Magee looked over at Anne. "You probably have regular work to attend to," he said.

"It can wait!" she said a little annoyed. "I think maybe we should discuss some more details." Magee looked up at Paul who smiled and threw his hands up.

"As I said, I'm going to make some calls to my friends to see how quickly they can come," he said. "I'll see you guys at 4:00 in Treatment." He turned and left. Magee looked back at Anne.

"I get the sense that you want to talk," he said. It was posed like a question.

"Of course, I want to talk," Anne shot back. "I wasn't worried about me being hurt. I was worried about you." She looked down at the table. "You're going to be poking around in the city, asking questions that probably someone doesn't want you asking. I want to know you will be safe." She looked at him expectantly. He smiled.

"You heard what I told Paul, right?" he said. It didn't seem to satisfy her. Magee scanned around the room and saw nothing that looked like a camera. Then he got up and closed the conference room door. He sat down in the chair beside her and twisted her chair around to face him. She was still looking down and not at him. He placed his hand under her chin and lifted her face to where he could look in her eyes. "Look, he said. I meant what I said about my friends. I've been working in that city for a long time. I've helped them, and they've helped me. They'll watch my back until I tell them it's not necessary." He saw her choke up a bit. She cleared her throat.

"It's just that...," she started and then paused. She reached up and wiped a tear from the corner of her eye. "I mean, I'm just getting to know you and already I can't stand the idea of something happening to you. I was looking forward to getting to know you a lot better." He smiled again.

"And you will. I'm going to get to know you a lot better, too," he said. "I'd try to do that right now if it wasn't for this little investigation *thing* we have to do first," he added. She laughed and then relaxed a little more. Then she reached over and kissed him again. This time it was just a short kiss, but still on the lips. He kissed back at the same time. "What do you say we go get some lunch," he said. "I'll buy." Anne laughed again.

"You know there wasn't any buying last night. The restaurant is free to all who stay here, including the staff. It's just one of the perks," she said.

"Okay," Magee said. "I'll pretend to buy. Then I'll interview you and find out everything I need to know!" Anne shook her head.

"I'm not *that* easy, Magee," she said as she stood up.

As they walked over to the restaurant, Magee talked about how much he enjoyed his walk this morning. He told her about being used to city sounds and never really living in the country. She smiled and told him she grew up in the country. She was from North Dakota, which was virtually all country and no city. She hadn't left for the city until she went to college.

"Where was that?" Magee asked.

"Harvard," Anne said. Magee looked impressed.

"Harvard," he repeated. "Pretty smart, huh? I guess you singlehandedly destroy the dumb blonde theory." She laughed.

"Oh, I did my share of acting dumb when I wanted to," she said.

"Why? Why would you deliberately act dumb?" he asked. She stopped walking and turned to him. He stopped with her.

"Really?" she asked. "Really, Magee?" she paused for a moment. "Most men don't like smart women. So, I played dumb when I was interested in someone until I figured out just the right amount of smart to be. If he turned out to be really smart, then I knew I could show that I was at least a little smart too. And if he wasn't, I just had fun until it didn't work anymore," she added, "which always came eventually." She began walking again.

"Is that what happened with your husband?" he asked.

"No, of course not," she said. "I wouldn't have married him if he wasn't a little smart, but he had a variety problem."

"What does that mean?

"He liked a variety of women, smart, dumb, tall, blonde, brunette, all of 'em, at once."

"Oh," Magee said, "that doesn't sound so smart."

"Worked out better for me in the end," Anne said. "I wouldn't be working for Dr. Klein if I had stayed with him. And I really like my job here."

"You seem very good at it," Magee replied. "You have a lot of responsibility and she does seem to depend on you." Anne nodded.

"Yes, I know," she said, "and that's one of the reasons I like my job because I'm helping her. I think she is doing great work here. Do you know how many of her patients she's actually helped become well enough to leave and live mostly normal lives?" Magee winced a little as he remembered his sarcasm when Dr. Klein told him about her success rate.

"Well, she did mention something," he said. Anne looked curious. "I made a little joke when she told me about it." Anne frowned. "But she made a joke right back after I did," Magee quickly added. Anne smiled again.

"I'm sure she wasn't offended," she said. "She's very patient with people."

"Yes," Magee said. "I saw the way she answered Paul earlier. But it's still weird to me that she calls him Mr. Rosner. She doesn't call you Ms. Farrow."

"Oh, I know," Anne responded, "but that's mostly because Paul was a patient of hers long before this clinic, in fact, one of her first." Magee nodded.

"I know. Paul told me the story."

"So, it's part of the way she thinks about him," Anne said. "When she's treating someone, she usually uses their first name. But once treatment ends, she always addresses the person formally. She told me it's a sign of respect as if it's a title they've earned."

"Interesting," Magee said. Then he looked up. "We're here."

They entered the lobby and Magee used his key to open the door leading to the restaurant. There were others seated around the restaurant, but not as many as had been there the night before. There was a buffet set up in an open area of the middle. Magee scanned the contents. It had an assortment of salads, two types of soup, multiple choices of bread and lunchmeat. A selection of fruits was at the end of the table. The soup was the only hot dish available.

"Everything looks pretty good, and easy as well," he remarked. Anne nodded.

"It's made to be simple," she said. "We don't have a lot of staff working in the restaurant. You've met Stan. He's usually around to serve dinner for everyone. But for the other meals, we focus on self-service."

"That's all I need," Magee said. Anne walked up and grabbed a dish and bowl.

"I'm going to take some salad and soup, and I'll meet you at that table over there," Anne said, pointing at a corner. "Don't forget to grab something to drink. You'll find that set up on the bar. Magee glanced at it and saw beverages lined up.

"Okay," he said. "I'm going to make a sandwich and see you at the table." He walked up and down the table trying to figure out exactly what he wanted.

She finished first and was already seated when he arrived. Magee looked around the rest of the restaurant before sitting down.

"Does Stan ever come in at lunch?" he asked.

"Once in a while," Anne replied, "but not usually. Remember, he's the manager. That means he has to do all of the administrative stuff even for the patients' meals, and then serve at night. He gets a couple of nights off a week, but other than that he's always around. It's a big job."

"I can imagine," Magee said. "But he seems very good at it. He learned well. I'd like to see how the new owners are getting along with his parent's restaurant." Suddenly Anne looked as if she realized something. She put her fork down.

"Magee," she said, "I just remembered. I meant to tell you this last night after we left the restaurant, but with all of your 'acting' and then asking me if we were still going back to your place, I forgot." Magee waited. She continued, "The restaurant he named for you to try, 'The Blue Lady'?" she said as if it was a question.

"Yes," he said.

"That was the reference he listed."

Chapter 10

The conversation on the walk to Anne's office after lunch was focused on Stan. Magee still wasn't sure if it was coincidence or something else. Anne had suggested that the restaurant had probably reopened under the new owners by now. Stan was probably just sending a customer their way.

Magee admitted that was a possibility. But he also told Anne that if people are working a scam, sometimes someone is placed close to the target for information purposes. He said It would be easy for him to check with the restaurant when he returned to the city. That would either confirm it as a coincidence or not. If not, he would figure out the next step.

"I'd like to use your computer for some research on the Devereaux's," Magee said. "Is that alright?"

"Of course," Anne replied. "I'm kinda interested in them as well now." She pointed at her chair. "You should sit there, and I'll read over your shoulder." Magee sat down. Anne leaned over and placed her hands on the keyboard. "I just have to log in." Her shoulder was brushing his while she typed. He could feel her warmth and smell her hair. He could hear her breathing softly. Part of him wanted to forget the research and the whole investigation for now. He wanted instead to take her in his arms and kiss her again. When she finished, she pulled back and stood just over his shoulder.

"Well I'm glad that's over," he said with relief. She gave him a curious look. "With you being so close, I didn't feel like working." Anne blushed and smiled.

"Waiting may be harder than we thought. You'd better work quickly," she said. Then she leaned down and kissed him on the cheek.

Instinctively, Magee scanned her office for cameras. She noticed and shook her head. "We don't have those in the offices. Only outside, and in some places where we deal with patients." He smiled and turned toward the computer.

He began the search by typing in Devereaux Holdings. The results appeared quickly. At the top of the list was a preview text under the heading of Devereaux Holdings, Inc. He clicked on the link that took him to Wikipedia. A long article appeared, and he began to read. Anne had her hand on his shoulder and was reading from behind him. She seemed able to keep up as he scrolled down through the summary and into the history section.

There, it explained the creation of the original company, Iron River Oil and Refining Company. It was exploiting a new thermal cracking process for oil refinement, based on a patent by Frederick Devereaux. Eventually, Frederick passed away and the company passed into the hands of Frederick Junior, his son. To honor his father, the junior Devereaux renamed the company Devereaux Oil. The son proved to be an extremely skilled businessman who believed strongly in the growth of assets and not necessarily always within the oil industry. After several years of aggressive acquisitions, he formed an overall holding company for several well-managed companies, across different business sectors.

For the most part, the details described a chronological picture of simple growth, as many of the companies were approached over time and succumbed to bids from Frederick Devereaux, Junior. Forty-four companies were acquired. Many were related to the original business of petroleum and refining. Chemical companies were an early favorite. Eventually, they included companies of many diverse types. Frederick seemed to find the ones that had great potential but were struggling. Typically, they lacked a solid management team.

In his youth, his father had required that he work during times he was not in school. He always had him doing small jobs around the company offices. He would later say his education at work was always more valuable than his degree programs at Massachusetts Institute of Technology.

The article went on for several paragraphs listing the acquisitions and subsequent changes to the structure of the holdings. Finally, it transitioned into the next section, one describing the environmental record of the company. Again, in this section, there was a list of details about a series of events that involved the units of Devereaux Holdings. The events identified specific units as being culpable for some amount of environmental harm or safety issues and described agreements for clean-up activities or fines of restitutions. The descriptions seemed to contain a significant amount of criticism of the company, but Magee concluded that the record, in general, demonstrated good corporate citizenship.

The following section was a list of political activities, including contributions to various political action groups or think-tank organizations. Magee found this section to be a bit out of place with most of the other information. It seemed to focus more on the individual family members' various activities and did not directly relate to the businesses. He noticed that three family member names were highlighted, indicating he could go directly to a page with information about those individuals. He started with Frederick Senior.

The article was not as lengthy as the one describing the holdings. There was a brief section about his early childhood describing him as the son of a Swiss immigrant newspaper worker and the daughter of a Texas rancher. His parents were not considered extraordinarily wealthy, but they were able to provide him with a comfortable childhood and good education, sending him first to Rice University in Texas and then MIT for a master's degree in Chemical Engineering.

Upon graduation, he found work for a growing Texas oil company, where he conceived of his thermal cracking process. Because of a dispute regarding the ownership of the patent, he left that company and worked for several years overseas in what was then the Soviet Union as a consultant.

Eventually, he was able to leave the Soviet Union and return to the United States. He married a girl he met at Rice. She was the daughter of a wealthy Houston oilman, who provided him with a loan to purchase Iron River Oil and Refining. His father-in-law also took an interest in the company but later gave his shares to his daughter as a gift.

Frederick Senior's experience in the USSR left him with a strong dislike for socialism and the heavy hand of a central government. Much of the political activity described in the previous article was devoted to causes that protected democratic ideals and capitalism.

In a description of his death near the end of the article, there was a quote from Frederick Junior stating that his father was always lecturing him on the evils of big government and the imposition of regulations on business concerns.

Magee returned to the previous article describing the holdings. This time he clicked on the link for Frederick Junior. The screen blinked and filled with a fresh article. There were similar descriptions for his childhood, and some of the same quotes found on the Devereaux Holdings page, including the one regarding his working education. Beyond that, it also talked about his Engineering degrees from MIT, one in Chemical Engineering, one in Electrical Engineering, and a master's in Business Administration. Magee looked back toward Anne, who was still standing behind him.

"It looks like he was even smarter than you," he said. She gave him a quick but light punch in the arm. "Ow," he said, pretending that it hurt.

"Right," she said, mockingly. "I'm lucky I didn't punch you harder. That arm is like a rock." He shrugged.

"I try to stay in shape," he said. Then he turned back to the screen and continued reading. Most of the information was very positive, describing him as a business wonder, and, also a very generous and deeply religious man. One article stated he had given more than one billion dollars to charity. There were several sources of descriptions from news sources or business reports comparing him to other, more well-known businessmen. Warren Buffet, Steve Jobs and Bill Gates were among those listed. The article also described several accomplishments, some of which were in the original article he read.

Toward the end of the discussion, there was information about his death. They both stopped reading and looked at each other, then back to the page. He had died suddenly. The cause listed was an Aortic aneurysm. Magee took his fingers off the keyboard and pushed back away from the desk.

"I suppose it could be genetic," he said. Anne nodded.

"Or it could be a coincidence," she said. Magee smirked.

"You know how I feel about those. Let's hope it isn't that'" he said. He was pensive for a moment, then turned back to the keyboard and opened another search page. "Time to go to the privy," he said.

"Isn't that a Navy term for toilet?" Anne asked.

"Yeah," he said. "But it's also something else I have to use from time to time." He typed the letters PIVN.pin into the search line. After a few seconds, a page appeared. It wasn't like most other web pages. It was simple. There was a plain box in the middle of the page with a line inside it. Magee positioned the cursor at the beginning of the line and typed a string of letters that did not appear to be a word. He pushed enter.

A moment later, another screen appeared. It had a similar box with a line. Magee typed again. This time only asterisks appeared as he typed. In a moment the screen refreshed with a four-digit number. Magee took out his cell phone and sent a text message to someone, using the four digits as the last part of the telephone number. His phone dinged as he received a reply. At the same time, a new page was delivered to the screen with the same type of box and line. Magee glanced at his phone and typed in the response he had received. The word "Welcome" appeared on the screen, along with a short-list of menu items. There was also text describing warnings about unauthorized use, details of punishments for violating Federal laws and so on. Magee paused for a moment and turned to Anne, who had a curious look on her face.

"The other information we were looking at was all the stuff available on Wikipedia," he said, "which is just public knowledge. It's great for a general view of whomever you are looking at, but if you need to go deeper, you need to tap into any significant research that has been done in the past.

"Once anyone becomes anyone, their lives are pretty much open season for cataloging information about them," he added. "And that's level one of information. It's mostly what everyone gets to see. But there is the next level, which includes things that most people never will know. Mostly the next level is made up of things that are just embarrassing, things that we don't want someone else to know about, but those things aren't illegal.

"Then there is the third level, Dark-Web, Silk-Road kind of stuff. Those are things that are illegal and could get someone put in jail or worse, depending on what it is. All of us have secrets of some sort. My profession is mostly about secrets. I spend most of my time trying to find out things that someone wants to know about someone else.

"Sometimes, they are good secrets, and sometimes they are bad secrets. But either way, it's my job to find out what they are, and then tell that to someone who is going to pay me for them." Anne frowned slightly.

"You're making your work sound a little, well, I don't know, sordid, I guess," She said. "It's like you're invading people's privacy." He nodded.

"I know. But you don't have to look at it that way. For example, Paul had someone do a background check on me because it made sense. You wanted to find out if I could do the job I needed to do because it was important to determine if there was some danger based on what happened. From what you told me after you reviewed the file, you thought I could."

"That's true," she said.

"And sometimes," he said, "you find out things you wouldn't like. If you were hiring an accountant, it would be good to find out if there was embezzlement in his past." Anne laughed.

"In your case, I could find out your first name is actually Abner," she said. A shocked look came over Magee's face. She suddenly realized she may have accidentally guessed his first name. She stiffened and looked worried. "But...but....but, that's not really it, is it?" Then it was Magee's turn to laugh.

"Got you," he said with a smile. She looked relieved. "Anyway, there is a website used by some P.I.'s where you can find out anything that any P.I. has already found on someone. But there are strict rules. Access is limited to a group of P.I.'s who have demonstrated they can handle the rules. Once in a blue moon, someone does violate them, and that person loses access for a very long time."

Anne watched as Magee selected the word "name" from the menu. A window popped up with a line for text entry. He typed "Frederick Devereaux" and pushed enter. A swirling circle indicated it was searching and a line of text appeared: No Information found. Magee sat straight up in the chair, put his hands down on his thighs and stared at the screen for a long time.

"This isn't supposed to happen," he said, shaking his head back and forth slightly. He placed his hands back on the keyboard pushed the back arrow. The menu appeared again. He repeated the process but got the same result. He repeated the steps but this time added Junior to the name. Still no results. Then he substituted Jason, Edward, Barbara and finally Robert, while trying again. Each time the result was the same. He reached for his cell phone and dialed a number. Anne remained quiet as he waited for someone to answer.

"Hello, Magee," he heard the voice from the phone say. "It's been a while!"

"Straight Cell, unsecured, Charlie," Magee said into the phone.

"Understood," was the reply. "How can I help?" Magee put the phone on speaker and laid it on the desk so that Anne could hear.

"There's a situation on the privy," he said. "Missing info."

"One sec," Charlie replied. They could hear keyboard clicks in the background. "Name?" Charlie added.

"Devereaux, Frederick, of Devereaux Holdings," Magee said.

"Hold on," Charlie said.

"Right," Magee replied. He pushed the mute button and turned to Anne. "The guy on the line is a technical support person for this site. He's the first level. Then there are higher levels if he can't solve the problem."

"What *is* the problem, Magee?" Anne said. Magee frowned.

"Well," he started, "this shouldn't be happening. I guarantee that Devereaux Holdings has been investigated before and info has been added. No one gets that wealthy without some level of investigation, and there is a group of people working for the organization that runs the network whose jobs are to research the sources and post the relevant information."

"Who decides what is relevant?"

"The same group," Magee answered. "There are strict standards about what must go on and what should not go on. But there is information on virtually everyone wealthy. Bill Gates, for example, has been investigated several times for different reasons. One of the investigations is rumored to have been funded by Steve Jobs. That isn't expressly stated on the site, though, because it's only a rumor. But in general, aside from attending a few raucous parties in his college days, the only things you will find out on privy are facts about how he made his wealth, and how he spends it. He's managed to stay pretty squeaky clean. Warren Buffet the same way."

"I suppose people are always curious about how people get so rich, figuring they must be doing something illegal," Anne said. Magee nodded.

"Yes," he said, "and there should be something on the Devereaux's. But if there was, it isn't there anymore. Makes no sense. I don't remember anything like that happening before." As Magee finished the sentence, there was a reply from the phone.

"Hey, Magee," Charlie was saying, "You're right. There seems to be a problem here. There should be info there, but I'm not seeing anything either." There was more typing. "I'm opening a case for you. But it may take a while before someone gets back to you."

"I understand, Charlie," Magee said. "Just text me the case number and I'll wait till they get back to me."

"Roger that, Magee," Charlie answered. "Stay safe." There was a click as he disconnected. Magee turned back to Anne.

"It might take some time to find out why this happened," he said. "But this case seems to be getting more and more interesting by the minute."

"Tell me more about what you were thinking you would find," Anne said.

"I was thinking I might find out more about the organization itself," Magee replied. "I mean, the details of an investigation would describe the individuals who are a part of the business, what their roles are, how long they have been in those roles. That kind of thing. Usually, the people at the top know something about the people they work with. They tend to socialize together at events. Families know other families. Husbands and wives of senior management form kind of a network of support for those who are doing the actual work. It would give me more people to talk to for leads."

"I guess that's sort of what happens here," Anne offered. "I try to get our people involved so we develop friendships. So many of the people are away from their families so we kind of stick together to support one another," she added. Magee nodded.

"Yeah," Magee said, "Sometimes I regret not working in that sort of organization. But I've almost always been a loner." Anne frowned.

"That's sad," she said. "But you've had some relationships you said. And there were some listed in your file."

"I hope that file didn't go into any details," he said with an attitude. Anne laughed.

"No, nothing like that," she said. "Although one seemed to last a long time." Magee's expression softened and he looked away. "Oh," she said, "I hope I didn't bring up something that you didn't want me to." Magee looked back and smiled.

"No, it's fine," he said. "It was a long time ago."

"Speaking of time," Anne said, "we'd better head over to the treatment center. It's almost Four."

Chapter 11

Anne led Magee down a hallway through the treatment center and into a small room. Klein and Paul were already there. It had a large window that allowed them to look into an adjacent room. There was a similar window on the opposite side of that room. Magee realized it was like a lot of interrogation rooms he had seen in police stations throughout his career. Both windows were mirrored so the room's occupants would not see the observers. He could see the outline of what appeared to be a door next to the window on the other side, and the reflection of a door from his side in the mirror. Two, comfortable-looking chairs were in the center of the room. Each had a swivel writing surface attached on one side. A wooden folding chair had been placed beside the one closest to the glass he was looking through. Klein was the first to speak.

"I will go in alone and get settled. Once I'm prepared, I will open the patients' door and allow him to enter," she said. "I have to determine who I am talking to before we proceed. Then I'll explain to him that we must ensure his rights are protected during the estate process following his brother's death and that we've hired you to investigate how it is being handled. I'll ask him if he is willing to answer a few questions from you." She paused to see his reaction.

"It sounds like a good explanation," he said.

"Fine," she added. "If he says no, give me some time to encourage him. I think he'll come around. You'll be hearing everything through a speaker, so I'll ask you to come in when it's time." Magee nodded. Klein picked up a tablet from a table as she opened the door and entered the room. They watched as she sank into the seat closest to their window. Just as the chair in her office had, it seemed to make her already small frame look smaller. Once she was sitting, she pushed a button on the tablet.

"She just turned on the speaker," Anne whispered to Magee. Klein pushed another button. "Now she's unlocked the patient door," she added. Klein put the tablet down and waited. A moment later the door opened, and Robert Devereaux walked into the room.

He looked fit again. He had dropped much of the weight he had gained in his admission photo. He had a serious look on his face but seemed relaxed. He was wearing light blue medical scrubs; the kind doctors or nurses usually wear. Magee turned to Anne.

"Why does he look like a doctor?" he asked her.

"That's what all of our patients wear," she said. "They're really easy to launder and we can buy them by the bulk, which is cheaper. Remember, I have to control the expenses," she added. "Otherwise, I wouldn't be able to hire high-priced investigators." Magee laughed and turned back to the window.

Devereaux's eyes were focused and alert as he scanned the room. He saw the folding chair next to the one Klein was sitting in and seemed to smile slightly before sitting in the chair opposite of her.

"Hello, Dr. Klein," he said. "How are you today?"

"Hello," she answered, "Who am I speaking with today?"

"It's me," he answered, "Mark Richard," Anne whispered to Magee.

"This is how she always starts a session."

"Well, hello, Mark Richard," Klein replied. "It's good to see you. How are you doing."

"The same as I was yesterday, and the day before that, and pretty much every day since my brother's death," he replied with a frown. Klein waited a moment before she spoke next.

"But you noticed the extra chair, didn't you?" she said. Mark Richard smiled.

"Yes, I guess you caught me," he said. "Is it possible we're going to have a guest today?" he added with a tease of excitement in his voice. Klein studied his face as if looking for something. Anne whispered again to Magee.

"It looks like she's evaluating whether he truly is who he says," she said. "She may not have anticipated that reply."

"How would you feel about that, Mark Richard," Klein asked.

"I guess it depends," he shot back. "Is it another doctor?" Klein shook her head.

"No, it's actually an investigator who wants to ask you a few questions," she said. "It's someone we have hired because we think it is important to protect your rights during the settlement process for your brother's estate."

"Is it an attorney?" Devereaux asked. Klein shook her head again.

"No," she said, "but it is someone who will investigate the details of how the settlement is being handled and write a report for us. Your situation is unique because of your admission to our facility. We want to be sure the appropriate actions are being taken to preserve your rights. And right now, we aren't sure that's happening." Devereaux looked puzzled.

"Why not?" he asked.

"It's complicated," she said. Magee couldn't help glancing at Anne when he heard it. Anne just kept watching the interaction between Devereaux and Klein.

"I'm sure you must have been exposed to some of the issues that come up when the attorneys settled your father's estate after his death," she said.

"Not really," he replied. "My brother handled everything. I mean, I knew some of the details, but I was busy with school, and he was already done with that. He had been working for the company for a while and was ready to take over for my father if something happened to him."

"Then it's probably important that you talk to the investigator we hired," Klein said. "Since you're here at this time, he's going to make sure we get all of the facts about how the settlement will occur, and we relay those back to you. Right now, you aren't considered legally able to make your own decisions. But I hope, based on your therapy, that you soon will be. Then you'll be able to decide how to proceed and you'll have a record of what transpired." Devereaux's eyes seemed to brighten at that thought.

"Okay," he said. "I'd like that." Klein smiled.

"Alright, I'll signal him." She turned to the window and motioned for Magee to enter. Anne touched his arm.

"Remember to call him Mark Richard," she said, "not his real name." Magee nodded. Paul had been standing by the door and was ready to open it.

"Be on your guard in there," he said. "Sometimes these patients can be tricky. I'll be right in there if anything happens," he added before pulling the door open.

Devereaux didn't move from the chair as Magee entered but kept an eye on him the whole time. Magee smiled and extended his hand as he walked in.

"Hello, Mark Richard," he said, "My name is Magee." Devereaux waited for him to reach his seat and held his hand out. Magee took it, but Devereaux's arm was limp. He wasn't actually participating in the handshake. Instead, he was letting Magee move his hand up and down. His face was placid, and he said nothing as Magee sat down in the folding chair.

"Thank you for taking the time to answer some questions," Magee said. Devereaux frowned.

"Did I really have a choice?" he asked sarcastically. "I'm stuck here until I can convince Dr. Klein that I'm okay now. So, I have plenty of time." Klein looked surprised.

"I thought you said you'd like to talk with him, Mark Richard," she said. "it's going to help you when you are better."

"I did say that, Doctor. But I can change my mind, can't I?" he replied. Klein sat up straight in her chair. Her face looked alarmed. Her brow was furrowed.

"Are we still talking to Mark Richard?" She asked with a concerned voice. Devereaux didn't answer right away. He sat back as if deep in thought. His face was slightly contorted. Klein and Magee watched as he shook his head back and forth several times. Finally, his face relaxed and he spoke again.

"Yes, Dr. Klein," he said. "I'm still here. Sorry about that." He smiled and then added, "We haven't actually had anyone else present with us in our other sessions, have we? I mean, other than other doctors. I guess it's just the stress of having to deal with something new."

"It's okay, Mark Richard," Klein said. "I'm pleased with the way you handled it. You *are* making progress." She added a smile. Magee took the opportunity to speak.

"I'm sorry if I've caused you any stress, Mark Richard," he said. "It isn't my intent."

"No problem," Devereaux said. "I think I understand what your job is going to be. How can I help?" Magee cleared his throat.

"Really, it's just a matter of a few questions to help me get started," he said. "I don't know any of the individuals who are involved with the settlement process yet. There is a man who identified himself as your brother's attorney. One of the staff here had a call with him." Magee pulled the index card from his pocket. "His name is Schwartzman, but other than that, we don't know who is actually handling all of the details. Does that name sound familiar to you?" Devereaux shook his head.

"No," he replied, "it isn't one of the people who worked on my father's estate. In fact, it wouldn't have been someone my father would have worked with. The name sounds Jewish, doesn't it?" Magee and Klein exchanged glances.

"Yes," Magee said, "It does. Would that have been a problem for your father?

"Well, yes. He didn't like them," Devereaux admitted. "I think it was something that got handed down to him from my Grandfather. He wasn't fond of Jews. I think that's because he was so Christian. He was very religious." Devereaux made a skeptical face. "But Jason wasn't. He doesn't care about any of that. He wants to have the best people that he can find doing the jobs that need to get done. He doesn't care about color, or size, or gender, or anything like that. He gets along with everybody. He..." Devereaux stopped suddenly. He looked like he realized he was referring to his brother in the present tense. Tears filled his eyes. Klein and Magee remained silent. After a moment, he started again.

"Sorry," he said, wiping the tears onto the sleeves of the scrubs. "I forgot for a moment why you are here," he added, looking at Magee. "Anyway, Jason was making a lot of changes at work along those lines. He had convinced my father that changes had to be made. My father didn't like it, but he was grooming Jason to succeed him at some point, so he gave him a lot of leeway."

"It sounds like your brother could have assigned Mr. Schwartzman as his personal attorney then," Magee said.

"Oh, yes," Devereaux agreed, "If he is good. Jason would have done his research to determine that. Is there some reason you would question it?"

"Well," Magee started, "yes. Just upon review of everything so far, I'm a little concerned as to why he didn't move more quickly to notify the clinic that your brother had passed away. Three weeks had passed between that and the call. It seems like it should have been the first thing he would do."

"I can't imagine why he would wait," Devereaux said, "but I'm sure if he was Jason's man, he must have had some reason." Magee nodded as if he agreed with Devereaux.

"Okay," he said. "Is there anyone else you can tell me about who may be involved with your brother's estate, perhaps others from the company perspective?" Devereaux looked pensive.

"Not so much on the estate side, but there would be others who would have been affected by Jason not being there. One is Anthony Rendon. He's the President of the holding company. My father had been both Chairman of the Board and Chief Executive Officer. Jason was the Vice President for Public Relations. He also was Vice-Chairman of the Board. When my father died, Anthony took over as acting CEO and acting Chair on the Board. It made sense at the time because Jason was pretty much devasted when Dad died."

"How about you?" Magee asked. "Were you in bad shape, too?" Klein shot him a glance that indicated it was not an appropriate question. Devereaux looked as if he was thinking of an answer. Magee added, "I'm sorry. That question really wasn't meant to disturb you. I was just trying to understand if you would have played any role in the business at that time." Devereaux shook his head.

"No. I was never really interested," he said. "I never really thought I had the head for it. I was more like my mother. I loved the arts." He smiled. "And sports," he added. "Did you know my mother was an Olympic swimmer?" He looked at Klein. "You know that, don't you Dr. Klein. We've talked about that before." Klein nodded in agreement.

"Yes, Mark Richard," she said. "You were always very proud of her accomplishments. I think she was probably very proud of you, too," she added. Devereaux smiled again and looked back at Magee.

"Besides Rendon," he said, "there is one other person I think you might want to talk to. That's Jason's right-hand guy, Tom Eagleton. He is likely the one who is acting for Jason right now. I can imagine that he's really busy trying to keep up." Magee wrote the name down.

"I just want to ask a couple more questions," he said. "How long did it take Jason to get back in the swing of things at work? I mean, did Rendon step aside and let Jason assume the Chairman position?" Devereaux looked pensive again.

"Well, no, not really," he said. "Rendon convinced him to be patient. Since my dad died suddenly, we couldn't be sure how quickly he would have turned over the reins to Jason. Apparently, there was concern among other board members about handing over the company to someone as young as Jason. Rendon suggested that it might be good if both he and Jason spent time working out ways to convince the board through specific activities Jason could take on."

"Do you know what he meant?" Magee asked.

"Yeah, Jason told me," Devereaux answered. "He said things like find an acquisition that was worthwhile and take it through the process." He made a face by scrunching up his nose. "I guess that probably means taking it back to the Board for approval. That way he would have a record to go on. I don't really know. But you could check with Eagleton. Jason would have discussed it with him."

"Ok," Magee said. "Just one final question. When your therapy is completed and you are released from here, do you think you will want to join the company at that point, or do you think you will want to pursue other things?" he asked. Devereaux pursed his lips and brought his hand up to his chin as if he was thinking.

"Hmmm," he said aloud. "I'll have to think about that one," he added. "I could probably tell you tomorrow."

"No hurry," Magee said. "I hope I'll be talking to the attorney tomorrow and my plan, for now, is to proceed as if you may want to become involved. He may have to counsel the people at the holding company not to make a lot of changes while you are here. I need to review what your brother put into his estate, and your standing at this point, but I'm guessing you own the majority of the stock in the organization. You should maintain the right to have input on any possible changes when you are released."

"Thank you," Devereaux said, "I agree." Magee turned to Klein.

"That pretty much wraps it up for me, Dr. Klein," he said. She nodded.

"Thank you. I'll finish up here with Mark Richard, Mr. Magee," she said. Magee turned and extended his hand to Devereaux again, who gave it the same sort of shake as before.

"Thank you, Mark Richard," he said, turning and walking back toward the door to the observation area. As it started to open, Magee suddenly stopped and turned back to Devereaux. "There is one more thing to ask," he said. "Dr. Klein mentioned to me that you warned your brother about something. Was it related to the company, or something else?" He looked directly into Devereaux's eyes, watching for the reaction. Devereaux's expression remained completely unchanged.

"It was about the stress," he replied flatly. "I thought that's what killed our father and I didn't want it to kill him too." Magee nodded and turned, continuing through the door.

After the door closed, Dr. Klein spoke.

"Well, I think that went very well, Mark Richard. Thank you for your cooperation," she said. Devereaux bent down and was fumbling with his right sock.

"Oh, it was no problem, Dr. Klein," he grunted as he was pulling something from the sock. "No problem at all."

From the observation room, Magee had joined Anne, and both were looking through the glass. Paul had just closed the door and as he looked through the glass, he saw the object Devereaux had pulled. It was a kitchen paring knife. They all watched as Devereaux held it up and grabbed Dr. Klein's arm. He pulled her small frame up out of the chair and dragged her toward the side of the room with the door. Paul whipped around and ran toward the handle of the door he had just closed, losing sight of what was happening on the other side of the glass. Devereaux had released Dr. Klein and had picked up the folding chair. As Paul pushed the door open and was running through it, Devereaux had stuck his foot out into Paul's way. Magee could see what was about to unfold.

"Paul wait!" he shouted, but it was too late. Paul had already tripped on the foot and was falling to the floor. Devereaux had dropped the knife and had both hands on the chair. He swung it quickly and brought the side of it directly across the back of Paul's skull as he was going down. His head continued down hitting the floor. Dr. Klein screamed as blood appeared from under where his head hit. Devereaux had recovered the knife and turned to come through the now open door. Magee had positioned himself between the door and Anne when Devereaux came through. He looked at them both. His face was angry.

"I guess I won't be telling you tomorrow," he snarled to Magee.

"You know," Magee said," I can't let you leave." Devereaux looked surprised.

"You're going to stop me?" he said. "I have a knife!" He brandished it in his right hand toward Magee's face. The blade was sticking up. Magee simply stepped forward toward Devereaux, grabbing his hand by the inside of the wrist. Devereaux was watching as it happened and didn't see Magee's right hand at all as the knuckles smashed his solar plexus. At the same time, the left hand was pulling down and toward Magee on that side, basically compounding the force at which the air was being forced out of his lungs. Devereaux's knees buckled and he dropped the knife. Magee twisted as Devereaux fell and allowed him to end up on his back on the floor. Magee's hand released the wrist and put his foot down on top of it as Devereaux gasped for air. Magee kneeled on him to make the process a bit more difficult. He reached over and picked up the knife. He held it pointed at Devereaux's throat and grabbed a handful of the scrubs, lifting him slightly off the floor as he stood. He dragged him over to the wall and propped him up.

"Go see how Paul is," he said to Anne. She rushed into the other room where Klein was now kneeling by Paul. She had turned him over and was resting his head on her lap. She looked up at Anne.

"He's going to be alright," she said. "It's just a nasty cut over his eye where he hit the floor, and he's starting to come around." Anne turned back toward the other room.

"He's okay," she said as she reentered the room. Magee had released Devereaux but was still facing him. "I have to go get a towel for Paul's cut." She left the room for a moment and returned leaving the door open to the hallway. She handed the towel to Klein, who held it to the wound over Paul's eye. He groaned slightly.

"This will need some glue," she said. Paul was becoming more alert.

"What happened," he said. "Did he get out." He made an effort to sit up but sank back down two times before being successful.

"No," Anne said, "Magee stopped him." Paul looked relieved.

"I told you he was our guy," he made a little smile. Anne smiled back at him.

"He's holding Devereaux in the other room right now," she said. She looked at Klein. "Are you all right?" she asked. Klein nodded.

"I'm okay," she said. "Nothing wounded but my pride. I should have seen this coming." Paul grunted.

"Seen it coming," he said. "How could you see it coming. How in the hell did he get a knife?" He started to stand. Anne took hold of his arms to help. He wobbled a bit before getting steady enough to walk into the other room. Devereaux was sitting on the floor with his back against the wall. Magee was standing over him. He was still breathing heavily but seemed to be recovering. Anne and Klein followed Paul into the room.

"What do we do next?" Magee asked.

"We're going to need to get Paul into the Infirmary to get him stitched up," Anne said.

"But first we need to medicate Devereaux and get him back into his room," Klein said. "I pushed my alert as soon as I could. Someone should have come by now."

"Where are they then?" Paul asked.

"I think I can answer that," a voice from the hallway said.

Chapter 12

Magee could see the gun in Stan's hand as he walked from the hall into the observation room. It was a Glock 19, nine-millimeter pistol. Stan was pointing it at Paul's chest and holding it with both hands, and his index finger on the trigger.

"Ok. Mr. Rosner," he said, "Please reach slowly behind and pull your gun out with two fingers. Then drop it on the floor and kick it over this way." Stan watched Paul intently as he followed the instructions. Magee considered making a move while Stan was engaged but ruled it out because he was a little behind Paul's left. There would have been ample time for Stan to realize what was going to happen and start shooting. He decided to wait for the right time. Paul's gun made a distinct thud when it hit the floor. Paul kicked it toward Stan, who was able to stoop down and pick it up while continuing to point the gun. He stuffed the extra gun into his pants under his belt. Then he turned to Magee.

"How about you, Mr. Magee," he said. Magee shrugged his shoulders.

"I didn't think there would be any real threats here, Stan," he said. "I guess I'm kind of surprised at this development." Stan laughed.

"Don't be," he said. "I wouldn't have thought so either. Under ordinary circumstances, it wouldn't have come down to this. But it turns out we live in interesting times." He looked beyond Magee and toward Devereaux.

"You alright, Bobby?" he asked.

"Getting there," Devereaux whispered. He was holding his hand across his chest where Magee's punch had landed. Stan looked back up at Magee.

"I thought you might be interfering with my plan a little," he said. "I knew right away you would be a wild card in the mix. But no one was supposed to get hurt." He glanced over at Paul. "I'm sorry, Mr. Rosner. I don't think Bobby meant for you to hit your head that hard. And the knife was mainly for show, just to be able to use to get out the door." Paul glared but didn't reply. Stan looked back down at Devereaux.

"Can you get up yet?" he asked. Devereaux rolled over and pushed himself up. He walked over and stood behind Stan. "I'm going to have to ask you four to move into the other room. We'll be leaving and I wouldn't want things to get messy." Paul finally spoke.

"Don't do this, Stan. Devereaux is sick. He needs help," he said.

"Oh, I know," Stan replied. "It's just that now we think we have others who can help him more than you can here." He waved the gun toward the other room. "Please," he said. "Really, the most important thing in the world to me right now is that I get him out of here safely. I'm dead serious." He waved the gun again. This time it was Magee that spoke.

"Interesting choice of guns, Stan," he said. "Simple and easy to use. Have you practiced much with it?" Stan frowned.

"Mr. Magee, I understand what you are doing," he said, "but let me clear something up. First of all, I am going to complete my mission. If I have to use this gun to do so, I will. And secondly, yes. There's a part of me that has practiced shooting a gun a lot, much more than you, probably." He glanced over in Paul's direction. "He told me you never served in the military," he added. "So, that's an assumption on my part. Either way, I'm the one holding the gun." Stan pointed toward Anne. "And I'm also pretty sure you wouldn't want to try anything that might end up hurting her by mistake." Magee was silent but knew that Stan was right.

"Now, for the last nicely said time, please make your way into that room." He motioned to Devereaux to go into the hall, and then also backed up until he stood in the doorway of it. Paul was still a little unsteady, so Anne grabbed hold of his arm and helped him make his way into the treatment room. Magee waited until Klein made her way through the door, and then slowly walked toward it.

"By the way," he said as he walked. "You never did answer the question as to why no one answered the alert." Stan laughed.

"Why do you think," he asked and then added before Magee could answer, "I disabled the system before the events started to unfold. I was just supposed to be waiting in a running car at the exit for Bobby to come out." He paused and looked at Magee as if he was studying him. "But something told me I might need to come in, just in case you were going to try something. I knew Paul would run in as soon as he saw Dr. Klein threatened. But I wasn't sure how you would react to the knife. Would it be enough, or would you somehow be able to disarm him? In the end, I thought it better to not take any chances." Magee smiled.

"Well," he said, "You're taking a chance that I'll come after you when you leave." Stan frowned again.

"I'll take that chance, Mr. Magee, rather than shoot you somewhere to disable you now," he said. "Like I said, I don't want to see anyone get really hurt." Magee nodded and walked into the other room. Stan started to grab the handle to shut the door. Devereaux grabbed his arm.

"Wait," he said to Stan. Then he turned to Klein. "I wouldn't have hurt you, Dr. Klein," he said, his eyes becoming moist as he spoke, "but I have to leave now." Klein looked back at him and smiled. Devereaux looked back at Stan and nodded. The door slammed shut. Magee looked over at Paul.

"How are you doing, Paul," he asked.

"I'm a little woozy," Paul answered. "Maybe it's from loss of blood." He took the towel off the cut on his head. "Is it still bleeding?" Magee shook his head.

"It actually doesn't look that bad," he said. "It's just that head wounds seem to bleed more than any other. You should still probably have stitches."

"I know," Paul said, putting the towel back on his head. "I saw enough of that in action. Jeesh," he said, under his breath. "I went through three tours and a lot of fights. Then I let some punk kid school me."

"I wouldn't look at it that way," Magee said. "Turns out it wasn't the kid we had to worry about."

"Go ahead and say it," Anne said. "You were right about Stan." She frowned.

"I'm not going to say that," Magee replied. "But I am going to say this proves that there is something bigger behind this whole thing."

"What do you mean?" Paul asked.

"I mean," Magee started, "we touched on the reasons why someone might be trying to run a scam on a rich patient. But now we know that wasn't what was going on. You heard Stan call Devereaux by a nickname, more than once. He was familiar with him before he got here, maybe even a friend."

"Okay," Anne interjected, "But what does that mean? If he was a friend, why would he want him to leave somewhere that he was getting helped?" Magee shook his head.

"Don't know the answer yet," Magee said, "and we won't know anymore unless we get out of here and catch up. We can't get back out to the Observation Room. What are our options?" Klein, who had been very quiet up to this point, spoke up.

"We just go back out through the patient door. We can go out any of the other exits." She said, calmly.

"Okay," Magee said. "Let's get Paul over to the infirmary for treatment. Then maybe I can get on the road and see if I can catch them. I'm assuming they'll be heading toward the city, and that's a three-hour drive. In the meantime, Dr. Klein, it may be time to bring in the police."

"I suppose you're right, Mr. Magee," Klein said. "I just don't know what we'll tell them. Whatever it is will end up being bad for the clinic."

"Wait a minute," Paul said. "There might be another way." The others looked at him, expectantly. "I have a confession to make. Remember at dinner last night you brought up the idea that maybe having to hire a new manager for the restaurant may not have been a coincidence?" Magee nodded. "Well, after I left you two, I got to thinking about that as well. I had already noticed that he always leaves for at least one night on his off days. I didn't really think about it before, but then I wondered where he goes. So, I decided to find out. I had an on-board GPS tracker in my car. After dinner last night, I took it out of my car and put it in Stan's."

"What does that mean," Magee asked.

"It means that unless Stan thought of checking for one, I can tell exactly where he is driving right now through an app on my phone," Paul replied. Magee smiled.

"Impressive," he said to Paul. "Where's your phone now?" Paul pointed toward the pocket of his sport coat.

"Right here," he said. He reached in the pocket with his free hand and pulled out the phone. He pressed his thumb to the button to unlock it and gave it to Magee. "It's on the first page. It says GPS under it." Magee found it and touched the icon.

"Okay," he said, "let's get Paul fixed up, and we'll watch where he's headed. Then we'll decide when and where to bring in the police." Anne walked over to the patients' door and opened it. They filed through and out into a long corridor. As they walked down the hall, an orderly appeared from around a corner. He stopped suddenly and looked at them with surprise.

"Dr. Klein," the orderly said. "Why are you here?"

"We have an incident, Mr. Williams," she said. "Robert Devereaux has escaped." The orderly looked more surprised.

"What happened to the emergency response?" he asked. "I didn't hear anything." Klein shook her head.

"No, you wouldn't have," she said. "It was disabled. Would you go take a look at the system and see if you can re-enable it as soon as possible? We've got to get Mr. Rosner to the infirmary." Williams nodded and hurried back down the hall the other way.

"Mr. Williams would have heard an indicator when we opened the door on the patient side," Klein said to Magee. "He was coming down to make sure Devereaux was going back to his room. This way." She pointed to a door with a keypad next to it. She walked up and punched the combination. There was a click and they went through to another hall. "The infirmary is up on the left," she said.

A moment later they were all together in what was a treatment room, with a couple of beds for patients. Paul laid down on one of the beds, while Klein went to a cabinet and got supplies. Anne went to a drawer and pulled out a clean towel. She wet it in the sink and returned to wash some of the blood off Paul's head and face. Klein washed her hands and put on some gloves. Then she started to swab the area around the wound with mercurochrome.

"This may sting a bit, Mr. Rosner," she said.

"That's okay, Dr. Klein," he said. "Just go ahead." Then he turned to Magee. "How's the signal holding up. You still got them?" he added. Magee nodded.

"They've been out from the main gate for about ten minutes now," he said. "It seems right now like they are headed back to the city. But they aren't using the main route going back. They've turned twice already." Anne spoke up.

"Shouldn't we alert the police now," she said, "and have them pick them up before they get far away? Won't it be easier for them to get lost in the city?" Magee thought for a moment before replying.

"It may actually be better if we waited until they get closer to it. Right now, they don't know we can track them. They probably figure we've gotten out by now and assumed we'd called the local police. But the local police don't have very many cars to respond with. They'll send one or two cars in pursuit and try to stop them as soon as possible. And as soon as Stan sees someone on their tail, he's going to run faster, because he knows what will happen if he stops. I don't think it's helpful to have them in a high-speed chase. It could end badly for them.

"If we wait a little longer, we can notify someone who can commit more resources and an organized response to stop them with a blockade. We'll be able to tell them exactly where they should go."

"So, you aren't still planning to try to catch them yourself?" Anne asked. Magee shook his head.

"Not if our plan is to get the police involved," he answered. Then he turned to Klein, who was still pulling stitches through Paul's skin. "Dr. Klein," he said, "I know I said we should contact the police now, but I also know you aren't crazy about involving them. The alternative is that Devereaux remains at large for a time. Is he a danger to others?" Klein stopped what she was doing and looked at him.

"I honestly couldn't tell you," she said. "In this situation, my ethical training says to get him off the streets as soon as possible. Not just for the safety of others, but for his own." She shook her head. "That should overrule what I said earlier about the damage to the clinic."

"But you talked about the progress he had been making and your thoughts about releasing him soon." Magee offered. Klein nodded at this.

"Yes, but remember at that moment, I was still trying to convince him he needed to talk to you," she said. "He was making great progress," she added, "but then again he regressed after his brother's death. And now, look what happened to Mr. Rosner!" she said. "I've already got that on my conscience." Paul reached up and put his hand on her arm.

"You don't even think about that, Dr. Klein," he said. "I'm fine. You didn't cause this cut. I was careless." Klein smiled.

"Yes, I can always depend on you, can't I?" she asked. "You rushed in to protect me, but you shouldn't have had to. I should have called off the session. I sensed something was wrong at the beginning but went ahead anyway."

"Was it something in his responses?" Magee asked.

"Yes," she replied, "his attitude was different. He was far more confident when he walked in than he had been in the sessions since his brother died." She paused as if looking for a way to explain it. "He was more alert. The last time I talked to him he just came in and sat down. He was apathetic. He didn't really care about the session. But this time, he came in and participated. It was almost as if he knew he was going to get out."

"Well," Magee said, "Stan must have prepared him for the escape. He probably gave him the knife and suggested how to take down Paul."

"Yes," Klein said, "You're probably right. But it doesn't matter. I still should have called it off the minute I had any concerns." She turned to continue working on Paul's stitches.

"Water under the bridge at this point," Magee said. "There is a reason I asked if he was a danger." Klein turned back to listen. He had Paul and Anne's attention too.

"Remember that Stan said he wanted to get him somewhere that could treat him better than here? If we alert the police when they have a reasonable chance to put up a blockade, and they stop him from getting where he was headed, we'll never know what that means." Paul raised his head.

"What are you hinting at," he said. Magee looked down at the phone with the location and smiled.

"They've turned a few times, but it looks like they're on track to get back to the city," he said. "When they do, they're likely to assume they got away clean and go straight to where they want to end up. And if we track them there, we should be able to find out more about who is behind this whole thing, and why." Everyone else was quiet for a moment. Finally, Anne cleared her throat.

"But they'll be miles away by then if they are in the city," she said. "And it would take you a long time to get there. Who's to say we could actually catch them there?"

"Well, you're right," Magee admitted. "They may decide it's too risky, particularly if they assume we've gone to the police." He paused for a moment. "Then again, I'm betting they won't clear out from wherever that is. They don't know yet that we're tracking them. Stan may stop at the intended final destination, drop off Devereaux, then drive the car somewhere completely across town – maybe even out of town – and dump it somewhere that it can be found. They'll want us to think they've ended up somewhere else, but we'll know where they stopped before that."

"Are they still headed in the same direction," Paul asked. Magee looked again at the phone.

"Yep," he replied. "They've turned a couple of more times, which means their progress is slow because they aren't using the easiest route, but essentially every turn has been corrected by another to keep them headed that way." He looked down again. "Wait a minute," he added, "they've stopped." Magee looked at his watch. "It's been less than 30 minutes since they left, hasn't it?" Anne looked at her watch.

"Yes," she said, "That's what I make it too. Why would they stop? You as much told Stan you would come after them before they left." Magee nodded.

"I'm not sure," he said. "It seems to be a small town."

"Maybe they need gas," Klein said.

"I wouldn't think that," Magee said. "I would think Stan would have thought of that and filled up so that wouldn't be an issue."

"Maybe they are meeting someone else there," Paul said. "If so," he continued, "they might transfer to another vehicle." Magee nodded.

"You're right, Paul," he said. "We should check it out anyway. Are you okay for a ride when the doctor is done?" he asked.

"Absolutely," Paul answered. He started to rise but Klein pushed on his chest and he went back down.

"Hold on," Klein said. "I'm not finished quite yet!" she scolded. She kept pulling a stitch through and grabbed the scissors. "There," she said as she tied a knot and cut the end. "Ok, Paul," she added, "you're good to go." Paul looked up at her in surprise. "What?" she said.

"That's the first time you've called me Paul since you finished my treatment," he said. Klein laughed.

"Well that's the first time you've been my patient again, Mr. Rosner," she said. Paul looked at Magee.

"Let's roll," he said.

Chapter 13

Magee offered to drive, but Paul said no. He said he had some things in his car they may need if they catch them. He told Magee to wait by the front gate and he'd be there in a second. He walked the other way from the gate, while Magee walked toward it. Now that he was alone, his mind was filled with checking the note pad.

First on the list was Stan. He had been right. Too much of a coincidence. He wished he had found out more about Stan, but everything was moving so quickly. He had arrived only thirty-six hours ago and yet it seemed like it had been longer. He was still absorbing the different things that seemed relevant. Most of all, of course, there was meeting Anne.

In his mind, he replayed the picture of her as he and Paul left Klein and her to deal with the explanations to the staff. He saw the worried look on her face. She told him to be careful. He had wanted to kiss her goodbye, but it was too soon for any affection in front of others.

He wasn't worried that both he and Paul would be gone. The mice wouldn't be back. They had wanted to talk to Devereaux, and he was gone. It was clear Stan and Devereaux weren't coming back. The car was still stopped in the same location. Besides, neither the mice nor Stan and Devereaux seemed like a real threat to others. The whole objective seemed to be getting to Devereaux somehow. But it was also clear that Stan didn't intend to hurt Devereaux. His mission was to get him out. Although it still wasn't clear how that would be better for him than the clinic would be. But Stan seemed confident about what he was doing. More confident than a twenty-five-year-old chef needed to be.

Magee heard a rumble behind him as he approached the gate. He looked over his shoulder and saw Paul driving up in a military-style Humvee. Paul stopped next to him.

"Get in," he said through an open window. Magee pulled on the door and jumped up into the Humvee. Paul pressed the remote in his pocket to open the gate and squeezed the Humvee through as soon as he could. As they pulled through, Magee looked over and saw his car where he had parked it the day before. It was going on dusk, but he could still see that one of the rear tires was completely flat.

"Looks like they didn't want you to drive anyway," Paul shouted. Magee nodded.

"This thing is noisy," he shouted back. Paul laughed.

"Yeah," he said, "but you get used to it after a while." Magee nodded. He grabbed a handle secured to the frame just in front of the door as Paul pushed the speed up as he negotiated the curves in the road. He looked toward the back. It was empty except for a box on the floor. Magee could see different weapons in the box.

"I can see what you meant about having stuff we might need," he said.

"Well," Paul said, "Stan took the gun I prefer to carry. I plan to take it back."

"Is this what you normally drive?" he asked.

"Yeah, mostly," he said with a nod. "A couple of other cars owned by the clinic are available to me if I need one, but this is all mine." He patted the top of the dash. "Got used to them on tours and bought one from an auction when I came home for good."

"Out of curiosity," Magee said, "why the GPS?" Paul made a face like it was a silly question.

"Are you kidding?" he said. "There are a lot of people that want one of these. It might get stolen. I'm a little paranoid about that even though it's unlikely out here at the clinic. But mostly, when I get some time off," he started then added, "although that's pretty rare," he emphasized, "I like to take it up into the hills around here, just to get away for a while. There are some pretty rugged trails. And if anything happens, I like to know exactly where I am so I can get out if I need to." Magee nodded.

"That makes sense," he said.

"More sense than this whole thing is making," Paul said. "I can't figure it out. First, we have the three guys who show up after the brother dies, but claimed they were going to bring him to visit Devereaux. Then there is Stan, who works his ass off for several weeks pretending to be someone he is not, and then takes Devereaux out." He shook his head.

"If it's any consolation," Magee said, "I haven't figured it out either." They rode in silence for a few moments until they reached the front gate. Paul took the remote from his pocket and opened it. He drove through and it closed after him. The road straightened out and Paul pushed the speed up again, this time to sixty. Magee knew that there would be a few miles before this road would meet the one that takes them toward the city. He crawled out of his seat toward the box in the back and started sifting through it.

"Be aware," Paul shouted back to him, "All of those are loaded."

"Thanks," he shouted back. "Which do you prefer?" he asked. Paul didn't hesitate.

"There's a Barretta M9 back there," he said. "I don't think I'll need anything more than that."

"I agree," Magee said. "I see this P229 back here. I'll take that one." He held one in each hand and made his way back up to the front seat. Paul waited until he was sitting again.

"Good choice," he said. He looked back and forth between the road and watching Magee as he did a press check. When Magee finished, Paul said, "Told you."

They drove on without speaking for a while. Magee checked Paul's cell phone periodically to see if the car had moved. Every so often, Magee would tell Paul to turn a specific way. Finally, they saw some buildings up ahead. It looked like the edge of a small town. Paul glanced at his watch.

"It's been about half an hour," he said, "that's just about right, isn't it?" Magee nodded. Paul slowed up. There were scattered buildings on both sides of the road, including some houses.

"It looks like we're still about half a mile away," he said, "but it's on this road." Paul slowed a little more. When he was about a quarter-mile away, he slowed and pulled to a stop on the side of the road.

"Stan's going to recognize my vehicle when I pull up," he said. "How do you think we should handle this?" Magee thought for a moment.

"From where we are right now, we don't see the car yet," he said. "So, they probably can't see us yet. But they probably aren't in the car." He stared ahead, still thinking about it, then added, "Wait a minute." He reached into his pocket and grabbed his cell phone. Paul couldn't see exactly what he was doing.

"I'm bringing up Google maps," Magee said. "We'll be able to see what types of things might be ahead. Even a street view, if we choose." He fiddled with the phone a little more, then stopped. "Oh, crap." He said.

"What?" Paul asked. Magee just shook his head.

"Keep going," he replied. "No need to worry about them spotting us." Paul pulled back on the road and kept driving.

"Why," he said. "What's up here?" He had barely finished when the buildings and houses ended and there was a clearing. There was a driveway and he could see a blue Prius parked in a parking lot by a small building. The sign on the building said Stanley Field. Beyond it, they could see a windsock and a flat grassy strip. There were some other buildings off in the distance that looked like hangers. Paul pulled up and stopped next to the Prius. There was a bumper sticker that read 'Fight the Change'. He gave a nod towards the car. "That's Stan's car," he said. It was empty. "Dammit," he said. They both sat silently for a moment until Magee finally spoke.

"Maybe they're still inside waiting," he said with a smile. Paul laughed.

"Yeah," he said, "it's not like this place is going to have a lot of flights they could just hop on." He picked up the Barretta that Magee had brought from the box. Magee still had the Sig Sauer in his hand. They each got out. Paul looked inside Stan's car to see if they left anything. The scrubs had been discarded into the backseat.

"Stan must have brought some clothes for Devereaux to change into," Paul said.

"Looks that way," Magee said. He pointed at the bumper sticker. "What does that mean?" he asked. Paul made a frown as he shook his head.

"It means fight climate change," he said. "What else would be on a blue Prius?" Magee laughed. He shoved the Sig into the waist of his pants and walked toward the building. A sign that said 'Office' pointed toward the field side. Paul followed as Magee turned the corner, found the door and entered. Inside was a small waiting area with chairs along one wall, and a counter. They could see a couple of desks behind the counter and the open door to an office on one side. A voice came from the office.

"I'll be out in a second," a man said. A moment later, he appeared. He eyed Magee and Paul with a frown. "What can I do for you guys?" he asked, still looking at them as if they didn't belong. Magee flashed a smile.

"Looking for some information," he said.

"Humph," the man grunted. "This is turning into a weird day." Magee and Paul exchanged glances.

"Why so," Paul asked the man.

"Well, I suppose you want to know about the other two who showed up earlier," he said. Magee smiled again.

"You'd be right," he said. "Is it unusual to get people coming in?" The man looked annoyed.

"Yeah," he said, "I'd say so. First, I get two young guys coming in, and saying they're waiting for their ride to get here." He waved his arm toward the window looking out on the grassy strip. "Then I get a chopper coming in and landing, and them getting on and taking off." He paused for a moment as if he was looking for understanding as to why that would be unusual. When neither Magee or Paul showed any surprise he added, "and then you two show up!" They still didn't react. He frowned. "I can go days without getting any traffic in here," he added with some emphasis. He seemed a little agitated.

"I guess that is unusual, then," Magee said. The man looked relieved to finally be understood. He started to relax. "Can you tell us anything about the chopper," Magee asked.

"Yeah," the man said, still a little angrily. "They didn't check in over the radio. I was on the job the whole time and they didn't even call. Then they just landed and didn't even stop the engine," he continued, waving his arm again and rolling his eyes. "And those guys just ran out and hopped in and it took off. Whole thing was maybe sixty seconds. I didn't even get a chance to get out from behind the counter and chase 'em down." He shook his head.

"Could you tell what kind of chopper it was?" Magee asked. The man nodded.

"I got a pretty good look out the window there," he said, pointing outside. "It was a Sikorsky S-76. One of those executive types. Seats six. Smooth and easy to fly."

"You seem to know your stuff," Paul said. "Did you serve?" The man nodded again.

"I flew in Nam," he said. "Part of Air-Cav." He seemed to stand up a little taller for a moment. "That's why I know my choppers," he added.

"Thanks for serving," Magee said, extending his hand over the counter towards the man, who took it and gave a firm shake back. "I met a lot of guys who served in Nam. Some were chopper pilots. I guess there's not much more you can tell us, huh?" he asked.

"Well, yeah, actually," the man said. "One of the kids said he'd be back for his car in a couple of days." Magee smiled. He took his wallet from his pocket, pulled out one of his business cards, and handed it to the man.

"If you're here when the kid comes to get his car, can I ask you to call me at the number on this card?" The man nodded.

"Yeah, sure," he said. "I'll be here. I own this place," he pointed at a plaque tacked up on the wall with the owner's name on it. Magee glanced at it. Willie Longbow, Proprietor, was etched on it. "I got a little apartment in the back here. I hope I'm able to catch the kid when he gets back. He needs to tell that chopper pilot he should have at least checked in on the radio," he added. Magee nodded in agreement.

"Well if you talk to him," Magee said, "please don't tell him that anyone was in here asking around." Magee looked at him expectantly. The man looked down and read Magee's card.

"Oh, Private Investigator, huh?" he said, stuffing the card into his shirt pocket. "Cool. You workin' on a case?"

"Yeah," Magee said, "The kid took something from where my friend works." He gestured toward Paul. "I'm helping him get it back." The man looked over at Paul.

"You serve?" he said to him. Paul nodded.

"Three tours in Afghanistan." He said. The man shook his head.

"Thank you for serving," he said. "What a waste, though. Just like Nam."

"I hear ya," Paul said. They turned and walked toward the door.

"Wait," he said. "There is one other thing. That chopper had a company name on the side, Iron River Properties." Magee turned back to the old man.

"Is that a local company around here?" he asked. The man shook his head.

"I ain't ever heard of something like that around here. That's actually only the second chopper I've ever had land here," he said.

"Who had the first one?" Paul asked. The old man smiled.

"Me," he said.

The ride back didn't seem to take as long, but it was dark before they finally pulled in. They had left Stan's car exactly how they found it. The old man had promised to call if Stan turned up to get it. Magee had called Anne as they drove to let her know the situation. She said she would alert Dr. Klein.

As soon as they passed through the second gate, she appeared from Klein's house. She was smiling and when Magee saw her, he smiled too.

"I'm glad you're back. We were worried," she said as Paul and Magee climbed out of the Humvee. "How's your head, Paul?" she asked. Paul made a face.

"It would be better if we had caught up to them," he said, "but it's okay." He pointed toward the house. "Is Dr. Klein inside?" he asked. Anne nodded. "Did anything else happen after we left?" he asked. Anne shook her head.

"Nothing here, but Al Marchioni called and asked if he could come back. I said yes because we need the help until we can get someone else," she said.

"What'd he say?" Paul asked.

"He's on his way. He should be here early in the morning," Anne replied. "And he said he's sorry. He didn't know what was going to happen."

"Who are we talking about?" Magee asked. Anne turned toward him to answer.

"He's the previous restaurant manager who recommended Stan," she said. "And he's willing to help by explaining how he came to make that recommendation." Magee smiled. Paul frowned.

"He'd better have a good explanation," Paul said. "Or I may have to bust his head, like someone busted mine."

"Before that happens," Magee said, "Let's find out what we can. I'm betting that somehow someone convinced him to leave just so they could position Stan. We may be able to find out who." Anne looked at him. Then he added, "I'm thinking there is money involved, a lot to get him to leave." Reluctantly, she nodded.

"You're probably right," she said. "He was very vague on the personal reasons that he told me when he resigned."

"I can give him the benefit of the doubt," Paul said. "I wasn't all that sad when he left. I mean, he was a good guy, but it was good to get someone new in. Stan was fun, for a while. How did the rest of the staff respond when they heard about Stan?" he asked.

"Those that worked with him in the restaurant were all surprised," Anne replied. "They didn't have any idea he would do something like that. And they all said that they'd keep doing their jobs to get the patients and others fed."

"Sounds like you've got a pretty good team here," Magee said.

Yes," Anne agreed. "They were all here before Stan got here. Some of them were surprised by how young Stan was, but they all admitted he knew his stuff. And they all said they thought he was a nice guy."

"Yeah," Paul said, "he was. I have to admit I liked Stan better than Al," he added.

"Well at least Al never helped anybody leave while he was here," Anne said. They all laughed. Paul turned to Magee.

"Looks like you're here for another night, Magee," he said. Magee nodded. Paul pointed at the house. "I'm gonna go in and check with Dr. Klein. If you want, I'll meet you over at the restaurant in a few and we can figure out our next steps."

"Sounds like a plan," Magee said.

"I'm coming, too," Anne said.

Paul left them and entered the house. Anne put her arm through Magee's and pulled just enough to get them started toward the restaurant.

"I'm glad you didn't have to do anything when you got over to where the car was," she said looking up at him while they walked.

"Well," he started, "I am, too. But the problem is now, we don't have much of anything to go on for our next step."

"What about what you said on the phone about the helicopter," she asked. "The name 'Iron River' suggests there's some link back to Devereaux Holdings, right? Magee nodded.

"Yes," he said. "But it doesn't answer any big questions like the motivation for putting someone here, and then pulling him out before he's released by the doctor." Anne thought for a moment.

"The only thing that really changed between when he got here and now is his brother dying," she said. "I guess that means you have to get back and check on that lawyer," she added.

"You're right," Magee said, "But at least I have one more night to get to know you a little better." He stopped and pulled her toward him in the darkness and kissed her hard. Then he took hold of her hand and they went into the restaurant.

Chapter 14

The restaurant was emptier than the night before. Anne explained that she had notified all of the staff that Stan had left, and the rest of the restaurant workers would try to keep up, but things would probably be slow. They sat at a table in the middle where they could flag down whoever came out of the kitchen.

"Who's in charge since Stan left?" Magee asked.

"That would be Carol," Anne answered. "She's good. I asked her to take over when Al left, but she didn't want his job. Too much responsibility. Plus, she would have to be telling people what to do all the time."

"Yeah, I know how that goes," Magee said. "I never wanted to be the boss over anyone. It's one of the reasons I'm a loner." Anne smiled.

"You are the boss of you," she said. "And you have an office back in the city. Did you have a secretary or anyone to help you with all of the paperwork, or appointments and things?" He frowned.

"Yes, but it didn't last," he said. Anne looked puzzled. He knew the next question was going to be 'why not', so he kept talking. "I decided she would make a better wife than a secretary," he added. Anne smiled.

"Oh," she said. "I was going to ask if you had to fire her." Magee laughed.

"Same thing," he said, smiling. Just then Anne saw someone from the corner of her eye and turned her head. It was a woman carrying some plates of food over to another table. Anne motioned for her to come over. The woman nodded, raised the plates and shrugged, then kept walking toward the other table. After a brief conversation, she walked to where they were sitting.

"Hi, Anne," the woman smiled, then turned to Magee and extended a hand. "You must be Magee," she said. He took her hand and gave a soft shake. Then he turned to Anne.

"Why is it everyone seems to know me before I know them?" he said. Anne pretended to be looking the other way as he was talking. The woman laughed.

"I'm Carol," she said. "Anne told me about you." Magee wanted to ask her what she had said about him, but Carol had already turned back to Anne. "If you want to get something to eat, tell me now because it's a little hectic back there." Anne nodded.

"Yes," she said. "And Paul will be joining us soon, as well," she added. "How are you holding up?"

"I'm doing okay," she said, "but for a while, the others were having a meltdown. I think we've got it under control.

"I knew you would keep things going," Anne said. "Al called earlier and he's coming back to help, at least for a while," she told her. Carol suddenly looked angry.

"Good," she said. "Then I can let him know just how crappy it was for him to leave that way. None of us even had a chance to say goodbye."

"I know," Anne said. "He said he'd explain it when he gets back." Carol smiled again.

"Okay," she said, "What can I get you kids. Keep it simple, okay? I'm no Stan."

"Right," Anne said. "I'll just have a cheeseburger, oh, and some water and a Diet Coke." Carol was writing it down on a tablet.

"Cheeseburger is good for me, too," Magee said, "with some fries, and if I may, a Jack Dan..." As Magee was speaking Carol started mimicking the words he spoke.

"Daniel's on the rocks," she said. "I know, Anne told me." Magee laughed. "Okay, cheeseburger with fries for you, but just a cheeseburger for Anne." Both Anne and Magee nodded. "Okay," Carol added. "Three cheeseburgers, two with fries," she repeated. Magee was going to correct her, but she held up her hand. "I know that's what Paul will order anyway. Be back soon," she said as she headed back toward the kitchen. They both watched her until she was through the door. Magee knew what was coming next.

"Well," Anne said, "nothing in your file said you were married, and it didn't come up when we talked earlier today." She looked at him, expectantly.

"I'm not," he said. "I mean, we never legally tied the knot. We just acted like we were married. She moved in with me." Anne seemed to be a little relieved. She leaned forward. "Was that the relationship that lasted more than a year?" Magee nodded and looked away.

"It's past tense, right? I mean you're not still living together, are you?" she asked. Magee shook his head.

"No, it was a long time ago," he said. The look on his face was the same one as Anne had seen earlier when they were talking about his past relationships.

"Oh," she said. "I'm sorry if I touched a nerve." She paused and bit her lower lip slightly as if she was deciding whether to ask another question. Magee could see it in her eyes.

"Well, you wanted to learn more about me," he offered, "so I don't mind." Anne smiled. She was about to ask another question when Carol arrived with their drinks. As she was setting them down on the table, Anne fidgeted. Magee watched as she looked up and made eye contact with Carol. For a moment it seemed if the two of them were having a conversation without speaking. Carol quickly finished placing the drinks and walked away without saying a word. Anne watched and when she was far enough away, turned back to Magee.

"You were in love with her, right?" she said. Magee nodded. "And she was your secretary?" she added. Magee nodded again. "Which came first?" she asked.

"The secretary," he answered, "although the attraction started with the interview. She was lovely."

"Oh, tell me what she looked like," Anne said. Magee smiled.

"A lot like you," he said. Anne blushed. He went on. "She was tall, thin, and blonde." He hesitated as if thinking about what else to say. "And she was smart," he added. "Maybe not as smart as you, but still smart. I mean, she didn't go to college right away. She took steno in high school and got a job right away after she graduated. She had a plan to save up enough money so she could go to school later. She wasn't even sure what she wanted to do with her life then." He stopped and took a drink. Anne waited.

"Anyway," he continued, "she got experience working at a lot of different places as a secretary. She started as a temp and people kept wanting to hire her. Sometimes she did take positions, but then she'd always get restless and want to move on. At the time I interviewed her, she was just looking for the next thing. I didn't have much of a business at that time. I only had a couple of clients from some recommendations people made for me. I had just walked away from a long-term working arrangement and was starting to get things up and running. All the smart people I worked with before said I should get an office, hang out a shingle, and hire a pretty secretary cause that's what PI's in the movies have."

"Of course," Anne said with a slight attitude. "Were any of these smart people women?" Magee laughed.

"No," he answered, "They were all tough guys. No women." Anne rolled her eyes. "But I would have hired her anyway." He continued. "Like I said, she was smart." Anne's brow furrowed.

"Well what happened then?" she asked. "It sounds like a pretty good arrangement."

"It was," Magee confessed. "She was the reason why the business worked. I already said I was a loner. Mostly I just liked the 'doing' part of the job. She did everything else to build it. Even when it came to finding clients, she was the one who found them. She arranged for advertising and she convinced my old employers to provide more contacts and she wrote letters of introduction to all of the ones she got. That turned into more clients, some which you saw in my file." He stopped and took another drink. Anne didn't wait this time.

"Okay," she started, "it's a pretty picture. The business took off. She was brilliant. You fell in love with each other but didn't marry. What am I missing here?" she asked. "Why didn't it last?" Magee didn't answer right away. Instead, he took a bigger drink than before. Then he looked into her eyes.

"She died," he said, matter-of-factly. The look on his face was stoic. He waited for her response. She gulped and tears filled her eyes.

"Oh, Magee," she started, "I'm sorry…..I'm so sorry. I---I didn't mean to, I mean---" she wiped a tear from her cheek. He reached over and took her hand and held it.

"Hey," he said, "It's okay," he added, rubbing her hand. "I told you, it was a long time ago. I've learned to deal with it. It's part of life," he said softly.

"Yes," she started to say, "but it's…"

"Am I interrupting anything, guys," a voice said. They both turned and saw Paul. Anne looked away quickly and wiped her face.

"No, Paul," Magee said. "We were just waiting for you." Paul looked at him curiously. "I just told Anne a sad story about someone I knew." Paul gave a little laugh.

"Oh, good," he said, "then the crying isn't about me showing up." Magee smiled up at him and shook his head. He kicked the chair next to him out a bit and signaled for Paul to sit down. Anne turned back and looked at him and managed a tiny smile. "You didn't eat yet," Paul added. "Then I'm not too late."

"Nope," Magee said. "In fact, we ordered for you." Paul looked a little surprised. Magee held up his hand. "Don't worry," he said. "We just got you a cheeseburger and fries, like you had last night. They're a little busy in the kitchen after what happened earlier." Paul smiled with relief.

"That's okay," he said. "It's just what I wanted." As he spoke the words Magee could see Carol coming from the kitchen with their dinners. When she arrived at the table, she placed the plates in front of Anne and Magee.

Oh, hi, Paul," she said, "I didn't know you came in. I left yours under the warmer." She looked at Anne and seemed to pause for a moment, then she turned back to Magee. "You need a refill, Magee?" she asked. He nodded. "Paul, you need anything to drink?" Paul pointed at Magee's glass.

"Same thing," he said, and then, "water, too." Carol nodded. She turned back to Anne.

"How about you, sweetie?" she said.

"No," Anne responded without looking up. "I'm okay with the water," she said.

"Ok, be right back," Carol said. Everyone was silent as they watched her head back and go behind the bar. They waited as she poured the Jack Daniel's and made her way back to the table with two glasses. It was only after she had set the drinks down and headed back toward the kitchen to get Paul's cheeseburger that Paul broke the silence. He grabbed his glass and held it up toward Magee.

"Here's to you, Magee," he said. "I knew you were good at what you do!" Magee raised his glass to Paul's and they made a clink.

"Just based on the whiskey I like?" Magee asked. Paul smiled and nodded.

"Mostly," he said, "But I had a feeling after our first talk. By the way, how did you disarm Devereaux? I was out on the floor when it happened. He had that knife." Magee smiled.

"Just standard stuff, Paul," Magee replied. "You know, step in when you have the advantage. He had the blade up." Paul nodded.

"Gotcha," he said back. Anne looked puzzled again.

"Okay," she said, "what does that mean, the blade up?" Paul laughed.

"It's basic physics, Anne," he said. "If the blade is up, whoever has it isn't ready to stab you," he added. "He's thinking it's enough to threaten you. In order to stab you, he has to be holding the blade somewhat horizontal, so it can either go right in or he can slash you." He grabbed a knife on the table and held it up vertically in his hand. "You can see," he said waving it back and forth, "to hurt you with it in any way, he'll have to turn his wrist and bring it down, one way or the other." He demonstrated how clumsy it would be to try to use it straight on from that angle. "Unless the guy was a midget," he added. "Otherwise, he'd have to start with the blade down in his fist. That way he could come in and stab you." Paul made a stabbing motion several times with the knife he held. Anne watched and laughed as she understood. Paul went on.

"Obviously, Magee knows that too. So, he would have a split-second before Devereaux adjusted to take him down, anyway that he could." He looked over at Magee. "How did you take him down?"

"Left parry, right up into plexus," Magee said nonchalantly. Paul laughed and raised his glass.

"Remind me never to be on the receiving end of that right," he said. "Devereaux's a big guy and it seems it took him a while to recover." He clinked his glass to Magee's one more time just as Carol was returning with his dinner. She set the plate down.

"Here you go, Paul," she said. "What's the occasion for the toast?"

"Just celebrating my instincts, Carol," he said. They all laughed except Carol who hadn't been around earlier to know the reference.

"Well let me know if there is anything else you guys need," she said. "I've got to get back into the kitchen to make sure things are getting done." She turned to speak directly to Anne, "I'll probably be here getting things organized for a while tonight. Let me know if you need anything, okay?" Anne nodded. Magee and Paul looked at each other as Carol walked away. Again, there was silence for a moment. Paul spoke up.

"Well, let's eat," he said. "Yours has been getting cold while we've been talking. Help yourselves to some of these fries, if you want." He pushed his plate a little closer to the center so they could reach. Magee and Anne picked up their burgers.

"How was Dr. Klein doing when you saw her, Paul?" Magee asked before beginning to bite his burger. Paul was already half-way through his first bite. He put down the burger and wiped his mouth.

"She looked tired," he said, "more tired than I've ever seen her look."

"Are you surprised?" Anne asked. It was more of a statement than a question. "She's been going through a lot these days. This whole thing is weighing on her."

"I know," Paul said sharply. "I've known her longer than you, remember." He took another bite and spoke in between chewing. "She needs a vacation, but there is no way she is going to take one."

"I'm sorry," Anne said. "I didn't mean it in a bad way, Paul. I know you've been with her longer than I have." Paul smiled at her to let her know it was alright.

"In the meantime," Magee interjected, "we still have a puzzle to unravel. At some point, we'll need to determine if Devereaux has to come back here so she can continue treating him, or if he needs to be elsewhere." Paul and Anne looked surprised.

"What do you mean, if?" Paul asked. "Of course, Devereaux has to come back. He's still her patient." Magee shrugged and shook his head.

"Someone thinks otherwise," he said. "Stan said as much when he talked about someone else helping him. "

"But his next of kin signed him in here," Anne offered. "Doesn't that mean that legally, Dr. Klein should be the one treating him?" Magee thought for a moment.

"Probably," he said. "But on the other hand, it may no longer be ethical for Dr. Klein to treat him. Whoever is handling his brother's estate could probably challenge it in court. The argument is that she would be biased after the events that took place. There was some physical violence involved, and she actually became a victim when he grabbed her. It would be easy to make a case that she shouldn't treat him anymore. It's sort of like a judge has to recuse himself if he has a personal connection to the parties involved." Both Paul and Anne looked pensive but nodded their heads. Anne turned to Paul.

"He's right, of course," she said, "but that will kill her if she can't finish the treatment." Paul nodded.

"She'll carry it with her, I know," he said. "She'll hold herself responsible." Magee frowned.

"Well, one, or both of you, or even all three of us, have to convince her that she isn't," he said. "Whatever is going on is something bigger, based on everything we've seen so far." He shook his head again. "I don't have any clue of where this thing is headed as of now. We know we have a sick patient on the run, a lawyer who may or may not be who he says he is, a chef who is more than who he said he was, and three weirdos who showed up and then went away when they couldn't get in to see a patient." He paused and waited to see if either of them had any thoughts. They were still thinking.

"Okay, then," he added, "Let me sum it up. We've got a lot of work to do. Are we up to it?" He looked at Paul then to Anne. She looked at him and then to Paul, who finally broke the silence and raised his glass.

"All for one, and one for all," he said.

Chapter 15

Paul was the first to leave after they finished eating. He said he wanted to go over his list of friends he thought could help. Magee could tell he was just being gracious. He and Anne had been having an important conversation when Paul joined them, and Magee knew Paul was leaving so they could continue where they left off. Anne knew it too. She seemed more reserved when Paul left. Her eyes were lowered toward the table. When she finally raised them, Magee saw that they were misty again. She looked at him as if she wanted to speak but couldn't find the words. He smiled and spoke.

"So, where were we?" he said. Her lip quivered. A tear streamed down one cheek. She reached up to wipe it away.

"It must have been awful for you," she finally said. "You must have loved her very much from the way you talked about her." Magee looked away for a moment and then turned back to her.

"I had a hard time initially," he said. He was looking down at the table and pushing his glass around with a finger. "I was angry. But I had my work to keep me going. The case I was working on at the time took an ugly turn and I had to bury myself into it. In the end, I think that helped me resolve my anger and be able to move on."

"Do you still think about her?" she asked. Magee raised his head. He glanced at the ceiling and then came back down toward her.

"Once in a while," he said. "Clearly when I'm having conversations like this," he added. "But I learned that life goes on. We're only here for such a short time. Some shorter than others. We need to live every moment while we can. So that's what I try to do. We only go around once. That's what she would say if she could." He smiled. Anne didn't say anything right away. Magee picked up his glass and finished the small amount of whiskey left. Anne became more relaxed and smiled.

"What was her name?" she asked. Magee paused for a moment before saying it.

"Jennifer," he said, "actually, Jenny." Anne lowered her eyes.

"I'm sorry," she said and then repeated. "I'm sorry." Magee shook his head.

"Don't be," he said. "I needed to tell you that. Now you pretty much know everything about me." Anne's smile grew.

"Not quite everything," she said. "I don't know your first name, but we should probably go somewhere more private to talk about the rest." Magee nodded.

"How about my place?" he asked. Anne shook her head.

"No," she said, "let's go back to my place. It's more comfortable." Magee agreed. They rose together and walked to the door. Once they were outside, she took his hand to lead the way. He wanted to walk slowly, but she pulled him along down the hall at a quicker pace. She pushed the numbers on the keypad when they reached the room and pulled him inside. When the door closed, she pushed him gently against it and held him there. She moved closer.

He put his hand under her chin and lifted her face toward him. Then he put his arms around her and kissed her. She kissed him back and then moved her hands to the buttons on his shirt while he kissed her neck, first on one side, then on the other. Once the buttons were undone, she pulled his shirt out from where it had been tucked in his pants. She put her hand on his bare chest and felt his skin.

She pulled away long enough to grab the sweater she was wearing and pulled it over her head, tossing it to the side. Then she leaned against him again. He kissed her again and turned her slightly so he could pick her up into his arms. He carried her into the bedroom and laid her on the bed, then laid down beside her. They were both on their sides, looking into each other's eyes.

"It's not too fast anymore, is it?" Magee asked. It wasn't really a question. It was more of a declaration. "Not anymore," he repeated. She smiled.

"No," she said, softly. "Not anymore." Magee kissed her again. He felt the warmth of her body, and smoothness of her skin. It had been a long time since he made love to someone he truly cared about, and he took his time. He was slow and deliberate, and when it was over, they both laid in bed sweaty and satisfied and fell asleep in each other's arms.

Magee slept on his stomach with his face partly smashed on his pillow. It was daylight when he opened his right eye. He saw a broad smile and two wide eyes watching him intently. Anne was lying on her side with her head propped up on her elbow.

"Morning, sleepy-head," she said happily. Magee opened his left eye and rolled on to his side.

"Morning," he mumbled. "What time is it?"

"Time for me to get over to the office," Anne said as she rolled the other way and got out of bed. She had already showered but was dressed only in underwear. Magee watched as she headed toward the closet. He appreciated the view as she moved gracefully and opened the closet door. Magee could see several dresses on hangers and watched as she considered one, then pushed it to the side. She repeated the process several times until she found one that she lingered over. She pulled it out and turned to him, holding it up by the hanger. It was bright red with white dots and a cinched waist.

"What do you think?" she said.

"Why don't you model it for me," he said, "that way I could tell better." Anne grinned.

"Sure," she said, "but don't get any ideas. I really have to get over to the office. I have this place to run." She pulled the dress off the hanger and put it on. She turned and slipped on a pair of shoes. The heels were higher than what she had worn when he saw her the first time. She turned back to him and did a quick twist while holding the skirt of the dress out. Magee smiled his approval.

"Now maybe you can take it off and come back to bed," he said. Anne frowned but walked to him. She sat down on the edge of the bed where he was laying. She put her hands on his shoulders, leaned down and kissed him.

"You know I have to go to work," she said. In a quick move, he put his hands under her arms, turning and pulling her over himself until she was on her back in the bed beside him. His arm was stretched across her chest. She was startled at first but started laughing as he pulled. He leaned up on his elbow and looked into her eyes. She stopped laughing and looked back, still smiling.

"Did I ever tell you how beautiful you are?" he asked as he pushed her hair back from the side of her face. She laughed again.

"Only 23 times when we were making love last night," she answered with a smile. He looked surprised.

"I didn't think you counted," he said, "but you're right." He kissed her again. "It wasn't enough," he added. She laughed again. Suddenly her phone on the nightstand rang.

"Don't answer," Magee said half-heartedly, knowing she would anyway. She rolled from under his arm and picked it up.

"Hello," she said. She listened. "Mhhm," she said. Magee saw her nod, reflexively, as she repeated it a few times. "Okay,", she said, "I'll be right down." She hung up. Magee sighed. She turned to him. "Al's here," she said. "He's already at the restaurant getting things organized. I need to go down there." She got up and headed toward the bathroom. Magee also got up from the bed.

"I want to go with you," he said as he watched her run a comb through her hair. "I want to hear his story." She nodded.

"Why don't you jump in the shower," she told him. "I'll go down and meet him. His number-one priority is getting the kitchen staff squared away and making sure the patient services are going smoothly, then we can talk to him about why he left." She turned and saw him standing naked in the doorway of the bathroom. For a moment she stopped and looked. He had kept himself fit, and she seemed to be admiring him, which he didn't mind. Then she walked up and kissed him again. She put her hands on his arms and gently turned him so she could move past him. "I gotta go before I decide not to."

He nodded.

"I'll be down in about ten minutes," he said.

"Okay," she answered. "By the way," she added, "I put your gun on the nightstand. It fell on the floor last night when things started moving quickly," she smiled. Then she quickly went through the door.

"It's Paul's gun," he shouted after her through the door. Then he turned to step into the shower.

By the time he arrived in the restaurant downstairs, he had stopped by his room and changed into clean clothes. As he walked in, he saw Anne sitting at one of the tables with Carol and a man he hadn't met. The man was shorter and older than Magee, and slightly overweight. There was a large manila envelope on the table in front of him. He walked to the table. Anne noticed him as he approached.

"Here he is now," she said to the others as he neared. Then she looked up toward him. "Magee, you already know Carol," she said. "This is Al Marchioni," she added, pointing at the man. Marchioni pushed his chair back enough to where he could stand and extended his hand across the table toward Magee.

"Pleasure to meet you, sir," he said. "Anne's told me about you." Magee shook his hand and nodded to him. Then he looked at Anne and smiled. She gave a small smile back. Al continued, "I hear it was good you were around yesterday to help."

"Things got a little crazy," Magee said to him. Anne interjected.

"Magee, I have one more thing to wrap up and then Carol can go and you and I and Al can talk about what happened," Anne said. "Okay?" Magee nodded. Anne turned back toward them and spoke about enhanced security measures she wanted him to put in place for those staff who served patients. When she finished, Carol stood up to go.

"I'm glad you're doing better this morning, Anne," she said. "You look radiant today." Anne blushed.

"Thanks, Carol," she smiled. "We'll talk later." Carol turned and headed back toward the kitchen. Anne looked at Al.

"Okay, Al," she said. "Why don't you tell Magee what you told me about why you left." Al cleared his throat and looked at Magee.

"I just told Anne I didn't want to leave here," he said. "I've always liked this job, and especially the people here." He paused again and looked at Anne as if he was seeking approval. She nodded and he went on. "It turned out, though, I hadda go take care of my brother. He got really sick. I didn't even know how sick until I got a call from his doctor.

"He told me my brother was dying. He had some kind of cancer that was going to take a while to kill him, and it'd be best if he had family members around him until he died. The rest of my family is gone, and I'm all he has left. He's all I have left, too. But I wasn't surprised he got sick. He's an alcoholic. Been on and off the sauce for a long time." Magee was still simply listening. He could see that Al's eyes were moist. It was best just to let him talk.

"The doctor said he had been placed in a private hospital near where he lived, and that I should come and see him as soon as I could. He would meet me there and give me all of the information I needed." Magee decided this was a good time to ask a question.

"Where does your brother live?" he asked.

"Down in the central valley by Red Bluff," Al answered. Magee nodded.

"I know Red Bluff," he said. "Jim Davis was born there." Both Anne and Al had a blank look. "He was a pitcher for the Cubs who struck out four batters in one inning in 1956," Magee added. Anne smiled and nodded her head.

"And that's why your file mentioned you were a huge baseball fan," she said, laughing. Magee smiled too.

"I knew I should have pushed for what else was in that file," he said. Anne turned to Al, who looked confused.

"Paul did a background check before we hired Magee to find out what was going on with the three men I told you about," she said. Al signaled that he understood and then seemed to relax a bit. His eyes cleared.

"So, anyway, I got there at this 'hospital,'" he said, using his hands with two fingers to demonstrate air quotes, "and it turns out my brother was the only patient." Magee raised an eyebrow and Al went on. "It was a small office building. The sign outside didn't even say it was a hospital. It said William's Center for Disease Research. When I went inside, the doctor was there. There was a receptionist and a woman in a nurse's uniform. There were a couple of offices, and one room that was set up with a hospital bed and a bunch of fancy equipment. I could see into it, and I saw my brother lying in the bed."

"What kind of equipment?" Magee asked.

"Things with screens on them that showed waves and stuff like that," Al replied. "There was one of those stands with a couple of bags hanging from it and the line going into my brother's arm. And he had one of those things sticking from his mouth. Do you know?" he asked, making a motion with his hand up by his mouth.

"A breathing tube?" Magee asked. Al nodded.

"Yes," he said, excitedly, "That's it. I could see he was unconscious, but I didn't get to go in and talk to him yet. The doctor said he wanted to explain things before he would let me go visit him. We went into one of the offices and sat and talked for about an hour."

"He told me a different thing from what he had said on the phone," he added. Magee leaned forward, placing his elbows on the table with his hands clasped together and resting against his mouth and chin. Al went on, "First, it turned out he wasn't his regular doctor. He'd been called in because he was a specialist. He said he was using a recently developed drug to combat the cancer. If it lived up to its promise, my brother would survive. I was relieved. He went on to say that the treatment required my brother to be put to sleep so it could do its work. He said it was sort of like inducing a coma." Magee dropped his hands to ask a question but then thought better of it. He signaled for Al to continue.

"Then he told me that it wouldn't be as deep as an actual coma. My brother would be able to hear things, mostly like he was dreaming, and that's why he asked me to come. He thought that my visiting him every day and talking to him from time to time would help him. It was supposed to keep him engaged so he would help his body fight alongside the medicine he was given. He threw a bunch of medical terms at me that I didn't understand. It was all pretty confusing. Then he finally got to a point where he asked if I had any questions." Al stopped as if he expected Magee to ask his question then. Magee waited and Al continued.

"I could only think of one at the time," he said. "How much will all this 'cost', I asked him. My brother doesn't have any money, and his insurance isn't that great. And I didn't think I would have enough to cover it either. But his response was surprising. He said the whole thing would be covered as part of a research grant funding the use of the new drug." He stopped again and looked at Anne. She turned to Magee.

"This is as far as he got when he was telling me," she said. Then she turned back to Marchioni. "Go on, Al," she said, "What happened next?"

"The doctor said there were stipulations, though. He pulled out a copy of a consent form my brother had signed and asked me to confirm his signature," Al said. "To be honest, I haven't really seen anything my brother signed for years, so I couldn't really confirm it," he added, sheepishly. "But I acted like I could. Then he pulled out a form that said 'Non-Disclosure' in bold at the top. It was also something my brother signed. He said since this was a research trial, 'it was important that it remained confidential.' He gave me a separate copy that I had to sign as well. Which I did." He turned to Anne. "That's why I couldn't tell you anything when I called you back to let you know I had to stay there." Then he turned back to Magee. "I actually have a copy of it here." He reached into the manila envelope in front of him, pulled out a sheet of paper and handed it to Magee for review.

"Based on a quick read," Magee said, "it looks legit." He handed it back.

"Well," Al started, "that may be, but the next thing that happened really surprised me. He said that since my brother had agreed to be a participant in the trial, there was monetary compensation. He passed this to me." He fumbled in the envelope again and pulled out a small piece of paper. He held it up. "Years ago, we added each other to our accounts so if anything happened to one of us the other could get quick access to whatever money was there. Not that either of us ever had a lot, but just in case." Magee nodded his understanding. Al passed the piece of paper to him. It was a deposit receipt for his brother's bank account. Magee let out a low whistle. The figure on it was one million dollars. Magee looked up at Al who added, "I checked it. That's really there."

"The hits just keep coming," Magee said. "How dangerous is this treatment?" he asked. Al shook his head.

"I don't know," he said. "But in the end, it doesn't matter." Magee frowned.

"Why not?" he asked. Al formed a huge smile on his face. Both Anne and Magee were surprised. "This must be good," Magee said.

"It is," Al said. "Because I found out later he wasn't sick.

Chapter 16

"Mind if I join the party," Paul said as he walked up to the table. They hadn't seen him come in and looked up at him still wearing surprised looks on their faces. "Whoa," he said, "don't look so shocked to see me." He held his hands up. "I do work here, too, you know."

"It's not you that we're surprised at, Paul," Anne said. "It's what we just heard from Al." Magee pointed to the chair that Carol had used earlier.

"Have a seat, Paul," he said with a smile. "Things just got interesting, again." Paul pulled out the chair.

Don't mind if I do," he said. "Good to see you, Al. How is your brother doing?" Both Magee and Anne laughed. Paul looked puzzled. They began to tell him what Al had revealed so far, starting with when he initially arrived where his brother was being treated, and ending with what Al had just said. When they were finished, Paul shook his head.

"No wonder you were surprised," he said. "I can't wait to find out where this story goes." He looked expectantly at Al, who suddenly looked sheepish again.

"It was as much of a surprise to me as to all of you," he said. "After the doctor was finished telling me all about how they were trying to cure him, I got to go into the room to see my brother. He seemed comfortable. I mean, he just looked like he was asleep. He didn't look sick, except for having all that stuff hooked up to him. The doctor said that is just how he was supposed to look. Normal, except that the medicine inside him was working to get rid of the cancer. He encouraged me to sit for a while and talk to him, which I did.

"Then later, the doctor came in and told me I should go back to my brother's house and come back again tomorrow. He said there would be a shift change later when another nurse would arrive, and then another in the early morning. He told me the treatment was going to have to go on for a while so I should try to establish a routine of coming in a couple of times a day. It wouldn't be necessary to stay with him all the time because the nurses would be there to take care of him."

"Wouldn't the doctor be there, too?" Anne asked. Al shook his head.

"No," he said, "the doctor said he would be there at least once a week to check on the progress, but he had other patients in other locations that he would have to tend to. So, I left and returned in the morning. The doctor wasn't there, and there was a different nurse. Later in the afternoon, she left and the nurse that was there when I showed up came in. I spent time talking to my brother, leaving to get some lunch, and talking again in the afternoon. Then I'd go home and do it all over again the next day. That's been my life for close to a month now. When I wasn't with my brother I was just back at his house, taking care of bills, having some people come and do repairs on it, stuff like that. He had let a lot of things go on it. Probably 'cause he didn't have much money to get it fixed up. Now that isn't a problem." Magee fidgeted a bit in his seat then cleared his throat as if he was going to speak. Al recognized it as a signal to get back to the main part of the story.

"Anyway," he continued, "The day before yesterday when I was leaving in the afternoon, the nurse stopped me. She said the doctor would be in during the morning of the next day, which was yesterday, and he had to do some tests on my brother to determine his progress. The tests would take most of the day, and then, depending on what they found, there probably would be some procedures done after that. She said I shouldn't come in at that time because I wouldn't be able to see him. She recommended I come in the evening, and then the normal routine would start again after that." Al looked at each of them to see if anyone had a question. When no one spoke, he started again.

"I was surprised when I showed up," he said. "It was shortly after seven o'clock. Usually, there's a nurse's car in the lot, but it was empty. The lights were on inside the building, though. I went inside and there was no nurse, only my brother, who was still in the hospital bed with all of the monitors attached. And there was this note taped to the side of the bed." Al took another piece of paper from the envelope and handed it to Magee for review. As he read the first line, he smiled and looked at the others.

"Ok," he said, "This is officially now the weirdest case I've ever had." He looked back down at the paper and began reading. "Dear Mr. Marchioni, I'm very sorry we had to deceive you, but I assure you, it was for a good cause. The good news is your brother is not sick. He does not have cancer, and although his health isn't great because of his alcoholism, he has several years left. Particularly if he can stay sober. The other good news is he's entitled to all of the money we deposited so he should be able to live comfortably for those years. There is a manila envelope on the receptionist's desk in the front office. There you'll find instructions for what to do next." Magee looked up at Al and pointed to the envelope. "I take it that's what you found," he said. Al shook his head.

"No," he said, "Actually, this is an envelope I got later. The police took the original envelope and everything else. But I made copies and that's what I passed to you." Magee smiled.

"Well at least that's something normal," he said. "What did you find in the envelope that was left there?" Al pulled another sheet out of the envelope he had and handed it to him.

"The instructions they left," he said, "just like they said." Magee took the paper and scanned it. Then he looked up at Al.

"They actually told you to call the police?" he asked. Al nodded. Then for the benefit of Paul and Anne, Magee began to read what was on the paper. "The first thing you must do is call 911 and ask for EMS to be sent to your location. The police should arrive with the ambulance. While the ambulance is on the way, make a copy of this instruction sheet and provide it to the Paramedics when they arrive. Below is important information about the treatment doses we've used so far and a reading of the last vitals we took. This will be used by doctors at the hospital to bring your brother out of the coma we induced." Magee could see statistics at the bottom of the page, along with a list of drug names and doses. "The police will want to take the original of this as part of their investigation. So, having the copy ensures the knowledge is passed immediately to the doctors when your brother arrives. We've already begun the process of waking him up, and they will continue the process at the hospital. I assure you he will recover fully. He'll be very weak for several days because he has been in bed for three weeks, but he should be fine under their care. Once again, I apologize for the inconvenience, Best regards, Dr. R. Schwartzman." Magee looked up again. "Well, whoever this Schwartzman is, he is certainly polite." Paul quickly spoke up.

"Magee, that's the name of the attorney I talked to," he said. Magee nodded.

"I know," he said, "Devereaux hadn't heard of him when I brought it up to him. Could be a coincidence."

"Or maybe he is both a polite doctor and an attorney, combined into one person," Paul said. Magee was still looking at Al.

"Is that all, then?" he asked. Al shook his head.

"No, Mr. Magee," he replied, "There's more. I accompanied my brother to the hospital. They told me it would take a few days to wake him up. They had to go slowly because the body would react to the withdrawal of the drugs they used. Plus, they were concerned about how long the breathing tube had been inserted and may need to do a different procedure to make sure there were no long-term effects of that. It was a lot of medical stuff and a little beyond what I could understand. But the bottom line was he was going to be there for a while. They recommended I go home, and they would know more by today.

"When I got back to my brother's house, I found another manila envelope between the front door and the storm door," he said. He picked up the envelope in front of him. "That was this one. Inside was another note and one thousand one-hundred-dollar bills." He waited to see if Magee reacted. But Magee just smiled. Al pulled the note from the envelope and passed it to him. Magee read it aloud.

"Mr. Marchioni," Magee read, "just some additional compensation for your time and any grief we've caused you. We left it here so you would not have to report it to the police. They would only take it from you as part of the evidence. By now they have already opened a criminal investigation for what happened to your brother." It was unsigned. "I don't suppose you still have the bills in there," Magee said. Al shook his head.

"No," he said, "I put them in a safe place. I really don't want to have to give that to the police. Is that wrong?" Magee shrugged his shoulders.

"The police would probably tell you it is," he started, "but I'm not going to say that. These people put you through a lot of grief. So, you are kind of entitled to something." Al looked relieved.

"What kind of people have that kind of money to give to people?" he asked. "Are they drug dealers do you think?" Both Magee and Paul laughed.

"I don't think drug dealers would be that polite," Paul said.

"He's right," Magee added. "You wouldn't be sitting here if this involved drugs. I mean street drugs. But there is someone else with a lot of money that just wanted to get you away from the clinic for a while. Out of curiosity, why did you return so quickly?"

"Well, after I found out my brother wasn't sick, I called Anne to explain things," Al replied. "I figured if these guys were doing something wrong, I shouldn't have to stick by this agreement they had me sign." He looked at Anne for confirmation and she nodded. "Besides, I felt terrible about having to leave so suddenly. And then Anne told me what had happened. I knew that meant she would need help. I mean, Carol is great at what she does, but she doesn't like to be a boss. And my brother won't be coming out of it for a while. So, I asked if I could come back to help get things going." Anne chimed in.

"You didn't have to ask twice," she said with a smile. Al smiled too.

"I drove most of the night to get here, and I'll stay as long as I'm needed," he said. "I'll go down and visit my brother once he wakes up. I told the police they can call me if they need more information." Magee sat back in his seat and looked at Paul.

"What do you make of it all, Magee?" Paul said. Magee tightened his lips as he thought for a moment before answering. He quickly ran down the list on his mental notebook.

"It's one interesting thing after another," he said. "I mean, they must have put in this plan to get Mr. Marchioni away from here well before the mice got here. They had to get Stan into the restaurant. Why even send the mice?" Anne spoke up.

"Can we think of a new name to call them?" she asked. "It's creepy that we keep referring to them as the mice. It sounds like we have a rodent infestation." Everyone laughed.

"Okay," Magee said. "How about the three amigos?" Anne smiled approval. "Alright," he continued, "so, why send them?" As the words came out of his mouth, his expression changed. His eyes grew wider and his jaw dropped a bit. "Wait a minute," he said. "When did the brother die?" Al's eyes grew wide.

"My brother isn't dead," he said quickly. Anne put her hand on his arm.

"No, Al," she said, "He means the patient's brother." Al calmed down. Paul spoke next.

"It was the end of the week before the mice," he stopped, "I mean, amigos arrived."

"And they came on a Thursday, right?" he said. Paul nodded. "And Dr. Klein called me on Friday, and I showed up Monday morning." Both Anne and Paul were nodding now. "Today is Wednesday. So basically, Stan had been in place before the brother died, and they had figured out this whole elaborate scheme with Mr. Marchioni's brother and had it up and running before they knew the brother was going to be dead," he said with emphasis on the 'dead'." He looked at them both to see their reaction. Their faces were both glum.

"I guess that means we're back to the idea that the brother could have been killed," Paul said. "Somebody was planning all of this. Maybe the brother found out and they decided to get him out of the way." Magee was pensive, and then finally shook his head.

"I hope not," he said, "I don't suppose we can rule it out, but it still could have been a coincidence. Maybe they planned for the brother to be there when they came out, but he died just before they made the trip."

"I thought you said you don't believe in coincidences," Anne said. Magee shrugged.

"I guess I'm starting to hope there are some," he answered. "I'm still going to be skeptical. But this whole case just keeps twisting every which way, I just might start believing in anything about now." As he spoke his cell phone rang. "One second, guys," he said as he pulled it out of a pocket. He stood up and walked away from the table before answering.

"Magee here," he said, pulling it to his ear.

"Charlie here," the voice responded. Magee walked a little farther from the table. When he knew the others could no longer hear him, he spoke into the phone with his back to them.

"What do you have for me, Charlie?" he asked.

"Good news and bad news," Charlie replied. "Isn't that always the case?" he added. "First, the good news. We did find out that someone got in and fooled around with the data. And, we were able to put it all back." He paused. Magee sensed he wanted a response.

"Great, Charlie," Magee said. "I can't look at it now, but I'll get back on later and follow up. What's the bad news?"

"Well," Charlie said, drawing the vowel for a longer time than usual, "we also found out who did it. Or should I say, we know whose password was used to do it." He paused again.

"Okay, Charlie," he said with irritation this time, "Who is it and why are you taking so long to tell me?"

"You're not going to like it," was the response.

"Try me," Magee shot back.

"Okay," Charlie answered, "It was Dig Smith's password." Then he waited. Magee knew why. He knew Charlie was expecting a reaction because of the name he just said.

"How is that possible, Charlie?" Magee finally asked. He could hear Charlie clearing his throat.

"We don't know exactly, Magee," Charlie said. "We both know he's dead. Maybe he passed it along to someone before he died."

"That would have been some forethought," Magee said. "He died so unexpectedly," he added. "I mean, I know he didn't think he was going to."

"I know that, too," Charlie said back. "You told me he said he didn't expect to die just before you killed him." Magee didn't respond. "But he could have had some plan in case it did happen," Charlie added. "He could have sent it to someone else with instructions on what to do if something happened to him." Magee shook his head, even though he knew Charlie couldn't see him doing it.

"No," he said, "that doesn't make sense either. How in the world would it get connected to a specific case I was on right now? He couldn't have left instructions to get rid of anything related to the Devereaux."

"Hmmm," Charlie started, "I suppose you're right. But I don't know how else to explain it. You know our passwords are ironclad. We've never had a breach before. And in this case, whoever used it did it correctly the first time. It wasn't as if they tried it until they worked out the bugs. It was one time, perfect, get in, wipe out the data, get out, clean," he said.

"Well, you guys better figure out what happened," Magee said. "Otherwise, the Privy is gonna be just that, a shit-hole." He knew Charlie could sense his anger.

"Okay, Magee," he said, "we'll work on it." He paused and then added, "there is one possibility. Someone on our tech team may have been compromised. It's a long shot, but it could happen."

"Find out," Magee said. "You were right. This is bad news. It may be a lot *worse* than you think, given that name is involved," he said. "So far, in this case, nobody has been seriously hurt. But I need to know who did this and why quickly before someone is." He heard Charlie agree and hang up the phone. Magee pretended to still be talking for a moment. He needed time to think, given the name that was brought up. Dig would have killed him if he hadn't killed Dig first. He turned around and looked at the table with Anne, Paul, and Al. The last thing he wanted was for anything to happen to anyone he had met so far, and especially Anne.

He started walking back toward them. Anne had turned and was watching him. She was smiling. Al and Paul stood up and were shaking hands by the time he reached them. Both of them were smiling. He forced a smile and saw Anne frown.

"What's wrong?" she asked as he neared.

"Am I that transparent?" he said to her. Then he made a real smile and she relaxed.

"To me, you are," she said with confidence. He kept smiling. He knew that was true and felt good about it. "Nothing's too wrong," he said. "That was Charlie on the phone, the guy from the Privy," he added. "Still hasn't found anything, which surprises me."

"You were talking to a guy in a privy?" Paul was laughing when he asked. Magee laughed and nodded.

"Yeah, Paul," he said. "I'll tell you all the details later."

"Not all the details, please," Paul replied holding his hands up. Magee looked at Al.

"I think we have everything we need," he said. "I suppose you're headed off to do some work now," he said, extending his hand. Al looked grateful as he took it.

"Y-yes," he stammered as he took it. "And thank you for understanding." Then he looked at Anne and Paul and added, "I didn't know whether you would blame me for what happened. I had no idea why Stan would do what he did."

"I understand," Anne said, "He seemed like such a nice young man." Al looked surprised.

"Young?" he asked. "Stan is old, as old as me. I knew him from when I got my first restaurant job. I worked at his parent's restaurant. So did he." Magee made a face and looked at Anne.

"What did you say, Al?" she asked.

"About Stan? I just said he was as old as me," he replied. "He worked at the Blue Lady. That was his parent's place. When they died, he inherited it and kept it open for a long time. I went on to other jobs and pretty-much lost touch with him for a while until he called me about a week before I found out about my brother."

"Why was he calling?" Magee asked.

"He was asking for advice," Al said. "He said he had to close the Blue Lady, but he wasn't ready to quit working. So, he was wondering if I knew of any places that might need help." Magee made a puzzled face.

"What did you tell him?" he asked.

"That I didn't know of anywhere," Al replied. "I've been working out here for a long time. I haven't kept up with the places in the city. But I told him if I heard of anything, I'd let him know." Paul spoke next.

"So, when you had to leave to take care of your brother," he said, "he was available to come and help. Somebody you would feel completely comfortable recommending." Al nodded in agreement. Paul continued, "Only it wasn't your actual friend that showed up. It was the young Stan. The people who sent him knew you weren't going to be around when he got here. No one here would know it was somebody else pretending to be who you recommended." Al looked a little unsure.

"I guess so," he said. Then he added, "All I know is that the Stan I recommended is old."

"The young Stan still seemed to know a lot about food and the restaurant business, Paul," Magee offered. "Everybody thought he was pretty good at the job." Anne and Paul agreed.

"He convinced me that he knew what he was doing halfway through the interview," Anne said. "Either he really was someone in that business before coming here, or they trained him well."

"Which would mean they had been planning it for even longer than we thought," Magee replied.

"I'm sorry," Al said. "I shouldn't have recommended him. I didn't know it wasn't going to be the Stan I knew that showed up."

"Believe me," Magee said, "It isn't any fault of yours. This doesn't have anything to do with you. This was just a well-planned operation." Magee offered his hand to Al again. "Thanks for your help. It was nice to meet you." Al shook his hand and walked away toward the kitchen. They all watched until he was through the door. Magee looked at Anne.

"Paul and I are going to have to go back to his office and meet for a while. I'm going to brief him on the Privy details, and we'll cover the security needed after I leave." he said, "I have to get back to the city and start talking to people." Anne suddenly looked worried.

"You're not going back without coming to see me after talking to Paul, are you?" she asked.

"Of course not," Magee said. Anne relaxed.

"Good. Then come to my office after," she said.

"Spoken like a true boss," Magee told her.

Chapter 17

Paul's office was pretty much the same as it was when he and Paul had left it two days ago. The paper with Magee's picture was still on the desk. The manila folder with the rest of his file was still off to the side. The glasses and the bottle of Jack Daniels were gone from the desk, but Magee could see two clean glasses on the credenza. He sat down again in the chair in front of the desk, while Paul took his seat behind.

"What's up, Magee?" Paul asked. "When you came back to the table there, you looked a little disturbed. But then, by the time you had talked to Marchioni, you looked fine again. What does it take to shake you?" Paul pointed at the file. "You didn't even blink when you saw how thick this was. And then when Stan was herding us into the treatment room, you had your blank face on. You were as cool as a cucumber when you talked to him." Magee looked over at the glasses on the credenza.

"You know," he started, "I was hoping to find my whiskey glass still here. Remember I promised not to let it go to waste. I'm regretting that I didn't finish my drink when we first met." Paul smiled. He pulled open the drawer of his desk and brought out the Jack Daniels.

"I didn't let it go to waste," he said, "and it's easy to fix." He grabbed the glasses and filled them up about a third of the way. Then he pushed one to Magee and raised the other one. "I'm glad you're the guy that came to the top when I asked around." Magee smiled.

"Me, too," he said, taking his glass up to Paul's to clink it. He took a swallow then brought it down in front of himself. He stared into it and swirled the whiskey around as if he was thinking of something far away. Paul didn't interrupt him. He took a swallow from his glass and just waited. Magee was content to let him wait. His mind was far away, in a different place, and at a different time. It was long before he met Anne or anyone else at the clinic. It was Paris, in the spring. He was working on a case, but not one that his secretary had arranged. His former employer had called and asked for a favor that would take him to France.

His first thought when he agreed was that he would take Jenny. Even though they hadn't gotten around to marrying, it could be like a honeymoon that they would never take because they were working to grow the business. So, there they were, sitting outside a small café on Quai de Montebello. On the other side of the street was the Seine and beyond that Notre Dame. They were having coffee. They were holding hands across the table.

"Are you glad you came?" he asked her as he reached with his other hand and brushed away a strand of hair that had fallen across her face.

"That's a silly question," she answered. "Of course, I'm happy." She took his hand as he started to pull it back from her hair. "This has been fantastic. I've never ever been somewhere like this before." She wore a broad smile on her face. He was smiling, too.

"Then I'm happy, too!" he stated.

"Good," she said. She rose slightly from her chair so she could lean across the table to kiss. He rose also and met her halfway. His napkin slipped from his lap and fell to the sidewalk. As he sat back down, he leaned over to pick it up. A popping noise from behind startled him. He thought maybe it was a car backfiring. When he came back up with the napkin, he looked back at Jenny and saw a stream of red running down the front of her dress.

She had an odd look on her face and her shoulders were pressed flat back against her chair. People around him were screaming and scrambling from their tables, running in different directions. It took him a minute to realize what was happening. He turned around and saw a man in a long coat on the opposite side of the street, limping slightly, but moving quickly away along the riverfront. The man turned his head and looked back.

Magee saw his face clearly and knew what had happened. For a moment, he wanted to run. He wanted to run as fast as he could to the man and put his hands around his throat and squeeze with all his might. He could picture the man's head exploding as he squeezed. But he knew he couldn't run. There was something more important to do. He turned quickly and caught Jenny as she was falling from the chair.

He laid her onto the sidewalk below the table and put one hand on her chest where the red was coming out and the other under her head to hold it. He pushed hard but the red didn't stop. It just kept coming out through his fingers. People were still running away. He screamed for someone to call an ambulance and held his hand firmly on her chest. He was shouting for somebody to help. Some people had stopped running and had turned back toward him. His eyes went from person to person as he pleaded for help. Then he lowered them to look back at her face. She was looking back and smiling as she attempted to bring her hand up to his face. He took his hand off her chest to grab hers and put it against his cheek. He felt her arm go limp as she closed her eyes and the smile faded away. He was saying no as it happened, then he closed his eyes and knew she was gone.

Paul was still waiting when Magee finally lifted his head. His eyes were moist. He looked down again at his glass, then quickly raised it and drank the rest of the whiskey in a gulp. Then he looked at Paul and pointed to the folder.

"You probably already guessed that my file doesn't have everything in it," he said. Paul raised his eyebrows.

"You're right," he said. "I figured that out a while ago when I saw how you handled yourself. You know how to fight. You know how to handle a gun. I mean, I know that a lot of PIs have those skills in case they need them. But most of the work I read about in your file wasn't dangerous. So, you wouldn't have needed them for those things." Magee smiled. "And in fact," Paul added, "I think a lot of PIs are working on surveillance stuff anyway, like cheating spouses, and things like that." Magee nodded but didn't speak. Paul went on, "So, what's the story." Magee cleared his throat.

"You knew from my file I didn't serve in the military," he started, "but in a way I did," he sat back in the chair and looked like he was relaxing. "I was an army brat, and you knew that," he said. Paul nodded. "But you didn't know that when I grew up and got old enough to enlist, they wouldn't let me." Paul frowned.

"What do you mean, the Army?" he asked. Magee shook his head.

"No, it wasn't the Army," he answered. "I mean it wasn't just the Army. It was the Corps, the Navy, and the Air Force, too." Magee laughed. "Hell, I probably should have tried the Coast Guard," he said, still laughing, "but I didn't think of it then," he paused long enough to shake his head, and then went on. "Anyway, I actually tried to enlist when I turned eighteen. By that time, my dad was high up in MIRC, and had been for a while."

"That's impressive," Paul interrupted.

"Yeah, I know," Magee continued. "Anyway, he apparently had a different idea. There was another group he thought could use me better, a civilian group. I mean, it's still a government group, but staffed by civilians, not military. To join, you couldn't even have a military record. You couldn't have even worked for the government. They had a shell company. And it was in the defense industry so the military could buy from it. But that was just a funding mechanism. It never supplied any products, only services." Paul was listening, intently, and Magee stopped only long enough to see if he had any questions. Then he continued.

"I know that the shell company was in my file. It's part of my 'official record.' It shows that I worked for them for fourteen years," he said. Then he added, "Well, the first year wasn't working. It was training." Paul interrupted.

"What kind of training?" he asked.

"Pretty much everything hard," Magee replied. "I did the twenty-four weeks with the Seals, and then I trained as a Katsa." Paul had a questioning look on his face. "It's a Mossad Collections officer, Magee said, "pretty much a field agent. The whole time in those situations, they had given me a different identity so that everyone I interacted with thought I was someone else. In a way, that was good training, too. In the job, I usually needed to make someone think I was someone other than who I really was."

"Well, you're good at that," Paul said with a smile. Magee laughed. He liked Paul. He had started to become comfortable with him, which was unusual for Magee. He knew he wasn't telling him everything, but just as much as he needed to know. He had always been a loner, never having any close friends. Growing up he made friends wherever he moved, but they were always temporary. He knew he was there for a couple of years max, so he never wanted to get too attached to anyone.

As he aged, he didn't have a chance to. In the on-base schools, he found himself being pushed into special classes where he was the only student. He learned subjects the others did not. Others were learning French, Spanish and Italian. He learned those, too, in addition to Japanese, Mandarin, Urdu, Farsi, and others. He learned basic math through trig but was told he didn't need calculus. They taught him basic science, but not chemistry or beyond.

His fitness classes gave him the discipline he needed to keep fit and included special movements that honed his reflexes. Through it all, he thought they were preparing him for a career in the military to serve his country. In fact, whenever he asked about why he was going through different classes than others were, his father would tell him that. The day he turned eighteen, his father was away on a mission. He wanted to surprise him by enlisting. He went to each of the recruiters and they all told him the same thing. Talk to your father.

At first, he was angry, but by the time his father got home, he was just confused. He met his father at the door and demanded to know why he went through all of the things he learned in school and then wasn't allowed to enlist. He still remembers the words his father used. Those who serve in secret are those who serve best. He understood that after his first mission for the organization.

Paul didn't need to know any more details. But he still had to brief him on the Privy so he could explain why he was worried about the call from Charlie.

"Well, anyway," he said when he started speaking again, "One day I just got tired of what they were asking me to do. So, I decided to retire and do something else." Paul held up his hand as a stop signal.

"Whoa, buddy," he said. "You haven't told me yet about what they were asking you to do." Then he waited for Magee to fill in the blanks. Magee shook his head.

"I will tell you that, just not right now," he said. Paul frowned. "I promise," Magee added. "I just need to tell you about the next part first because it may become a problem." Paul stopped frowning and became serious. He leaned forward to listen more closely as Magee continued. "When I quit, I went into P.I. work. A lot of people who worked for that group did the same thing. In fact, a lot of ex-military do, too, or at least some sort of security work. But you know that. That's what you did when you got better." Paul nodded.

"Yeah, it's true," he said, "Gotta make a living some way."

"I was lucky," Magee continued, "Because of my dad, I knew about another group of guys who provided a service to people doing investigative work. These were computer geeks. They were ex-military, too, but they took what they did in the military and created a sort of library for Private Investigators. It's just a side business for them. They made a whole bunch of money selling an app to Microsoft, and then they used some of that money to start a network for P.I.'s." He stopped. Paul was still leaning forward and listening.

"Their URL is PIVN.com, and I use them a lot," he continued. "Basically, they aggregate data from all investigations that P.I.'s do, so you can get a lot of info without having to do it all yourself. It only works, though, because the P.I.'s add the info after they're done with an investigation. I was trying to use them yesterday to find out more about the

Devereaux, but anything that had been put up there by anybody else was gone."

"What do you mean, gone?" Paul asked.

"I mean not there," Magee answered. "Poof. Vanished," he added while using his hands to convey something disappearing. Paul looked puzzled.

"Maybe there was never anything put there," he said, more like a question than a statement. Magee shook his head.

"The Devereauxs have too much money, and too much fame to be blank. I knew someone would have done an investigation on them before now," he said. "I called and reported it as a problem. And, in fact, when I received the call yesterday, they told me there was a breach and all of the info was put back."

"Then that sounds like good news, right?" Paul said. "Why is that a problem?

"It isn't," Magee replied. "The problem is who erased it," he added. Then he paused for a moment to think about how to explain it. He had told Paul some things about the job he did before becoming a P.I., but not any other details about what he did for them. Now he had to tell him about why the missing information was dangerous. That part had nothing to do directly with the Devereaux. Paul was still waiting when he started again.

"Actually," he said, "It isn't so much who erased it as it is the ID that erased it." He pulled his hand up and scratched his head, then continued. "These network guys are good. They know their stuff. They had to. They worked with top-secret stuff and they all had that clearance. They have a password system on the network that I don't think anyone could crack. They don't think so either." He paused again. Paul seemed very focused, listening to every word he said. "But somebody, somehow, got hold of a password, and in the process used it to get in. The ID was for a real person, but it was someone else that used it."

"How do you know that?" Paul asked. "I mean, it's all done over the network, right. Maybe it was really the person who had some sort of reason to get in there and muck with the system." Again, Magee shook his head.

"Not possible," he said. "That person is dead." Paul's look went from questioning to surprise.

"For how long?" Paul asked, but didn't wait for Magee to reply. "Was it recently?" he added. Magee's head shook again.

"No," he said. He died a long time ago." Paul frowned.

"Then why was his ID even still active?" he asked. "They should have taken it down when he died. That would be the first thing they did if they knew their stuff. Sheesh," he added with emphasis. Magee laughed, but then got more serious.

"Well, they don't do that in certain circumstances," Magee said. He could tell Paul was waiting to hear the kinds of circumstances. "These are all guys that served in some way. If someone dies while they're still on active duty, they leave the ID active, out of respect. Although they probably will change that now."

"Well, then," Paul said, "Maybe the guy isn't really dead." Once again, Magee had to shake his head.

"No, he's dead, alright," He said. "I know that for a fact!"

"But how, exactly?" Paul said. "I knew a guy who went missing and was presumed dead for a couple of years, and then suddenly he turned up."

"Not possible for this guy," Magee said. "I killed him, and I made sure before I left him in a gutter in Paris."

Chapter 18

Paris had been three years before Magee received the call from Dr. Klein. He had done several cases in between, but this was the first time he had said anything to anyone about what happened there. He had long since buried it in his mind and focused on his work. But it was always with him. And now he was forced to think about it again.

He had no plan to share the details with Paul yet. Perhaps after the case was resolved he would. For now, he simply closed his eyes again and let himself remember what had happened, and what came immediately after.

Jenny had been gone for twelve weeks. Magee was still in Paris. He had no reason to leave. He did have a reason to stay. He stood looking down from a window off Rue des Barres, not far from Notre Dame and the other side of the Seine where she was killed. The handler in the organization had told him the kill was approved and said Magee would find Dig in a rented apartment somewhere along that street. They couldn't be sure exactly which one.

Magee had gone to the top to obtain approval for the operation. He insisted on complete control. There would be no team, no formal plan either. Too many of the previous plans had broken down. People had been lost. Still, he was surprised when management agreed completely to his demand. Perhaps they knew that it didn't matter what they said. He was not officially working for them. He had left the organization two years earlier. His presence in Paris was because they asked for a favor.

In the time since his Jenny had been shot and before he started staring down at the street below, their investigation had identified the person who had been conspiring with Dig, and the fact that Dig had been living in Paris for some time. They provided him with the address of Dig's apartment.

They left Dig's accomplice in place on the job with no reason to suspect he had been discovered. They monitored the individual's communication and when he sent what appeared to be a coded e-mail, picked up and read from a French server, they had dug up the remainder of information needed to allow Magee to proceed.

France was the location for the first attempt to take out Dig. Magee had been on that first attempt. When the operation went south, it ended with French authorities getting involved. International agreements between allies allow for certain situations to be 'covered' before they become public knowledge.

The assassination of one of your own citizens on the foreign soil of an ally is explicitly forbidden but still required at times. Drones are often used when dealing with an adversarial country, but they couldn't be used in the case of an ally. Those cases required a human agent that could make decisions in the heat of the moment. The organization works very hard to develop an appropriate plan, so it avoids discovery. However, there is a process for handling the situation if authorities find out what has happened. Attempting and failing also has a process. And each discovery comes with a cost.

A non-involved panel of arbitrators is convened from three other allied nations. They review the circumstances and agree on an appropriate punishment for the offending country. Over the years that the process had been in place, several decisions had been handed down. Sometimes substantial fines had been paid. Sometimes other arrangements are suggested. Rarely has any country objected to the decisions of the arbitrators.

In the case of the first attempt on Dig, France insisted no new attempts be made on an American citizen for at least three years. There was a fine and a promise to make at least one attempt to lure citizens out before conducting future operations. It made sense that Dig would stay in France for as long as that agreement was in effect. He had ventured outside of France to conduct his business activities. He was vulnerable then but always could rely on his ally in the organization to keep him informed if a new attempt was going to be made. He slipped in and out of France several times during which he was able to take revenge on three other team members who had tried to take him out.

He knew the time was running out and soon he would be in season again. So, the sham operation had been planned to give him the opportunity while in France. He knew he would not be hunted, which allowed him more freedom to choose his time and place for the executions.

Two other agents had died but chance interfered with his revenge on Magee. Now it was Magee's turn to seek it.

Magee had researched the area in which Dig lived. He had rented two apartments on the same street, in the same block. Using his training to convince people he was someone else, he had disguised himself as an old Jew. He dressed in a long black suit, traditional hat, and gartel. He let his beard grow out and dyed it white, along with his hair worn with sidelocks. He shuffled on the street like one would expect a very old man to shuffle.

The location was a few blocks from the Shoah memorial and every morning Magee would shuffle there and back. While inside, he would watch those who entered to see if he had been followed. If Magee aroused suspicion as a new neighbor, he expected Dig would follow him to the museum to see what he did there. After a week, he was not concerned that Dig suspected.

When he wasn't performing his museum trip, he would spend alternating times watching and photographing from the windows of the two apartments. Each gave a different view. He kept track of the time he spent at each one, recording the direction that he watched, the lighting conditions and detailing possible suspects. Dig had similar skills regarding disguises but when Magee saw him leaving the scene of the shooting, he was himself.

Magee couldn't be one-hundred percent certain that Dig could be found in the location they had given him. But it was the easiest place to start. And he knew Dig. He knew that Dig would have been emboldened by his success. Dig always had a cocky side. When you have a perfect record, you begin to think you're infallible. He was hoping that Dig would believe that just a little longer.

It took four weeks of watching. He had identified three possibilities. All were the size and build of Dig. All had slight limps on their right sides. Dig's limp was the result of Magee's shot on the first attempt to stop him. He recovered, but he was no longer untouchable. Now it would be what Magee would use to identify him as the man who killed Jenny.

The next step would involve narrowing it down to just Dig. He needed to be certain and to be that absolutely, Magee would need to get close, very close. It would be a risk. He would be face to face with someone who knew him for who he was. Convincing people that you were someone other than who you are is fairly easy when they don't know you. Not so much when they already do. Dig would look in his eyes and realize immediately who he was looking at. Magee began to relish that thought. He wanted Dig to know. He needed Dig to know.

The difficulty would be that he would get only one chance. Whatever occurred at the instant that Dig became aware would determine if Magee would succeed or not. Magee would have to kill him at that point or watch him vanish underground and never surface again. Dig had that ability. He had a network of support built up and enough money squirreled away to let him live quietly in a very nice place, unsought, unknown, and untouched.

Magee reviewed the notes he had made looking for something that might help him differentiate between the three ahead of time. He decided he didn't have to have absolute evidence of who was who. He only had to have something to prioritize which one he would confront first. He decided to change his observation point to street level. There was a small café in the path of each man's daily journey. He made it a point to spend time there, sipping coffee and reading the Israeli Daily Hayom. From the cafe, he was able to take additional photographs of each man. After a week, he felt he had enough to review and prioritize.

He copied the pictures of the three men to a computer where they could be enlarged and enhanced. He also had photographs of Dig from his days as an agent. He started with a full-body picture of Dig in stride and brought up a picture of each of the three men in stride to compare against it. He ignored the limp entirely and focused on other comparable items, starting with the hands. Dig had very large hands.

The distance across the knuckles on top of Dig's hand was over four-and-one-half inches. The fingers were thick and not long. When he gauged the three hands together, one stood out distinctly. The fingers were long and narrow. The hand itself was thin and delicate. Magee imagined the owner to be a concert pianist or master of some other instrument. The hands were unscarred and well cared for. He set this person aside.

The other two were very similar and Magee found little to base his opinion on. He moved on to the face. He found the likeness between the two faces to be alarming. Each had a broad nose, deep-set eyes, and thin lips. The facial hair was similar as well. Magee examined each component of each face, looking for anything that would help.

Each one looked old when compared to the original he had of Dig. Magee opened software that allowed him to age the face to what would be Dig's current age. It seemed to give one of the men a slight advantage. The decision became clearer when he examined the ears. The lobe in one picture was longer than the aged picture of Dig. The other matched exactly. Magee understood that ears and lobes continue to grow as people age. It was as much as he needed. He decided that one was Dig. He would confront him first then make the final decision after confirming.

The next step would be the confrontation. For that, Magee decided that he would change his observation schedule. He intended to determine the appropriate time for the confrontation. He would prefer that it happen at a time when few people were on the street with them. It would make things simpler, not only for the organization but for him to ensure that Dig understood what was happening. He would take as much time as he needed to confirm the death. Then he wanted to walk away and move on with his grief. He hadn't mourned yet. He knew it would be coming as soon as he left France with the knowledge that Dig was dead.

It took six more days to determine that the best time would be between midnight and two AM. Dig made a nightly visit to a street not far from his apartment known as a hangout for local prostitutes. Magee had followed him a few nights in a row. Each night Dig would walk to the street, choose one of the local working girls to escort into a hotel, and then return home later. Magee determined that the seventh day would be his last.

As night fell on that day, Magee had packed his belongings and left two suitcases in one of the apartments he had rented. He would call a number later that would prompt someone to pick up the bags and ship them to a destination in the south of France, where they would conveniently disappear soon after. He carried with him the gun he planned to use, a Beretta M9A3 fitted with a silencer, and an MTech G10 folding knife. The gun was to incapacitate Dig if necessary. The knife was to allow him to bleed out at a reasonable rate so that he knew it was happening, and Magee had an opportunity to watch as he realized it.

He wore the same disguise he had been using, the long black coat and hat, with the gartel. Not that it would matter. He would announce his presence to Dig at the appropriate moment as Dig was returning home. He had selected the spot carefully, allowing him to remain unseen for as long as possible. Dig would be walking through a small passageway, connecting one street with another.

Magee waited near the café that had served as his observation post, concealed in a small alcove. As Dig passed, he counted the seconds until it was safe to step out. From there it was only a matter of keeping just the right distance, so Dig did not spot him. He watched as Dig entered the passageway and waited the appropriate time before entering himself.

There were doorways along the passageway. Magee had chosen one in which he could stand back and wait for Dig to pass as he was walking back to his apartment. He envisioned that from there, he would step out to wrap an arm around Dig with the gun firmly placed at his back.

Once he pulled him back into the doorway, he would spin him around till his back was against the wall, put the gun to his right shoulder and pull the trigger. As the momentum of the bullet pinned him to the wall, Magee would remove his knife and slit his throat, then ease him down to the ground. He would kneel on his left arm and hold his head up from the ground so he could look in his eyes, just as he had held Jenny's head as the life drained from her. Dig's right arm would be useless. Magee would put his mouth close to Dig's ear and tell him the final words he would hear. When is revenge not revenge? When it also serves a higher purpose.

Magee entered the passageway. Dig had already exited the other side. Magee knew he would have a good view of Dig chatting with various girls once he reached the end. As he neared it, he slowed. He leaned cautiously around the side.

There was a blow to the side of his head that knocked him back and up against the wall. He could feel a pair of hands grabbing his coat and pulling him first, then pushing him, which slammed his head against the wall. The motion was repeated, and things were starting to go black when his training kicked in.

His knee rose by instinct and found its target between Dig's legs. It wasn't much but was enough to interrupt his push. Magee's head had cleared enough for him to use it. He brought his forehead down on Dig's nose and could hear it crack. Dig released his grip and grabbed at his nose. Magee pushed Dig's right shoulder as he grabbed his left and spun him. His left arm came up and wrapped around Dig's neck, pulling him back into him. His right hand dropped to his pocket and took out the folding knife. Dig had slowed with age, and the knife found its target before he could bring his arm up to shield it. Magee made a clean cut on the right side. He avoided the esophagus and focused only on the artery.

The knife moved quickly into his left hand and completed a cut on that side. Blood spurted straight out, reaching to the wall on the other side of the passageway. Dig released his nose and put his hands on the sides of his neck as if he was going to stop the bleeding. Magee released him. He staggered for a moment and then sank to his knees. Magee moved behind him and twisted as he pulled him over to lay him down on the ground. Their fight had spilled partly out from the passage. Magee dragged him back in and to the nearest doorway. He propped him up against it and scanned both ways along the passage. No one had entered from either side. Magee took a knee alongside him and moved his face close. He took off the hat and looked in his eyes. Dig's eyes grew wide as he looked back, then he smiled.

Magee had intended to speak to him. He wanted to ensure Dig knew why it was him who came. He wanted Dig to speak back and say he understood. Instead, he realized it wasn't going to happen. He simply watched and waited until the last bit of life drained out onto the cobblestones of the passageway and into the sewer.

Chapter 19

By the time Magee opened his eyes again, the surprise had faded from Paul's face. He understood the reaction. It wasn't that Paul thought Magee hadn't killed anyone. Once Magee had explained the training that he had, Paul would assume that he would have used it. No one gets that kind of training unless it's needed for the work you were going to do. Odds were that somewhere during his years on the job, he would have needed to kill. But it was his description, particularly the emphasis on 'gutter,' that Paul would have considered surprising. Magee hadn't filled in any of the details for Paul. He only knew that Magee had killed the guy with an ID used on the privy. But the use of the word gutter would let Paul know that the killing was motivated by revenge.

Paul himself had killed on tour. He also could describe, even with a very brief statement, when it was personal. Soldiers are trained to kill in battle when it is necessary because the enemy will kill them if they don't. It isn't personal. It's only work. Sometimes, it turns personal. When you watch your friends disappear one by one in the heat of battle, you get angry. You start having a different reason to kill. It's part of being broken, which Paul had talked about being the first time they met. Paul's look of surprise was replaced by one of empathy. Paul had been in those shoes.

"We haven't known each other long," Paul started, "but from what I know about you right now, I'd say the guy deserved it." Magee smiled. "I used to read a lot when I was on tour, pulp suspense stuff," Paul added. "I read one by a guy named Mumma. It was called 'Some People Just Need Killing.'" Then Paul reached over and picked up the Jack Daniel's bottle. He poured a little in each of their glasses.

"I did have a reason," Magee said. They both sat silent for a moment. Paul looked at his whiskey.

"Something tells me we may have to lay off this for a while," he said as he raised his glass and held it, waiting for Magee to raise his.

"You're right, Paul," Magee replied, bringing his own glass up to touch Paul's. They both gulped down the contents. Then Paul put the bottle back in the drawer and shut it.

"So," Paul said, "what's our next move?" Magee was still thinking about how to respond when his cell phone rang. It was an unknown caller. Paul nodded and motioned for him to go ahead and take it.

"Hello," Magee said.

"Hello," a man's voice on the other end said, "is this Magee?"

"Yes," he replied.

"Good," the man said. "This is Deputy Thomas Lane, from the Sherriff's department in Mendocino County. Do you know a...," there was a pause before he began again, "Willie Longbow?" Magee thought for a moment.

"Maybe," Magee answered, "Is he the guy that works at the airport, the little one called Stanley field?" he asked.

"Yeah," Lane said, "he had your card in his shirt pocket."

"Yes. I just met him yesterday," Magee said. "I gave him my card."

"Yeah, I found your card. He had it in his shirt pocket," Lane repeated.

"What do you mean had?" he said.

"Well, he's dead, Mr. Magee," Lane said. "I was searching his body as part of the call." Magee knew what he meant. Lane would have been among the responders who had been called if there was an emergency.

"Hang on a sec," Magee said back to Lane. He pushed the mute button on his phone. "The guy at the airport is dead," he said to Paul. Then he pushed the speaker option on his phone and placed it on the desk. He put a finger up to his lips to signal Paul not to speak. He grabbed the paper with his picture on it and flipped it over, and then took a pen from his pocket. Then he rustled the paper into the phone so the deputy could hear it.

"Ok, I got some paper, I wanted to write this down," Magee said into the phone, putting his elbow on the table and resting his forehead against his fingers. "Now, what was your name again, Deputy?"

"My name's Lane, L-A-N-E," he said with an attitude. He sounded as if he didn't think Magee was very smart. "I came across your card when I was searching a body, William Longbow" he added. "We got an EMS call about an hour ago from the guy that found him. So, you did know him, Mr. Magee?" he asked.

"I didn't know him well. I only met him yesterday," Magee replied. "That's when I gave him my card. Do you know what happened?"

"Before I go into that," Lane said, "This card says you have a current PI license. That accurate?"

"Yes," Magee answered, "that number on the card is up to date."

"Then you know the drill," Lane responded. "We're gonna want you to come in and make a statement as soon as you can." Magee looked at Paul and rolled his eyes.

"Of course, Deputy," he said, "I know. But by your statement, I take it the death wasn't natural. What happened?"

"No sir," Lane said back. "It wasn't natural. Somebody put a bullet through the back of his skull, sort of execution-style." He waited for a response, but Magee stayed silent and took in the news. He put the tips of his fingers up to his forehead and he was glancing at Paul when Lane continued. "You know any reason why someone would want to do that?"

"No," Magee replied, "not at all. But what does the scene look like? Robbery maybe?" Lane gave a short laugh.

"Nothing like that," Lane said back. "Nothing's messed up here. I don't think he knew what was coming."

"When I talked to him yesterday, he stayed behind the counter the whole time," Magee said. "Is that where you found him?"

"No," he said. "He was found just outside the front door. It looked like he was headed toward the field." Magee pursed his lips as he recalled the layout.

"So, someone maybe was waiting for him to come out and shot him as he went past?" Magee asked.

"I'd say that's a pretty good bet," Lane replied. "He fell flat forward. I had to roll him over when I searched. That's when I found your card in his shirt pocket." Lane paused for a moment, then he added, "Listen, Mr. Magee, your card says your office is in the city. But it really would help if you could get up this way and make that statement quickly. This is kind of unusual for us in these parts. The guy that found him was a local guy who was learning how to fly. He was pretty upset when we got here, but we didn't have any reason to hold him, so we let him go home. By now, he's prob'ly started spreading the news around here. People are gonna get spooked. Frankly, you're our only lead at this point."

"I understand, Deputy," Magee answered. "I'm actually not far away right now, only about half an hour. I've got some business to finish up where I'm at right now, but I'll be headed back to the city after that. I'll stop there later this afternoon. Where will you be?"

"I have to accompany the body over to the Coroner's office," he said. "It's in Covelo off 162."

"Perfect," Magee replied. "I'm at a client's in the mountains east of you. I'd be taking 162 back anyway. I'll meet you there." He hung up and looked up at Paul.

"Have you checked your phone for the location of Stan's car lately?" he asked. Paul shook his head. He dug his phone out of his pocket and pushed on the screen.

"Forgot to look with all of the discussions we were having," he said as he scanned it. "Uh-oh," he added, "he's on the move, headed back towards the city. Moving pretty fast, too. Almost back. From the timing, he could have been at the airport about the time Longbow was killed." Magee nodded his understanding.

"Things just got a lot riskier," he said. "What about your friends you were gonna call. Did that happen?" Paul nodded.

"Yeah," he said, "I've got two guys on their way right now and another guy coming day after tomorrow."

"Are they good?" Magee asked. Paul smiled.

"Silly question," Paul replied. "They saved my ass more than once over there. Best I ever worked with against anything that got thrown at us." Magee didn't return the smile.

"Good," he said. "I'm not even sure anything will happen, but it's good to know you've got back up if you need it. This morning I didn't think anything was going to be dangerous. Everything till now has been weird, but nobody got really hurt. Now somebody's been killed." He stopped for a moment as if he was thinking. "I just can't figure Stan doing it. He didn't seem the type. Especially after his speech yesterday, even though he was pointing a gun at us."

"You're right," Paul said, "Stan's no murderer. Maybe he isn't even involved in it. Maybe our friend at the airport was into something else. You know, we used to have a lot of drug problems up here. Maybe the airport had a whole other business going on." Now Magee smiled.

"You mean it was a coincidence that we were there yesterday, chasing a guy that had a gun, and today the guy was murdered by somebody connected to something completely different?" he asked. Paul gave a weak nod and half-smile. Magee laughed.

"You know how I feel about coincidences," he said. "Still, it probably wasn't Stan who did it. I doubt if they would have brought him back by chopper. It's more likely he had to have someone drive him back to get his car. Someone we don't know, but someone who wouldn't have any problem with getting rid of a witness."

"That would make Stan an accomplice, though. Right?" Paul asked. Magee shrugged.

"Maybe," he said, "or maybe Stan left, and the other person stuck around to take care of loose ends. Paul conceded the point. "Either way, we're going to have to be very cautious going forward."

"What will you tell the Deputy?" Paul asked. Magee made a face.

"I'll think of something," he replied. "Right now, he thinks I was alone at the airport. I didn't mention you at all," he paused for a moment to collect his thoughts. "I can't lie to them, but I'm not ready to tell them everything yet. They wouldn't believe it anyway." Paul laughed.

"Hell, I wouldn't either if I didn't live through it," he said. "So, after you talk to him, you plan to head back and start digging?" His reference to digging reminded Magee that he had not finished telling Paul what he needed to know.

"You just reminded me," he started, "that I had something else to tell you." Paul leaned forward to listen. "The guy I mentioned earlier, the one I killed, worked for the same organization as me and did the same job. He had the same training, too." Paul kept listening intently. "His name was Dig…Dig Smith. Dig is short for Digby. It fit him also. He had a reputation for never giving up. They used to say he always kept digging until he got to what he wanted. In fact, he had a perfect record with his assignments. And he was called untouchable. Not because he was like Eliot Ness. But because he had never been hurt on a job. Nobody else had the kind of record he did. Even me." Paul interrupted.

"Excuse me," he said, "but you haven't told me yet what you mean by assignments. What, exactly, was your job?" Magee looked away for a second, and then back to Paul.

"We killed people," he said, matter-of-factly. He watched as Paul raised his head back and stiffened his neck. Then he pursed his lips, exhaled slowly, and brought his head back down.

"Assassin?" he asked, waiting for confirmation. Magee nodded. Normally, he would have left it at that and not felt compelled to explain further. He wasn't ashamed of his previous occupation. It was done in service to his country. But he had come to trust Paul in the time he spent over the last few days.

"We called it auxiliary action," he said. "Sometimes it was in support of what you guys did. We took out guys that you couldn't get to. Sometimes it had nothing to do with what you did. It just dealt with a different kind of bad guys." Magee stopped and laughed, as if he thought of something funny. "It was never women," he continued. "Why was it never women?"

he asked, not really expecting an answer. Paul couldn't offer one anyway. "There was always a rational reason given when an assignment came down, some bio on the guy that let you know who you were taking out. By the time you got the call, it had been sanctioned all the way up the chain. There was a support team in place. You got briefed on the details and then executed the plan.

"Sometimes things didn't go the way they were supposed to, and you had to improvise. But, mostly, you just followed the plan." Magee paused and looked away. If Paul's office had a window. he would have been looking out it. Instead, he focused on one of the bookends. "I knew Dig. He was a legend when I joined. Like I said, a perfect record. But he went rogue. It happens sometimes." He stopped again. Paul spoke up.

"What do you mean 'rogue'?" he asked. Magee turned back to Paul.

"It means he went on his own," he replied. "Started working for himself," he added. "It took a while for anyone to catch on. He did four or five jobs before they knew, but eventually, they figured it out." Magee shook his head. "It's a no-no," he said, "for a lot of reasons." Paul nodded his understanding. Magee continued.

"Anyway, somebody on the inside tipped him off that they knew," he said, "so he never came back in. They had to send a team out after him. It took a few years to track him down. I was on the first team that tried to take him out. It didn't go well. The details aren't important. But after that, I decided to hang it up. I quit and started my business. I put all of the rest of it behind me." Magee took a breath. "But now, a part of it is coming back."

"But eventually, you killed him, right? You said you left him in a gutter in Paris," Paul said. Magee nodded. "What happened between when you quit and then?" Paul asked next. Magee wasn't ready to tell him about the early days of his business, his near-marriage, or what happened at the café in Paris.

"I got a call from one of the assignment handlers asking for a favor," Magee started. "I'd been building my practice for three years by then. Things were going along well. But this guy just needed some surveillance done and thought I might be interested. He said it wasn't dangerous or anything. They just needed to make sure someone stayed put for a few days while another operation was going on.

"At first I told him I wasn't interested," he continued. "But then he said he was asking as a favor. He didn't have anyone else. He kind of pleaded with me, and I finally said okay. Next thing I knew I was on a flight to Paris."

"And that's when you took out this Dig guy?" Paul asked. Magee shook his head.

"Technically, no," he said. "The job didn't have anything to do with Dig. It was watching one of the Saudi Sheiks just to make sure he stayed in Paris. They didn't even fill me in on the details of why. I didn't really need to know. And the job was a piece of cake. You know how those guys travel with a big entourage. Everything they do involves a production. We had a three-person team set up across from the hotel where he was staying. I only had to take one shift a day. I knew the other two guys from before. They had quit, too, so it was kind of a reunion. After it was done, I stayed in Paris for a few days, just as a little bonus vacation," he added.

He looked down for a moment. When he looked up again, he could see Paul studying his face. He knew it was giving away what he was feeling as he was remembering. He decided to get to the point.

"Turns out," he said, "it wasn't what I thought it was. The whole thing was a sham. The guy who had called me turned out to be the guy who tipped off Dig about the team coming for him. The other two guys with me had been on the next team sent for him. They didn't make it out of Paris alive. Dig was making a point of taking out everyone who had ever come after him. He had a chance to take me out too, but I bent down to pick up a napkin just as he took his shot. He missed me but..." Magee paused for a moment and started counting in his head. It was his ten-second rule.

He made it up as a child when he moved from base to base and had to make a stand with a new bunch of other kids. In addition to the counting, he'd bring his right hand up to his left shoulder and stretch his left arm behind himself, as if he felt a twinge. He'd be looking at it, and then he'd frown as if it was uncomfortable. Then he'd pull his right arm back and turn to whoever was listening and start again. Ninety-nine percent of the people listening to what he was saying would wait politely for him to finish so that he could go on. By the time he got to ten, he was completely composed again. He had become comfortable with Paul, but not so comfortable as to let Paul see him get emotional.

"Anyway," he started again, "he missed me, but the shot took out an innocent bystander. And then he was gone. After that, I felt responsible. So, when the organization finally sorted out what happened, they let me have the next assignment on him."

"What about the other guy?" Paul asked. "Did somebody get him, too?" Magee laughed.

"Yeah," he said. "That guy was in management. He wasn't a field operative. He was in the organization because of one of the people he was related to. He was a guy who had been a mid-level bureaucrat for a long time. He thought he should be running the whole thing, but he kept getting passed over for promotion. He finally decided he'd get even and make some money at the same time. He knew Dig made a lot of money; so, he teamed up with him. But he didn't get killed. I know he's in a cell somewhere with a lot of people who think he's there because he was a pedophile." Paul smiled.

"I'm sure he's having a great time," he said. "So, this Dig is dead. He isn't a threat. Are you worried about whoever erased the stuff on Devereaux?" Magee nodded.

"That's the problem," he said. "If it's someone who knew Dig, and someone who knows the Privy, then it's potentially a field guy from the organization."

"So, it's someone like you," Paul said.

"Precisely," Magee said. "And you said earlier that I'm good at convincing people I'm someone other than who I really am." Paul nodded. "And so that's why you have to be really careful after I leave," he added.

Chapter 20

It was a short walk from Paul's office to Anne's, but she wasn't in it when he got there. He took out his cell and texted her, asking where she was. The reply came back quickly and said she was updating Klein. It was followed by another text that said he should come to Klein's office. He traced the route from Anne's back over to Klein's residence and reached her office. The door was slightly open, so he tapped a couple of times and pushed it all the way.

Anne was sitting where he had been sitting during his first discussion with Klein. She smiled when she saw him. Dr. Klein was sitting in the overstuffed chair near her. This time she looked even smaller than it had made her look the first time he met with her.

"Hello, Mr. Magee," Klein said. "Anne has been updating me on everything that has happened since Mr. Devereaux left. Magee smiled and thought about last night with Anne. He assumed she hadn't told everything.

"Yes, Dr. Klein," he said, "Things have continued to get more interesting. In fact, I told Paul and Anne that it is the most interesting case I've ever had." Klein smiled.

"Well, I'm glad you're the one who's working on it," she said. "Yesterday, I forgot to say thank you for being there to take the knife away from Mr. Devereaux. I didn't actually see what happened because I was trying to help Mr. Rosner, but Anne tells me it was quick and effective." Magee smiled again.

"He actually wasn't much of a threat," he said. "He didn't really know how to use the knife effectively."

"Still, I'm grateful," Klein replied. "I honestly don't think he's dangerous, but I suppose we can't take a chance now. We're going to have to bring the police in, aren't we?" She looked at him expectantly. He knew that she had a legal obligation. If Devereaux was violent and managed to hurt someone now that he was out, she and everyone else involved could be liable for whatever happened. It had been important to protect the clinic from publicity, but all of that changed with Devereaux's escape. He nodded.

"I'm afraid so, Dr. Klein," he said. "I may be able to influence how they get the search going, but they won't want to wait too long before they put out the word. I'm going to stop by the Sherriff's office on the way back to the city this afternoon. It's actually right on the way."

"I trust your judgment, Mr. Magee," Klein said, "but I don't know what you could tell them to keep them from alerting other authorities to help them find a patient that escaped from a mental institution." Magee nodded. "When are you leaving?" Klein asked.

"As soon as I meet with Anne," he answered. "I need some information about Stan and Mr. Devereaux's attorney." He looked at Anne, who then looked over at Klein.

"Do you have any more questions, Dr. Klein?" Anne asked.

"I suppose not," Klein answered. Then she looked at Magee. "Please call us back and let us know what the police say as soon as possible, Mr. Magee." He nodded. Anne stood up and turned to go. Magee let her go first through the door and then shut it behind him.

"Dr. Klein looks really tired," Magee said to Anne. She nodded in agreement but remained silent. They walked further down the hall toward her office, still in silence. Finally, Magee stopped and took her arm. He turned her toward him and looked into her eyes. They were moist.

"What's wrong?" he asked. She looked away. He put his other hand on the side of her cheek and pulled her gaze back to him. He wiped a tear that was dropping from her eye and he smiled at her. "You know I'll be back soon," he said. "I have to get back and figure out why all this happened, but I promise, as soon as I have something, I'll be coming right back here." She nodded slightly and forced a smile. Magee wasn't about to tell her about the call from Lane, or what happened at the airfield. He made a mental note to tell Paul not to tell her either. They started walking again.

She went into the office first, then reached behind him and closed the door after he entered. She put her arms around him, pulled herself close and buried her face into his chest. He reached down with a hand and lifted her chin. They kissed while she clung tightly to him. When the kiss ended, she didn't let go. He pressed the side of his head against hers. His arms were around her. He could feel her softness and her warmth. He breathed in the smell of her hair. Everything seemed to fit perfectly as they stood there.

He let his mind wander back in time to before Paris and the only time he had been so close to someone else. He remembered the same feeling, everything fitting perfectly together. He had missed it. All his life he had been alone, except for then, and for now. He wanted it to last. Part of him wanted to take her away and just be, the two of them, wherever they ended up. He sensed that she felt that way, too. But another part knew that he couldn't. Not yet. Before Lane called, he could have. But now things had changed. Until he knew who had killed Willie Longbow, and why, he couldn't be sure who would be safe.

He felt Anne relax her arms and took it as a signal. He relaxed his and let the gap between them grow. Their eyes met and he could see the tracks of tears that had rolled down her cheeks. She smiled again as she brushed the wetness away.

"I've made your shirt wet," she said. Magee smiled.

"It will dry," he said, "and I'm not going to wash it again until we're back together. That way, I'll have a little bit of you with me till then." That made her laugh. She pushed him slightly so she could move around him to reach her desk.

"Now, Mr. Magee," she said, playfully, "what was it you told Dr. Klein you needed from me? Information on Stan and the Attorney?" Magee laughed.

"Yeah," he said, "let's start with Stan's last name. I don't even remember it." Anne pulled a folder from the drawer of her desk, but at the same time started to answer.

"His last name is Smith," she said. Suddenly she stopped opening the folder and just held it in her hand. Her eyebrows furrowed. "Now that I think about it," she added, "I don't really know if that's his last name or not." Magee made sure his expression remained the same. He didn't want to reveal anything about his past to her yet. Or anything about Smith. He understood it could be a coincidence but didn't really think that. Smith was once the epitome of aliases, right up there with John Doe. "I'll write down his cell phone number, and his address, and the name and number for the attorney also," she added.

"I've got his name," Magee said. "Paul gave it to me." Anne looked up.

"Is there anything else you think will help?" she said. "What if I came with you?" she said, suddenly excited. "I can probably help in some way."

She had a broad smile and it was hard for him not to agree. He didn't speak but gave her a small smile.

"The best way you can help is to stay here where I know you'll be safe," he said. "Paul has some friends coming in to help. I don't really think anything is going to happen, but just in case. Besides, after I talk to the Sherriff's office, they may send someone up to take a statement. I'll call you and let you know what I told them, just in case they do." Anne's smile turned to a frown as her excitement drained.

"Ok," she sighed, "are you leaving now?" Magee shook his head.

"No, not yet, he said. "I want to use your computer to look at the Privy again. Charlie said everything was back." Anne's smile came back and she pulled the keyboard toward her and began to log in. Then she moved to the side and pointed for him to sit behind the desk. He slid into the chair and she stood behind him. She draped her arms around his neck and leaned on his shoulders as she watched him navigate to the Privy site. Soon, he had pulled up a page with an index of Devereaux investigations and was scanning each synopsis.

"That's more like it," he said to her. "Mostly I see what I expected. Some of these are official, like this one about possible bribery in another country," he said, pointing at the screen. "Others are more personal. Here's one where Devereaux Industries did an investigation into one of its Vice Presidents who had been accused of Sexual Harassment." Magee continued scrolling down the page. "But overwhelmingly," he added, "every one of the investigations comes down to a positive report on the part of the company. It makes them look squeaky clean. They're almost too good." He put his elbows on the table and drew a hand up to his face, resting it across his mouth while in thought.

"Does that mean something is wrong with the reports?" Anne asked. Magee paused for a second, then shook his head.

"I don't think so," he said. "I think it means that Frederick Devereaux was actually a very ethical guy. He made a lot of money, but he also tried to live a good life. It looks like there were times when people questioned it because it's easy to paint people who have a lot of money as somehow evil. But that's not automatically true. Buffet is another example of someone that seems to just be principled."

"Well, the father is dead," Anne pointed out, "the mother is dead, and even Devereaux's two older brothers are dead. But it was a company helicopter that picked up Stan and him when they got away. So somehow, someone is doing something unprincipled. I mean, Devereaux still needs treatment." Magee conceded her point with a nod.

"Sure," he said, "but don't forget that Stan said there were 'others' who could treat him better than what he can get here. He said, 'they had others', plural. I think that means another team of doctors or another hospital."

"Well, why didn't they just come and ask us to move him?" Anne said, indignantly. "I'm sure that we would have agreed." Magee shook his head again

"Not that simple," he said. "Legally, he had been transferred here by his brother. Remember he became the guardian. The brother was dead. They would have to wait till the attorneys sorted everything out, and then they would have had to go back to the court and get agreement. I'm sure the court would have granted it, but it would all take time. There must be some reason they didn't want to wait." He paused for a moment to think. "Why is it they wouldn't wait?" he asked himself.

"Maybe the company had something big in the works, something like an acquisition, and there would be questions about moving on it without getting agreement from the controlling shares," Anne said. "It may have been worth a lot of money getting it done quickly." Magee smiled.

"You paid attention at Harvard," he said. Instinctively, he drew his arm up and grabbed her wrist before she could swing it to punch his arm. "Remember, last time you hurt your hand when you did that." He stood up and pulled her to him and kissed her again. Then he pulled back. "I have to go," he said. She put her arm around the back of his neck.

"I know," she said, "but you'll be back soon, and I'll be here." She pulled him close for one more kiss and then took him by the hand and led him to the door. Once it was opened, she dropped his hand and they walked out into the hall. "I had housekeeping pick up your suitcase from your room and put it in your car," she told him. "They fixed your tire. too."

"Thanks," Magee said. "I'm going to bring a bigger suitcase when I come back," he told her. They left the building and walked out into the courtyard. He turned back to her. "I have to stop and see Paul one more time before I leave," he said. "Would you do me a favor?" he asked.

"Sure," she said with a smile, "anything."

"Would you walk back into your office as if we were done?" he said. Her smile faded. He knew she wanted to walk all the way to his car with him. He looked into her eyes. "If you are with me when I get to the car, it will be all I can do not to grab you and kiss you deeply before I leave," he said. "No doubt, someone will see that. Are you ready to take this to that level yet?" Magee could see that she was starting to say yes, so he added, "It may not be the best timing now that the police are going to get involved and things are going to go very public." She looked confused.

"I…" she started, "you think that it would be bad somehow?" she asked. Her look turned to disappointment. She backed away slightly. Magee wanted to take it back, but he knew there would be publicity after the police were involved. Somewhere out there was a person who was linked to Dig. He didn't know if that person was someone to be feared or just someone playing around with the network. He did know there was someone who was dead at a place not far away. He had been there and talked to the man. He left his card in his pocket. Whoever killed him may have even read it. He didn't want to take any chances that would put her in danger. Too many unknowns right now.

"First thing, when I get back, I'll take you right here, in this spot and I don't care who watches," he said. She blushed. Magee knew she was listening. "But right now, you have to trust me. We should wait until then." She finally smiled. It was small, but Magee thought she understood. She backed away a little further and squeezed her lips together. Then she turned and walked quickly back inside. He watched her till she was through the door. Then he turned and went into Paul's office.

"How did it go with Anne," Paul asked when he saw him come in. Magee let out a long breath and sank down in the chair in front of Paul.

"Okay, I guess," he said. He leaned forward and put his elbows on the desk. You know, I didn't tell her anything you and I talked about." Paul nodded.

"I figured you didn't. It took a while for you to tell me," he said. "Probably still wouldn't have if you didn't have to warn me." Magee laughed.

"Yeah, but I did tell you," he said. "I just wanted to make sure you don't tell her," he added. "And definitely, don't tell her about Longbow." Paul nodded.

"I won't," he said. "I care about her, too, you know."

"Thanks," Magee said. "Ok, back to business. Can you check on where Stan is?" He pointed toward Paul's cell phone. Paul picked it up and checked the screen.

"Looks like he's parked," Paul said. "A parking lot on Illinois street, between twentieth and twenty-second. Says it's Dogpatch area."

"Dogpatch?" Magee asked, "That's all old warehouse and pier stuff down there. Just big buildings with lots of space. What's he doing down there?" He wasn't expecting an answer. "I'm gonna head out, Paul. Can you just keep an eye out, and text me if he moves?" He stood up. "Oh, and I'll call you and let you know what I tell the Sheriff." He started for the door.

"Magee," Paul shouted. Magee stopped and turned back.

"Be careful out there," Paul said. "We don't know what you're going to find. You don't have to be alone anymore. You need help – you call." Magee nodded and walked out.

Chapter 21

Covelo was a small town on 162 not far south from the place where Stan and Devereaux had turned off to go to Stanley Field. A population sign as he entered the main part listed the number as 1,255. Magee passed a strip mall with several vacancies. The anchor was a discount store. On one side was a nail salon. The other side had a tattoo parlor. Most of the other fronts were vacant with for lease signs in the window. A little farther down the road was the business district. Several old buildings, a few churches, and a couple of small restaurants dotted the road. Magee knew he had passed through the town on his way to the clinic but hadn't really taken notice of anything.

He imagined that at one time this had been a thriving agricultural community. There were still local wineries in the area, and the surrounding hills had plenty of recreational activities. But the core of this town had been hollowed out, much like towns all across the country. Up ahead he saw a sign pointing toward the Sheriff's office. He made the turn and pulled into the parking lot. As he walked from the car into the office, he still hadn't thought through what he would say.

Once inside, he took a minute to look around the office. Lane had told him this was the Coroner's office. He didn't see anything that mentioned the Coroner, but the building was large enough to have it in another part. There was a counter separating the entrance area from several desks behind it. A white-haired sergeant was seated on a stool behind the counter, rifling through a stack of papers. He looked up.

"Can I help you, sir?" he asked, looking over the top of his reading glasses. Magee stepped over to him.

"Looking for a Deputy Lane," he said. "He told me he'd be here." The sergeant nodded and pointed to a bench against the wall. He picked up his phone as Magee walked over and took a seat.

"Hey, Tommy," he said into the phone, "I've got a guy out here looking for you. Okay." He hung up. "He's on his way out," he said to Magee and went back to the stack of papers. Seconds later a young officer in a uniform came through one of the doors on the side of the room. He was tall and thin. His uniform was crisp. He looked around the office until he saw Magee sitting on the bench, then walked toward him.

"Mr. Magee?" he asked. Magee nodded. He extended a hand. Magee shook it. "I'm Deputy Lane. I'm glad you could come in. Why don't we go in the back? I have an office to use when I come here." He pointed to the door he had come through. Magee followed as Lane led back through it. They walked down a hallway with offices on both sides until they came to one marked 'visiting deputy.'" Lane went behind the desk and pointed to the chair in front of it. "Please have a seat," he said.

He reached into a drawer and pulled out a pad of blank forms and a pencil. Magee could see the words 'Witness Statement' at the top of the first page on the pad. He pushed the pad across the desk. He slid a cup full of small pencils next to the pad.

"Before we're done," he started, "I'll ask you to write down anything that you can tell me about your time at Mr. Longbow's airport. But, first, why don't you just tell me why a PI from down in the city is up here in Mendocino?" The chair squeaked as he crossed his arms and leaned back to listen. The body language and tone of the question implied that Lane believed Longbow's murder was tied directly to Magee's presence. Magee couldn't blame him. He suspected it as well, but he still found it hard to believe that Stan would have done it.

"On the job," Magee said, matter-of-factly. He waited to see Lane's response, but none came. Magee knew a lot of cops, of all sorts and sizes. Their personalities were rarely black or white. They fell somewhere in between on a spectrum. He knew some were talkers, and some were listeners. The talkers told you about things you should know and hoped that led you to share. The listeners sat back and waited until you told them what they wanted to hear. Some were both, but talkers don't usually hear everything you say because they are too busy talking. He wasn't sure about Lane yet, but he seemed to be a listener. Magee preferred the talkers. He started slowly.

"I'm doing an investigation for a medical facility up in the hills. It's called the Klein Institute for Dissociative Identity Disorder. They handle people with personality disorders. Ever hear of it?" he asked. Lane shook his head. "They've been up there eight years," Magee added.

"It's a big county," Lane said. Magee nodded his agreement.

"They don't handle a lot of patients," he said, "but some of the ones they have are pretty well off, and sensitive to a lot of publicity." Lane shrugged.

"It's California," he offered. Magee laughed. Lane was engaging a little. It was a good sign. He still had to decide how much he wanted to tell Lane. On the one hand, he had an obligation to tell him everything, considering that there was a murder. It was part of the Code of Ethics for P.I.'s. On the other, once news reports started getting out, the clinic would probably get more and more attention. Whoever was behind getting Devereaux out would get spooked, and trails would be made cold, very fast. And whoever was using Dig's ID could be gone, too.

"Yeah," Magee said, "what a world, huh?" He waited again, but this time Lane didn't bite. Magee took the next step. "Anyway, they had some strange visitors, and the head of the clinic called for my help." This time Lane took the bait.

"What do you mean, strange?" he asked. Magee thought about how to describe it. He knew that he could keep some things back until it became absolutely necessary not to. He had an ethical obligation to his clients to maintain privacy, as long as it wasn't material to a police matter. Everything that happened up until the incident with the knife was weird, but not something that absolutely demanded police attention. After that point, things would be a little gray. Magee had to weigh the circumstances. Little harm was actually done, except for the cut on Paul's head. And Magee had signed a non-disclosure form that required him to protect a patient's confidential information. He decided he'd use what Paul thought of earlier.

"Well," Magee started, "three men showed up wanting to visit a patient they said they knew. They didn't have any authorization from the patient's family. One of them claimed to be the patient's brother, but the staff at the clinic knew he wasn't. It turned out, though, the patient's brother had died the week before." Lane perked up and leaned forward.

"Killed?" he asked quickly. Magee shook his head.

"Nope," Magee answered. "He died of natural causes, an aneurysm." Lane looked a little disappointed and leaned back in the chair again. "Anyway, only two of the three actually came into the office to register as visitors. The other was wandering around outside the buildings, sort of scoping things out." Lane leaned forward again.

"You mean he was casing the place?" he said. Magee nodded.

"Seemed that way to me, too, when I heard it." He said. "All three of them had to be escorted off the premises by the head of security there," he added.

"Did they report this to us?" Lane said expectantly. Magee shook his head. "Well, why not?" he asked. "That's what we're here for." He frowned.

"Yes," Magee said, "but remember I said the place has a lot of people who were very concerned about publicity. The men didn't cause any real problems and left quickly when they were told to. They decided they could hire someone to look into it, to make sure it would stay discreet. That's where I came in." Lane leaned back again.

"What have you found out so far?" He asked.

"Nothing that provided anything concrete," Magee replied. "At first I thought that someone might be setting up a scam. All those rich patients. Maybe it would be some sort of blackmail. But then, their security guy suggested something else. Because it's a medical facility, and maybe because it's particularly a mental treatment facility, it stores a lot of drugs." Magee paused to check Lane's reaction. It was what he expected. He was listening closely and putting two and two together.

"So," he added, "I thought if someone was going to lift a whole load of stuff, they would want to get it out of the area quickly. They wouldn't want to be driving around with it." Lane was nodding his head now. Magee continued. "So, I checked around and found out that Stanley Field was close by. I decided to run by there and find out if that was a place they might use." He paused again. He knew the next statement he made would be crossing a line. He took a moment to mentally ask for Longbow's forgiveness.

"I got the sense that he was agitated," Magee said. "It was a little unusual for someone to be in there to ask him questions. I mean, I don't know if he had anything to hide, but he did seem a little indignant." All of the years Magee had spent, first training, and then working, had taught him how to mask his feelings. He knew what he was saying wasn't a lie, but it was not the whole truth. He didn't think Longbow deserved it, but he'd attempt to make amends for it later. Lane seemed excited to have something.

"This kind of makes more sense now," Lane said. "At least it's a start. We had nothing till now." Magee knew that it was only a delaying tactic. Lane would run down this road for a little while at least. "Did the people at the clinic give you a description of these three guys?" he asked. Magee smiled.

"They have pictures," he said, "And recordings of their voices." That made Lane smile. "Their Security guy is pretty good. He can give you all the details, too."

"Perfect," Lane said. "Can you give me the address? I'm going to take a run up and get all those things." Magee ripped a page off the pad of forms in front of him and turned it over. He pulled a pencil from the cup and his cell phone from his pocket. He copied down the main number of the clinic from his phone, the one Klein had called him on originally. He pushed it over to Lane.

"Better yet," he said, "I'll call their security guy right now so he can get you in past the main gate when you get there." He activated the speaker button on his phone and pushed Paul's number. Lane started to say something, but the number was already ringing. Magee could guess that Lane would have told him not to do that. He had sensed that Lane was good at his job. He knew that he would have preferred to show up without any introduction and get the feeling on his own. He laid his phone on the desk. Paul picked up.

"Hey, Magee," he said, "what's up?"

"Hi, Paul," Magee answered, "I'm sitting with Deputy Lane, the one I told you called earlier today about the murder at the airport I went to. I just told him about the men who came to the clinic, and he put two and two together about this being drugs, and maybe the visitors had a deal cooked up with the guy at the airport. You remember that was what you kind of thought, too."

"Yeah, I remember," Paul said. "Am I on speaker?" he asked. Magee told him he was. "Hello, Deputy," Paul said, "This is Paul Rosner. I'm head of security for Klein institute. How are you?" Magee pushed his phone toward the center of the desk. Lane cleared his throat.

"I'm fine," he answered. "Mr. Magee was just speaking very highly of you," he added. He didn't wait for Paul to comment. "Look, I'd like to come up and get some details from you about those visitors you had," he said. Paul didn't miss a beat.

"Okay," he said. "How about 9:00 AM tomorrow? Did Magee give you the address?"

"Um," Lane said checking a notebook from his pocket, "I have court until 11:00 in the morning, but I can make it around Noon unless I have to respond to a call on the way," he said. Then he added, "He also said you have some photos of the men who came to your clinic."

"Of course," Paul replied. "I can get some copies for you to take. Tomorrow then, sometime after Noon. When you arrive, you'll pull up to the outside gate first. I'll be monitoring the cameras and will open the gate.

Just drive through and up the road to the inside gate, and I'll be waiting there for you."

"That sounds good," Lane said. "I'll see you then." Magee pulled the phone back over.

"I'm going to be on the road for a while, Paul," he said. "If I get back before it's too late, I'm going to try that restaurant tonight, the one our friend recommended. You know, the Blue Lady. But you may need to find out for me where it is again. I didn't write down the address."

"No problem, Magee," Paul said. "I'll have to find him to ask, but I'll call when I do." Magee smiled as he hung up. "Someone told us about a really good restaurant in the city that was reopening after being closed for a while," he said to Lane. There was no reaction from him. Instead, he pointed to the tablet in front of Magee.

"Could you take the time to write up what you told me now," he said. "I'll get a witness to sign it and then you can be on your way. I'll be heading home after we wrap this up." Magee nodded as he picked up the pencil again and started writing. It took about three minutes for him to fill in the spaces and write down the information on the blank lines. Lane watched intently as he wrote. When he finished, he picked it up and seemed to be reading very carefully. He wanted Lane to think he was very serious about getting it right. When he finished, he passed it to Lane, who read it just as thoroughly as he saw Magee doing.

"Seems to be just what you told me," Lane said. Magee nodded. Lane picked up the phone and dialed an extension. He asked the person who answered to send someone back to witness a statement. A moment later the door opened and the sergeant from the front desk came through. He looked at Magee and picked up the statement form.

"This your statement," he grumbled. Magee nodded. "Tell me in words. Don't just nod," the sergeant said with a frown.

"Yes," Magee answered, "It's my statement." The sergeant put the statement down on the desk and pulled a pencil from the cup. He signed in a box at the bottom of the form. Then he pushed it over to Lane and turned and walked out abruptly. Lane laughed.

"We don't have a lot of staff," he told Magee. "He has a lot to do every day. Doesn't like to be interrupted when he's in the middle of something." He laughed. Magee laughed, too.

"This is a big county," Magee said. "I bet you have a hard time trying to cover it all." Lane nodded.

"County has over eighty-thousand people," he said. "It's over thirty-nine hundred square miles, and we have about seventy guys patrolling it.

At that moment, the phone on the desk started to ring. Lane picked up. "Lane here," he said. He nodded and said yes, a few times as he listened. "Okay," he finally said, "Thanks," he added as he hung up. "That was the coroner's assistant," he said to Magee. "The autopsy is done, and they recovered a lot of the bullet," he said, looking at Magee. "It was a 9-millimeter." He kept his eyes on Magee looking for a reaction, but Magee didn't register anything other than a casual acceptance. Lane waited a few seconds longer and then spoke again. "They pegged the time of death at around 9:00 AM." Still no reaction from Magee. "So, you are headed back to the city tonight. Do you think you'll be back up this way or is your investigating done for now?" Magee shook his head.

"Oh, no," he said, "Not done. I still have to write up a report, and I'll be spending some more time coming up here and advising on some new procedures they might use to help beef up the security. I want to make sure they get their money's worth." He stopped and smiled. "After all, they are spending a lot of money on me and I want to give them as much service as they think they need," he added. Lane made a slight frown.

"Everybody's got to make a living, I guess," he said. Magee could tell he didn't like the response. Lane was a good cop. He wanted to catch bad guys and keep people safe. His opinion of Magee dropped a bit because it sounded like Magee was milking the job. But this was exactly what Magee wanted him to think. He wanted Lane to focus on the mice, and not on a PI who was simply trying to make as much money on a job as he could.

Lane was assuming there wasn't really anything left for Magee to do. His job was already finished at this point. It was Lane's job now to catch the mice, which would involve putting out the notice, matching up the pictures to real people, and running down any leads that popped up. That should keep him busy until Magee could catch up to Stan and Devereaux. He had two, maybe three days to get things wrapped up. Magee wasn't sure what would happen after that. But he did know that somewhere out there was someone who knew Dig. And that made everything else unpredictable.

Chapter 22

Magee glanced at the clock as he left the office. It would be rush hour in the city. There was none in Covelo. The streets were as empty now as when he drove in. As he pulled out from the parking lot, he took out his phone and dialed Rosner. It took a while for him to answer.

Hey, Magee," Paul said, "hang on a sec." Magee could hear him telling someone he had to take the call. In the background, there were men's voices and laughter. "Okay, I'm back," he said.

"You got a party going on there, Paul," Magee asked. Paul laughed.

"My guys showed up," he said. "Haven't seen them for a while. It's sort of a reunion."

"Don't party too much," Magee said. "If we are up against one of Dig's people, you won't see him coming. If you do, it'll be too late. Those guys need to have your back."

"I know, Magee," Paul said. "They will. We're good. It's not really a party. No one has had anything to drink. It's just the last time we were all together at the same time, we were facing down forty-two Taliban fighters in a cave outside of Spin Buldak. We were just rehashing how the hell we got out of there."

"Okay, Paul," Magee answered. "I guess I'll meet them when I get back. Right now, I'm headed down to the city. I need to know where Stan's car is."

"I'll look," Paul said. Magee had to wait for a minute till Paul returned. "Still in the same place. You said it was some kind of warehouse district. Hasn't moved since it got there."

"Ok, text me the exact address, I'll start with that and work around it until I find him," Magee told him. "As far as Lane goes, I think you caught on to what I was telling him. I got him thinking that the mice were looking for drugs, and Longbow may have been involved or not, but he's got suspects. He'll chase them down."

"I got that," Paul replied, "and, also that you didn't tell him I was at the airport with you."

"Right," Magee said, "and nothing at all about Devereaux and Stan. So, you'll need to brief Anne and Klein. He might ask to talk to them."

"Roger that," Paul said, "but I'm assuming your gonna give Anne a call while you're driving. I took these guys over to meet her when they got here, and I could tell she was upset. I think she misses you already. She may have even been crying."

"Okay, I'll call her now," Magee said, "but you brief her all the same when you get a chance. I don't know how my conversation with her is going to go."

"Got it, Magee," Paul said. "You're a lucky man, you know," he added. "Be safe," he added before he hung up. Magee didn't call right away. He needed some time to think about what he would say. It would be another half hour before 162 would put him on 101 back to the city. He decided he would use it to check his mental note pad. A lot had happened in the three days since he came from the city.

He had come to know more about the incident that caused Klein to call him. He reviewed the details in his head. Three men showed up to see a patient who suffered from multiple personalities. What in the world had they hoped to achieve? He assumed the obvious once he found out the patient was a member of one of the richest families on the planet. It was all part of a scam to bilk the family out of money. The mice had referred to 'others' in their conversation.

They claimed to know the brother of the patient when they made the appointment. But he was no longer around to verify that, having died of natural causes before they showed up. One of them pretended to be the brother and wanted badly to still talk to the patient but was easily convinced by the others present that it was not feasible. Instead, they simply left and have not been back.

Since that time, someone else helped the patient escape. In the process, though, he had professed that the patient still needed help and he would be taking him to others who could provide better help. Were those the others the mice had referred to? Were they originally there to take the patient out? It was a possibility. Perhaps they did know the brother and, if he had accompanied them when they came, they would have left with the patient at that time. Was Stan simply a back-up in case the other plan didn't work? It was a possibility. Maybe they knew the brother was sick, and they made arrangements in case something happened before he could physically go to the clinic.

Magee had asked Klein if an aneurysm could be used to commit murder, and she had told him no. But perhaps he asked the wrong question. Maybe he should have asked if you can predict that a person will die of an aneurysm, or even if you can tell someone is at risk of one soon. This was a possibility. If they knew the brother might not be available to remove the patient, they may have come up with a back-up plan. He made a mental note to ask Anne to check with Klein when he called her. Suddenly, he was thinking about a different event that had happened in the last three days. It was at that moment, in his car on the drive back to the city, that he realized he was in love with Anne.

The attraction had come first, just as it had with Jenny. He sensed that she was attracted to him, too. But it quickly became more about the time they spent together. She was playful and coy. She tried to find out more about him, the person, not the detective. He tried to be his loner self, only to regret not letting her get to know him better. She turned up the heat by making herself beautiful and he slowly decided to open up to her. Since then, he spent as much time as possible with her. He suddenly regretted that she wasn't with him. He hadn't reached 101 yet but decided to make the call.

"Hello, Magee," she answered. The voice was tentative.

"Hello, back," he said. "I miss you." There was silence for a moment.

"I wanted to come!" she finally stated with emphasis. Magee nodded, even though he knew she couldn't see him.

"I know," he said. "I almost said yes," he added, "but I thought it might be dangerous. I don't know what I'm walking into yet. Did Paul come and brief you about my talk with Lane?"

"Yes," she said. "Why didn't you tell me about the man at the airport?" Magee didn't answer right away.

"I didn't want you to worry," he finally said. "I don't think it's connected." He bit his lip as he said it, but she couldn't see that.

"Hah," she said. "You think it's a coincidence, right?" she said back, sarcastically. "I know you're lying just because you think I can't handle it. Well, maybe you're right. Maybe I can't, but you're not giving me a chance." Magee regretted that he didn't tell her everything while he was there. It would have been better to talk about it face to face instead of him being so far away.

"You're right," he confessed. "I was wrong. I should have let you know before I left. But you need to know that I thought you might try to make me stay, and that would have made it too easy for me to say okay. I had a hard time leaving when I did."

"I thought I was having the hard time," she said, softly.

"No," Magee answered, "It was me. I didn't want to leave because I am in love with you." There was silence. Magee waited. He thought he heard sniffling. Finally, he asked, "Did you hear what I said?"

"Mmhmm," Anne said tentatively. He waited. More silence.

"Anne," he said, "the number one thing I want to do at this point is to finish this investigation and get back to you. Do you understand?"

"Yes," she said. He heard her sniffle again.

"I needed to go to get it done," he added. "And I needed to know you were going to be somewhere safe while I was gone. Paul has some guys that he brought in. You met them, right?"

"Mmhmm," she said.

"They're going to make sure that you and Dr. Klein, and everyone else at the clinic, for that matter, are safe if anyone should come to try anything. I'm going to find Stan, and whoever he is working for, and find out what they know." Anne finally spoke.

"Do you think Stan killed the man at the airport?" she asked.

"No," he answered. "Stan may be someone other than he said he was, but he's no killer. In fact, he might be in danger now. So, I need your help from there. Are you in your office?" He could sense her sitting up straight in her chair.

"Yes," she said. Her tone was different, more excited now. The sniffling stopped. "Okay. What do you need?" Magee let out a breath.

"I need two things," he started. "First, I need you to ask Dr. Klein a question. Can you know ahead of time that someone is going to have an aneurysm?"

"What?" Anne said. "You mean like a stroke or something?"

"Sort of, yes," Magee answered. "but more specific, an aortic aneurysm. It's when the aorta ruptures. I'm trying to find out if someone knew how sick Devereaux's brother was. It would help explain a few things." He sensed she was writing it down and waited for her response.

"Got it," she said, "What else?"

"Ok, about finding Stan," he started, "here's what we have. Paul texted me the address where Stan's car is parked. I don't expect that Stan is in that car, but apparently, the car hasn't moved since yesterday. And if he was delivering Devereaux somewhere, then it's probably to a place around there. Hang on one second." Magee saw he was approaching 101. He pulled into a gas station near it. He put the car in park and forwarded the address to her. "Did you get the text?"

"Yes," she said.

"Good," he told her. "Can you start searching around to see if you can come up with the names of the places around there? I know the area and there are a lot of old warehouses down that way. We need to determine if any of them are likely candidates for where Stan might end up taking Devereaux. Maybe something around there is owned by Devereaux Industries."

"Okay," she said, "It may take a while."

"I know," he said, "but it's all we've got for now. I've still got almost 3 hours on the road to get down there. So, at least give it a shot for a while and see what you come up with. Then call me back."

"Okay," she said, "I'll get started right now." There was silence again for a moment. Then she asked, "Magee, did you mean what you said a minute ago?

"Every word," he answered.

"I love you, too," she said. There was the click of the phone being hung up. Magee smiled. It had been a long time since he had someone to go back to. He started driving a little faster after getting on 101. He had a job to do and then he could go home. He was, indeed, a lucky man.

He would stay on 101 until I-580. Then it would be down on the east side of the bay through Berkley and over the Bridge into the city. It would be late when he arrived so he knew the traffic would be gone. But it presented a different problem. Everything would be closed up by then. It would make it harder to check out places where Stan might be. On the other hand, Magee assumed Stan took Devereaux to some sort of hospital, or clinic. In that case, there would likely be staff there all hours. It should be lit up. It may make it easier to find.

Then again, Magee reasoned, Stan and Devereaux were lifted out by helicopter. He couldn't even be sure that Stan returned for his car. Whoever killed Longbow could have been lifted in by the same chopper, just like Stan and Devereaux were lifted out. Then he could have just taken the car to get back to the city. Magee started working through the different scenarios in his head.

He could picture a chopper landing out in front of the small office building and dropping a passenger. He imagined Longbow trying to rush out to catch the pilot to give him a courtesy lesson. At some point, the person who shot him was behind him. Someone who got out of the helicopter could have just waited at the door until Longbow came rushing out. As soon as he passed, the person waiting could have taken him out with a kill shot to the head. Magee knew precisely the kind of movement that takes. He had used it before.

But that would mean there was at least one witness, the pilot. That would complicate things. Magee was still ruling out the possibility that Stan could murder someone. None of the others had thought so either. The scenario Magee had considered implied that at least two people were okay with murdering someone, the pilot and the one who did it. If the pilot wasn't at all complicit, he would have been reporting it to someone quickly after the fact. It would have gotten back to the Mendocino County Sheriff's office and the conversation Magee had with Lane would have been entirely different.

It was possible the pilot wasn't complicit but had been threatened in some way. It would have to be a deep threat to stick once the murderer was out of the chopper. It would be possible if the killer had reach, meaning the ability to make good on threats if needed. But it wasn't the most likely scenario. That left other scenarios. The pilot could have told people in his organization, in the management chain. They could be making decisions about the next step. Most organizations have nothing to hide. They simply want to have a purpose and take action to fulfill that purpose. If someone in their organization committed a crime or did something that might hinder their ability to pursue their purpose, they would deal with it swiftly. In the case of a crime, they would get it into police hands as quickly as possible. Any lapse in time would raise liability issues and perhaps expose them to criminal charges.

If it wasn't a normal organization, that raised a lot of other serious questions and challenges. The scale could run from very close to normal, and therefore mostly ethical, to being at the other end, and completely unethical. Devereaux's companies had all seemed mostly ethical, based on what he reviewed. It would be a stretch to conclude their management would condone murder. Still, helicopter or no helicopter, it would be too much of a coincidence that the murder occurred roughly the same time that Stan's car was being retrieved.

Magee decided that he didn't know enough about the timing or other factors to conclude how the killer arrived, or if anyone might have witnessed it, or even why it would be important to take Longbow out. If he was lucky enough to find Stan, and hopefully Devereaux, too, he would be walking into something unknown.

He was on I-580 now, making good time and just passing Point Richmond. He had less than an hour to go. He was starting to plan his approach. For now, he knew his main goal was to get to Stan first, hopefully alone, then extract what he could to make sense of everything. Beyond that, he could take whatever steps were necessary. It struck him that he was feeling uncertain. Only once before had he felt it.

Even when he was a child, moving from camp to camp, he hadn't known that feeling. He could always predict what the next camp was going to be like. Or the types of other kids he'd meet. The rules and regulations he would need to follow. And how he might have to act to get through it until the next camp. He was always certain on his first job too, certain someone would die, maybe even him. There was always a support team on board too. He knew they were not supposed to intervene if things went wrong. They were there to observe. But he also knew that out there in the field, beyond the eyes of the handlers back in the office, men did what they needed to do.

He met his secretary soon after he left that job. She helped him work through the scenarios of a case to the point that he could predict how the investigation would go down. Cases became somewhat routine, until Paris. And in those moments when he held Jenny in his arms and screamed for help, he felt uncertain about the future. He didn't know what would happen to him without her.

He had gotten used to working alone since she died. Cases remained routine and predictable until this one. This case had been anything but routine. He told people he was always a loner, but he realized it wasn't exactly true. Except for now, at this moment. Instead of a well-planned situation, he would have to improvise at the moment he caught up with Stan. His cell phone interrupted that thought. He had just reached the Bay Bridge. It was Anne.

"Hello, Magee," she said. She sounded happy. It made him happy too.

"Hello, back." He replied.

"Where are you now," she asked? He described the city skyline to her. He could see Coit Tower off to his right, not far from the Trans-America Pyramid. "Sounds like a nice view," she said.

"It is," he said, "but I'd rather be looking at you."

"I hope that you will be, soon," she said. "I think I found something that can help," she added, "but first, let me tell you about what Dr. Klein's answer was. I wrote it down verbatim." Magee could hear Anne picking up a piece of paper. "Okay, here it is, 'Yes, aneurysms can be diagnosed. When he asked me about aneurysms before, it was in the context of Mr. Devereaux's brother. I told him it wasn't something that could be used by someone to kill someone else. But we were talking about ruptured aneurysms. That's what killed Mr. Devereaux's brother, and Mr.

Devereaux's father, for that matter. The aneurysm itself is just a weakening of the wall of an artery, sometimes a bulge, if you will. If people have certain symptoms, Doctors can usually prescribe a scan to see if an aneurysm exists. Once they know, they may want to try different things to reduce the risk of it rupturing.'" Anne paused for a moment. "That was the main part of her answer. She would have talked longer but I stopped her because I wanted to get back and work on your other question."

"Good choice," Magee said. "I'm sure she could have gone on for a while if you would have listened."

"Does that make a difference in how you're thinking about something?" Anne asked.

"Yes," he said. "It means that whoever had started this whole thing could have known the brother was at risk. The original plan may have been that the brother would come with mice. At first, it made sense this was all some sort of scam going on, a typical attempt to get money from someone who's family had it. But everything that happened since I got involved has kind of thrown a monkey wrench into that idea." He paused.

"Everything?" Anne asked, playfully. Magee laughed.

"No," he said. "Not everything, but at least those things related to getting Devereaux out. For example, now I'm thinking Stan was put there as part of a back-up plan, in case the other one failed."

"Hmmm," Anne said back. "I see what you mean. I guess that's possible, but I still don't see how Stan is involved in the murder of the man at the airport. I just never would think he was capable of that."

"I agree, so far," he said. "None of us think Stan is like that, but I'm still gonna be very careful when I find him. So, any luck with the buildings? I'm getting pretty close to Dogpatch."

"Yes," Anne replied. There was excitement in her voice. "There is a building at the corner of Michigan Street and Twentieth, about a block from where the car is parked. A year ago, it was purchased by Iron River Properties. It's a big place on the outside, but I can't give you any details about what it looks like on the inside."

"That's okay," Magee said. "How did you find that out so quickly?" he asked.

"My husband owned a real estate development business," she answered, "I worked there when I met him. One of the things I did was find properties that the company could turn around quickly. Most municipalities keep records online about the ownership, and the records are open to the public if you know how to get to them."

"Smart girl," Magee replied. "It's really helpful because it means they own a building outright, which gives them a very public persona. On the drive down, I was playing with different ideas about Longbow. Since they used a helicopter with that name on it to pick up Stan and Devereaux, they didn't have any idea that he would have been murdered soon after that pickup. Too easy to be seen and get linked back. If someone from their organization is truly responsible, it means that person likely went rogue." He stopped suddenly. His use of the word rogue reminded him of Dig. Anne would know nothing about him or Magee's previous occupation.

"What does that mean?" Anne asked. "Someone killed him for no reason?"

"No," he answered, "that's not what happened in this case. Whoever killed him had a reason, based on how it happened. It was deliberate."

"But you don't think this company had someone do it on purpose," she said. She would have seen him nod if they were together.

"Right," he said, "they are a legitimate business. It doesn't mean they can't do unethical things, but murder wouldn't be smart for them."

"So, where does that leave us," she said back, with emphasis on us. "If it isn't related to Devereaux in some way, shape or form, is it a coincidence?" Magee laughed. He knew she chose the word purposely.

"We'll need to work on that once I've talked to Stan," he answered. As he said it, he was pulling into a large parking lot with several parked cars. He drove along the aisle off the main entrance until he spotted a blue Prius with the bumper sticker. "I'm here," he told her. "I've found his car." He continued driving until he could loop around on the other side and park in a spot facing it. "They don't have a lot of lights on around here. I can see a big building from where I am, and it has windows. But they look like they've been painted over with black paint. I can't tell if there are any lights on inside the building. I'm going to scope things out. I'll call you in a little while to let you know what I find."

"You'd better," he heard her say. He hung up and reached for the glove compartment. He still had the Sig he had taken from Paul's collection in the Hummer. For the moment, he stayed in the car and looked around, checking for any activity.

He couldn't tell whether the lot was being monitored. Because there were no lights, it was unlikely. It looked like it served several buildings, not just the one that belonged to Iron River. After ten minutes, he decided it was time to move. He quickly got out of the car, so the light did not remain on long. He stood by for a minute. Still no activity. He moved toward the building. As he got closer, he could see small indications of light. One of the windows at the top seemed to have a scratch, and light was clearly showing through. It was a good sign. At least he might find someone inside.

He reached the corner of the street and peered around the front. About twenty feet away, he could see an entrance door. Across the street, he saw a fence running about halfway down the block. It would give him cover while he watched for any activity at the door. He walked around the corner toward the door itself. When he was close, he pulled on the handle. The door didn't budge. On the wall next to the handle was a badge reader. He turned away from the door and kept walking down the street. As he reached the end of the building, he crossed the street and moved behind the fence to take up a position. Then he waited. It took about twenty minutes, but his patience paid off.

Chapter 23

Magee noticed a car driving into the parking lot where he had parked. It was only one at first, but then two more appeared and a fourth was close behind. The cars were parking. People were exiting and heading toward the entrance to the building. Other headlights were headed toward the parking lot. He glanced at his watch. It was approaching the hour. Shift change, he thought. He counted the number of people so far. There were the first four, and now at least three other cars were pulling in.

He considered his options. There were two. He could intercept someone on the way in and see if they would cooperate in an attempt for him to enter the building. Cooperation could be as simple as holding a door open if they see another person about to go through it. Or, depending on the level of importance management decides to place on security, a person may hold the door but ask to see his ID or tell him to swipe his badge. He may be able to talk his way past a diligent employee because he knows he can be a nice guy when he wants to, or he could simply flash his gun to persuade the person. Either way, he was sure he could convince someone. The other option was intercepting someone on the way out and expecting similar cooperation. Both options had problems related to timing. He couldn't know how many would be coming or going. It would be preferable to isolate someone and have them assist, versus creating a scene with multiple people.

He decided to follow someone in. In his opinion, people usually are focused on getting into work. They may be early, or they may be late, but once they have committed to getting on the job, that becomes what they focus on. They would be more inclined to hold the door open for someone focused on the same thing. People who have finished their job for the day will typically take their time, making them more likely to question a person who is trying to get into the building they are leaving.

As he thought about it, two more cars entered the parking lot. Others had left, driven by the people who had come out of the building. He noticed one that was leaving had stopped near one that had just parked. In the dim light, he could see that someone was leaning on the edge of the car by the driver's window. He concluded they were having a conversation. He could see no other cars pulling into the lot. The last person from the other group had already entered the building.

Finally, the remaining car started to pull away and the person talking made his way toward the door. Magee decided this was his opportunity. He waited till the man had turned the corner and was approaching the door before moving quickly across the street. He took his position close behind the man and waited until he swiped the badge. As the door was swinging, Magee caught the handle just before it closed. He stepped inside.

The man turned slightly and glanced over his shoulder at Magee. This would be the moment. If the man challenged him, he would have to ask for his cooperation, nicely, or at the point of a gun. He looked back at the man and smiled.

"Sorry," the man said, "Didn't see anyone behind me." He turned away and kept on walking. Magee kept walking, too, in the same direction but more slowly. He was in a hallway that kept going straight for about thirty feet. He could see that as the hallway ended, he would turn either left or right. When he saw the man make a left turn as he reached the end, Magee decided he would turn right.

This hallway was longer. The first things he noticed were security cameras mounted just below the ceiling at various points along the hallway. He hadn't seen any of them outside in the dim light, but they were clearly visible on the inside. The red dot on each indicated they were active. He was probably being observed as he walked.

On both sides, there were doors with glass windows and signs identifying what appeared to be a purpose. While the exterior of the building had been old and not updated, the inside appeared to be relatively new construction.

Each room that he passed was fully lit up. Many had people working at desks with computers and phones. Some that he passed seemed to be laboratories. Men and women in lab coats were reviewing numbers and images on large screens hung on the walls. There were spinning machines that held what looked to be test tubes.

The signs on the doors identified the purpose in scientific terms. Some were simply labeled, such as 'Neuroscience", or "DNA Correlation'. One was called "Discovery Indexing". Others were more, obtuse and Magee was unfamiliar with the meaning of words like 'Corpus Callosum'. Approaching the end of the hallway, he could see that it branched again in opposite directions. A sign going toward the right said 'Residential'. The sign on the left said 'Administrative'. He turned left. At the end, he could see a double door. There was a badge reader on the wall to the side. He wondered if it meant that he needed to turn around, but as he neared, he saw the doors beginning to swing open.

A tall man stood on the other side. His hands were clasped together and held in front. His eyes were focused directly on Magee, who kept walking at the same pace. When he reached the door and began to pass through, the man extended his hand.

"Welcome, Mr. Magee," he said, "we've been expecting you." Magee extended his own hand. The man's grip was firm, and the handshake vigorous, as if it was heartfelt. "We're pleased to finally meet you." Without stopping the handshake, the man stiffened a bit and shook his head. "No, I mean, I am glad to meet you. That's more appropriate for now." Magee remained cautious as the man released his hand and turned slightly, pointing toward the hallway behind him. "Let's go where we can have a comfortable discussion, shall we?" he asked. Magee simply nodded and joined as the man began walking. "You've probably already guessed we run a twenty-four-hour operation. I believe it's pretty impressive when you grasp what we've accomplished in a short time. I know you must have many questions to ask."

"Like who you are," Magee offered. "You seem to have an advantage since you know my name already." The man smiled.

"You're right, of course," he said. "I know more about you than you do about me right now. But that's why we're going to chat. I'm going to tell you a story you will find hard to believe." They continued walking until they reached the open door to a small room. On the wall next to the door was a sign that read 'Orientation'. The man put one arm on Magee's shoulder and used the other to offer that he go first into the room, closing the door once both had entered.

Inside there were two large, comfortable chairs with a coffee table in between. On each side of the room, and along the back wall, stood large bookshelves filled with books. He recognized many of the titles as reflecting classical works across the ages. One wall contained everything from Homer and other Greeks, to Romans and early theologians, early

Renaissance scientists, and philosophers. Another wall contained many of the Eastern classics, from the Upanishads and Bhagavad Gita, through the Buddha, and into Chinese philosophers, including Mao Ze Dong. The third wall contained what appeared to be strictly related to scientific pursuit. The authors ranged from Newton to Hawking, along with a representation of social and economic writers as well.

The chairs were arranged so that both occupants would be looking at each other and beyond that directly at one of the walls containing a bookshelf, with the door of the room either on their left or right side. Magee chose the chair that faced the eastern philosophy bookshelf. The man took the other chair by default.

For a long time, neither spoke. They just looked at each other, as if they were evaluating what they saw. Magee was simply studying the demeanor of the man. He was younger than Magee, perhaps the same age as Anne, but he held himself with impressive ease. He was showing no sign of fear of Magee. He maintained a slight smile the whole time. Magee judged it to be genuine.

The man seemed to be studying Magee as well. He had already known Magee's name, which did give him an advantage, but Magee was wearing his 'no surprise face', as he had done when Paul pulled Magee's large file from his desk drawer. His objective was always to let the other person take the initiative, and then determine the motivation from where he takes it. Finally, the man spoke.

"You know," he began, "we call this room the orientation room. We bring those who are joining us to this room to help them adjust to their new situation." He paused. At that point, most people would ask for an explanation about which situation. Magee was content to let him go on.

"But I like to think of it as an observation room," he continued. "I like to observe how people react as we discuss why they are here. I even like to see which chair they choose because, of course, on one side their view is of things western world. On the other, it is all about the east. Have you read many of these works?" he asked while making a sweeping gesture around the room with his arm. Magee shook his head to indicate no. The man continued, "I've read quite a few." He added, "although some of them only when I need something to help me sleep." He smiled as if he expected Magee to share in his joke. Magee didn't react.

"I'm a bit partial toward the Eastern side, but I like to think that whatever side people choose is a matter of comfort for them. Of course, that doesn't apply to you," The man said. Again, he stopped and waited. Magee thought briefly and decided this was the time to engage. He leaned forward in his chair.

"Why doesn't it apply to me?" he asked. "I like books," he added. The man's smile broadened.

"Of course, you do," he said, "but you're not here for the same reason most people are."

"What *reason* are they here for?" Magee asked. The man cocked his head as if it was a strange question.

"As I just said," he replied, "adjustment. They've all experienced significant trauma. Some find it hard to adjust to it, which presents a lot of problems. Take Robert Devereaux, for example."

"Is that what happened?" Magee asked, calmly, and still leaning forward. "Some sort of trauma that he couldn't adjust to made it necessary for you, or someone connected to you, to get him out of a hospital where he was being treated, and bring him here to help him adjust?" The man nodded.

"That is precisely what happened, Mr. Magee," he answered. "There were few who understood what exactly had happened to him. And I know he was getting excellent treatment, but it wasn't likely to help in the end. We had to get him back here to make the adjustment, and then he, and we could move on with the work we have to do. It was in his best interests."

Magee was puzzled. It seemed like the man had concluded that Robert Devereaux was an important part of some work that had to be done. What could a young man who had been diagnosed with DID be able to contribute to? How could it be in his best interests to be taken away from treatment? It seemed almost selfish. He decided to ask.

"How would you know?" he asked. "How is it in his best interests when he was beginning to respond to the treatment there?" The man frowned.

"In due time I'll answer that, Mr. Magee," he said. "We'll get back to talking about Robert in due time. First, I want to ask you a few questions. Let's start with what you just mentioned about Robert. He was being treated for DID. What do you know about it?" Magee thought about it before answering. Of course, he knew what Klein had told him. He understood that real cases were rare.

"Not really that much, I'm afraid," he said. "I only know what Dr. Klein told me. I didn't need to know details because it wasn't what I was hired to investigate." The man smiled and nodded.

"Ah, yes," he said. "You're a private investigator, aren't you? You must be very good to have gotten here so quickly. I know you didn't follow the helicopter that picked Robert up and brought him here."

"I caught some lucky breaks as I started to investigate," Magee said.

"Still, I'm impressed," the man said. "Is it something you like to do?" It seemed to Magee to be an odd question. The man had just commented on how good he was. He knew he was good. Didn't that mean he must like what he does? He thought back to his recent work, before the clinic.

He had many jobs demonstrating his effectiveness. Paul had obtained a complete file with glowing recommendations. That must have meant he was enjoying what he did. But the more he thought about it, the more he wondered. He couldn't say he was happy doing them. The work filled the days and sometimes the nights. But he was mostly alone as he did it. He had been happy when he first started, especially with Jenny. After she was taken, the job had become something else. It was just what he had to do to get from one day to the next.

He had been happy before that, too. His old job was different, but it had a purpose. It called for only one person to take the risk, and he was willing to be that one to do it. He realized, though, that a part of what he liked about it included the team of people who supported him. He had liked doing that job up until the time he saw those people being taken out also. He would have stayed in that job then if he had been able to go after the person responsible. But instead, the organization had to make a deal that allowed Dig to stay alive in France.

So, he moved on until that day in Paris, when Dig was trying to take revenge on him as he had done to others on the team. After that, he was going to take out Dig regardless of whether they sanctioned the kill or not. He realized that his case for the clinic was the first time since then that he had truly liked his job. At every turn, the case became more interesting. But it was more than that. He realized for the first time in a long while, he was not alone. There was someone else to share his work with.

"I do," Magee said, coming back to the question he was asked, "at least on this case. Although, I'm not sure that is always necessary to do a good job." The man nodded.

"I agree," he said, "but I think it makes doing a good job a bit more rewarding. What is it about this case that causes you to like your job?" Magee had no intention of sharing what he had just thought about it. That was one of the things he believed made him effective in his work. He let others drive the conversation and expose more of themselves first before he would open up, if at all. But he also understood he needed to give them something to take up.

"Well," he started, "Its weirdness. It makes it interesting." The man laughed. "It's a lot different from the usual cases I get. Every time I think I understand it, something weirder happens," he added. "Even this place is weird." The man laughed a little harder.

"We haven't even discussed the most interesting part yet," he told Magee.

"That's exactly how this case started," Magee replied, "with Dr. Klein telling me about the 'more interesting parts' when I met her. I can't wait to hear what you are going to tell me. Maybe you could start by telling me your name, or at least your connection to this case."

"Fair enough," the man said. "for now, you can call me David. Let's just say I'm connected to the Devereaux's in a way that I'll explain later. And as far as this place is concerned, it's their money that funds it. You probably already know that it's kind of a research facility. You could say we're researching DID, but with an entirely different focus from the established medical community.

"It's quite complex, you know. Most of the time, the initial diagnosis is wrong. There's an ongoing debate about what causes it. Some professionals think it's the result of previous trauma. Some believe it's brought about by improper psychological treatment on the part of therapists, and newer ideas think it might be related to something in the way memory is processed. Even disrupted sleeping patterns are supposedly a cause.

"Regardless, of the cause, the technical answer always comes back to the presence of two or more distinct personality states in one individual. But there isn't any way to look inside someone and see a personality state. If you want to treat an individual who presents with DID, you're going to be dependent on at least one of the personality states that is contributing to the illness. I'd say that makes it pretty tough to deal with.

"When do you ever know whether the person you are working with is actually pretending to be someone he or she is not? You can never be sure that what you see is what you get, or more appropriately who you see." Magee smiled at the comparison. He had made a career of being someone other than who he really was. And he worked with a whole group of other people who were trained to do the same.

"I was under the impression," Magee said, "that people with DID aren't pretending. They really believe they are other people." The man nodded.

"You're right, of course," the man said, "they believe it. But people believe all sorts of things, UFO's, ghosts, mind-reading, Santa, at least when they're young. I'm really only saying that it's a complex problem." Magee nodded.

"From what I've observed so far," he said, "I agree with you." The man smiled.

"Okay," he said, "we're making progress. What do you know about death?" Magee smiled back. He knew a lot about death. He had faced it, and dealt it, and seen it happen to those who didn't deserve it. His smile faded with the last thought.

"More than I like," he answered. The man was looking in his eyes as Magee spoke. He seemed to sense that Magee had known death at a very personal level.

"Have you ever died?" he asked. The question caught Magee off guard. He made a noise of surprise.

"You mean, as in died and been resuscitated?" he asked.

"No," David said, "like died completely."

Chapter 24

Up to that moment, Magee had relaxed. He had gotten comfortable in the soft chair. The lights and position of them had been selected to encourage people to relax, to open up and become 'adjusted', as David had put it.

Now, alarms were going off, and the case had become even weirder. He had been sitting with someone who had seemed completely rational, having a semi-normal conversation, but the question just posed had been completely irrational. He didn't react immediately to David's question. Instead, he calmly moved his hand closer to the pocket where he had kept the P229 he had taken from Paul's stash. David had noticed his hand move and frowned.

"I think you may have misinterpreted my question," he said. "I just mean whether you have felt completely dead. For example, if something happened to you that was so horrible that it became too difficult to cope, emotionally at least." Magee relaxed again and moved his hand back to the arm of the chair.

"Thank you for not pulling the gun out," David said. "I didn't mean to startle you with the question." Magee was surprised that David knew. He was confident in his ability to control his reactions. It was part of his training. At this point, however, David already knew why he moved his hand.

"You seem to be a keen observer," Magee offered. "But I'm sure you might understand why I was concerned about your question."

"I saw the bulge earlier and assumed it was normal for a private investigator to have one. I suspected you grew a little concerned about your safety," David said, matter-of-factly, "perhaps as if a life-threatening something was about to happen. I can assure you that you are completely safe. I, and in fact, everyone in this building, have no desire to harm anyone. I understand that Robert did hurt one of the staff at the clinic, and I am very sorry about that. I had provided strict instructions that no one was to be harmed." Magee snickered.

"Well," he said, "there was a lot of gun-waving that went on, too." David smiled.

"I understand from my associate who was there that you were a wild card, Mr. Magee," he said. "We hadn't planned for you. Fortunately, the situation was resolved without further harm."

"Unless you count Longbow," Magee said. David looked surprised.

"Who is Longbow?" he asked. Magee paused to gauge David's reaction before answering.

"William Longbow was the man shot at the airport this morning," he continued. "He was shot in the back of the head, right around the time that your guy was going back there to get the car he left." David shook his head.

"I can't believe my associate had anything to do with it," he said. "I believe you know him, don't you?"

"Are you talking about Stan?" Magee asked. David nodded. "Then, yes, I know him."

"Do you think he would be capable of murder?" David asked.

"Well, he was the one waving the gun around," Magee replied.

"Still, he isn't," David said. "None of us are." Magee was puzzled.

"You know," he said, "I'd concede the point on Stan. He doesn't seem capable of committing a murder. But what does that mean?" he asked. David sighed.

"I'm afraid I wasn't completely honest with you a few minutes ago," David said, "but it was necessary given the reaction I got from you." The statement didn't help. Magee was just more puzzled, unsure of which thing David was not honest about. David seemed to sense it, too.

"Look," he started, "We've talked a lot about DID. The idea that one individual could have more than one personality." Magee nodded, and David continued. "We also talked about death. I think you know about death, too, in a very personal way. You've been affected by it." Magee found himself struggling not to react. David seemed to be very perceptive. Any indication would be more than Magee wanted him to know. He began to count in his mind. David continued before Magee had reached ten.

"As have we," he said, "Stan, myself, others in my organization, even Robert," he added.

"I'm still not following you," Magee said.

"My question earlier," David said, "the one about you ever completely dying was sincere. I walked it back only because of your reaction toward your gun. But I've asked that same question in this room with over one thousand people. And they've all answered yes." Magee was calmer this time. He did not move his hand toward his gun. David did not appear threatening. There were only the two of them in the room and the door was closed. He was just trying to comprehend David's meaning.

"How should I interpret the question then," Magee said. "If it isn't 'emotionally' as you implied, what is it?"

"Remember I said to you earlier that I was going to tell you a story you would find hard to believe?" he asked. Magee nodded. "Well, this is that story. I did die. Physically. Completely. Dead." He waited. Magee didn't say anything. "And I'm not the only one," he added. Magee made a face.

"But your death didn't include resuscitation as I had asked earlier," he said. David shook his head. Magee shook his head back in the same rhythm. "So how can you be here, conversing with me?" he asked. David smiled.

"Through the grace of another person, and God, of course," he answered. "When my physical body died, my consciousness seemed to move from that body to another body that was still living."

"What about the person who happened to be using that body at the time?" Magee asked. "What did he have to say about that."

"He accepted it," David replied. "I mean, we didn't actually have a conversation about it. It just became something we both knew."

"I hope this is the most interesting part," Magee said, "because I don't know how much more 'weird' I can take." David laughed.

"I know," he offered. "That's what I thought at first, too. But just think about it hypothetically for a moment, as if it might be true. Maybe think about it if it happened to you. How weird would it be? One moment you're dead. You see this light ahead. You figure, okay, go into the light." David made a gesture of moving forward with his hands as he was talking. Magee laughed.

"Okay, that part all makes sense," Magee said. "I've heard it described like that by the people who have been resuscitated."

"Right," David continued. "But then you close your eyes because the light is bright. And when you open them again, everything is different. You're in a place you don't recognize. Maybe it's a normal room. Maybe it's inside a car. Maybe you're on a merry-go-round. For a fraction of a moment, you think this must be heaven, and then suddenly you sync." Magee gave a questioning look.

"What does sync mean?"

"It means you synchronize. You realize that you know where you are. Wherever it is, you went there to be there. And you realize you aren't alone. You're really two people inside one body. You know everything that the other person knows, and still everything you used to know. Whatever childhood experiences each one of you had, you know them as if you've known them your whole life. You've synchronized all of your knowledge with all of someone else's knowledge."

"It must make you twice as smart!" Magee said. "Smart enough to know it's impossible." David shook his head.

"It doesn't exactly work like that," he said. "I mean, you are smarter in the sense that if one of you knew Calculus, and the other didn't, now you both do because you can recall the same learning. But it doesn't help you with things that one of you didn't already know. Except that you do know it's possible because it is happening to you. And it improves your judgment because you have an entirely new set of experiences to draw on to make any judgment."

"But why, how?" Magee asked. David shook his head again.

"We don't know that yet, but we have an idea," he said. Magee was looking at him expectantly. "We think it's related to DID."

Magee sat back in his chair and considered what David had said in the way he would always approach a problem. He considered different options. He had judged the man to be perfectly sincere in his statement. Whatever the truth was, David believed what he was saying was true. But how was it possible?

David appeared to be comfortable waiting for Magee to process what he had just said. He had looked away to let Magee have his moment of thinking it through. He adjusted his body in the chair. He picked a piece of lint from his pant leg. He brushed it away again as he had dropped it on the arm of the chair. Finally, he looked back at Magee and waited for a response. Magee didn't have one yet.

The most logical explanation was that it did relate to DID. The person sitting in front of him had the very same thing Robert Devereaux had but functioned at a much higher level. Robert had been institutionalized because of his erratic behavior, roaming the streets of Palo Alto, believing himself to be a homeless person. In Magee's brief discussion with David, he displayed nothing erratic. He seemed very intelligent and articulate. He wished, for the moment, he could be back at the clinic to ask Dr. Klein to evaluate David.

"Let's assume," he finally said, "that you are right. What's the relationship? David smiled again.

"We don't know precisely," he answered. "That's why I created this research lab." Magee leaned forward again.

"With the Devereaux's money," he said. "Which may tie up some loose ends for me," he added.

"How so?" David asked. Magee smiled.

"I've been looking for the angle on this case," he said, "I've suggested from the beginning that this case was somehow related to Devereaux's money and getting a piece of it. I know you set up Stan at the clinic so you could get Robert out. Were you also responsible for the mice?" David looked surprised.

"What mice?" he asked.

"Sorry," Magee replied, "That's a nickname that people at the clinic gave them. I'm talking about three men who showed up at the clinic wanting to see Robert."

"Oh," David answered, "yes, we sent them. That was the first plan. We had arranged to send them there to bring Robert out and bring him here. But then Robert's brother died, and we had to figure out something different. Stan had already been put in place to assist for two reasons. One was to survey the clinic and give us information on what we might expect when we arrived. The other was just in case assistance was needed."

"Which they could have used, obviously," Magee offered, "since they were unsuccessful."

"True," David said, "but that's because of just what I said. Robert's brother died before he could go with them. He was scheduled to go. If he had been there, it would have been different." Magee thought about arguing the point. He doubted that Klein would have approved of them taking Robert out. But Robert's brother had guardianship from the court. If the brother had been there, perhaps she would have had to comply. If she didn't, Paul would not have allowed anyone to take Robert.

"You're talking about Jason, right?" Magee asked. David nodded.

"Yes," he replied. "He had a ruptured aneurysm. It runs in the family. Killed his father, too." He paused for a moment and looked at the floor as if in thought. "So, there was no way that Dr. Klein would have allowed anyone to take him unless it was a newly appointed guardian. And that would take a while. And I needed Robert to be back here so we could continue our research."

That had been Magee's thinking as well. It would have taken time to go through the legal mechanisms to get Robert out. He had said that before to

Anne and Paul. But he didn't understand what David meant about continuing the research. He had been thinking that he wanted Robert out for the money.

"How could Robert help with the research?" he asked. Magee smiled.

"Because he represents a link in the chain," David replied. Magee shook his head.

"That doesn't help," he said. "What does that mean?" David didn't answer right away. He seemed to be weighing what he wanted to say.

"Because, Mr. Magee," David started, "Because…" he paused again, "we share the same DNA. Robert Devereaux is my son. I am his father, Frederick Devereaux. And I represent someone who woke up in someone else's body, David's to be exact. Robert represents someone who woke up with someone else in his own body. It gives us a chance to study the genetics of this from both sides and find out if there is a link."

Magee sank back into the chair again. He realized he was tired. It had been a long and stressful day. It was late. His mind was wrestling with several questions. He was sitting with someone who could easily be called crazy, yet David didn't appear threatening. And based on his surprise regarding Longbow, he didn't believe David would have wanted that to happen.

"What about Stan?" he asked. "Is he someone who woke up in someone's body, or did someone wake up in his?"

"The former," David said. "And believe me, we've run tests on him, and more tests on me than I can count. Robert gives us a direct comparison with the same genetic material. It really could be the key."

"Is Stan here at this facility?" Magee asked. David nodded. "Can I talk to him?" Magee added.

"Yes," David answered, "But it's late now. He would be sleeping. He was up early to go retrieve his car."

"Did he mention anything about Longbow when he returned?"

"No," David said. "but you can talk to him first thing tomorrow morning and find out what he knows. You may want to consider getting some sleep as well. This has to have been a long day for you, too." Magee knew he was right. There was a lot to think about.

"If I go home now," he replied, "will all of this still be here in the morning? Or will I come back and find everyone has gone and the whole place cleaned out because the scam is over?" David laughed.

"No, Mr. Magee," he said. Everyone will still be working here. I'll still be here. Robert and Stan will be here as well. You can stay here if you like. We have plenty of extra rooms. We're not that much different from the clinic you're working for. Just bigger, with more resources." Magee considered the offer.

"Okay," he said, "but a couple more questions first." David nodded. "You've been able to convince other people that you are Frederick Devereaux, or at least enough to get others to open the Devereaux money supply. How did you do that?" David smiled.

"It wasn't too hard, really," he replied. "I only had to convince Anthony Rendon. He's the current CEO of Devereaux Holdings. He and I go way back. We were friends from school, really. And I know things about him that no one else knows. More importantly, I left instructions for him before I died.

"About this possibility?" Magee asked.

"No, of course not. But instructions if I should die unexpectantly. I was always thinking ahead. I built my business on it," he said with a tone of pride. "He knew my intentions toward the leadership of the business. I had been grooming my son Jason for that leadership eventually. But if I died before Jason was ready, I wanted to make sure Anthony knew what I wanted to happen until he was. I wrote everything down and gave a sealed copy to my attorney. Anthony knew about it.

"And the attorney delivered it to him the day I died. Inside the instructions was something only he and I knew. It was something we did as kids. It was something we both used throughout our working together to convince each other something was real. In the case of the instructions, it was there to convince him they were truly what I wanted.

"After I died, I showed up at the funeral. Well, I mean David showed up at the funeral. I only had to get close enough to tell him one word to get his attention. After that, it still took a while to convince him. But he's completely on board now. He wasn't the only one I had to convince, but he was the most important. I died suddenly, and I didn't have the opportunity to talk to my sons first. The people closest to my sons were people in the company. Anthony was still in charge there, and he was working to protect my sons, and not let anyone intrude on their privacy."

"So, once you got him on board, why not call a press conference, and let the world know what was going on," Magee offered. Devereaux laughed.

"We could have done that, I suppose," he said. "But I'm not sure how ready the world is for this news. Plus, at first, I didn't know if I was the only one. If I was, people would spend all sorts of energy trying to prove it was a hoax. The company would be in chaos. There would be a lot of problems. Anthony was the one who suggested we take a scientific approach first. He wanted to see if we could find others and determine what caused it. The more actual knowledge we gather to share when it does go public, the better people will accept it.

"He and I laid out plans and created a subsidiary group so we could fund the research. We gathered some of the top medical researchers in the world to look at the physiological questions. We had me as a patient to study. We started searching for others. And we started finding them, lots of them with similar situations. We had outlined the criteria we wanted.

"We started building a network of sources. Other cases were out there, but we were the only organization with enough resources to start pulling everything together. All of that took time, though. And by the time we were ready to bring my sons on board with what had happened, Robert had his experience. And Jason had already had him transferred to the clinic. So, we waited until we could collect enough evidence to introduce Jason to the concept. We just started gathering everything we could.

"Once we began to compile it all, we discovered something interesting. The oldest documented case we found that fit most of our criteria happened in 2012, in China. But as we gathered more data each year after that, we discovered the number of cases was accelerating. In the early years, there was only a trickle each year. But over the last two years, the number has grown substantially in each one. The growth seems to be greatest in countries with the largest populations. We've developed more than a few theories about it, but it would take a while to explain them all. We're still in the early stage of exploration, but we know a lot more now than we ever did before."

"Do you think there is some sort of correlation between high populations and incidents of DID?" Magee asked. David shook his head.

"Not DID in general," he said, "Only DID in the sense as it relates to what I have experienced. Remember that I don't think I have DID. I think that I died, left my body, and moved to someone else's body. The same is true in all of the cases that I say we have documented. That includes all of the ones in populous countries. Consider one theory that has been proposed. What would happen if people stopped dying altogether?"

"The population would increase unless you figured out a way to keep people from reproducing," Magee answered.

"Exactly," David responded. "And if the population increased exponentially, it would have significant effects on the world." Magee nodded. "Eventually, something would have to be done to relieve the pressure. Either people would have to become less fertile, or something else would have to be done. Becoming less fertile is kind of an evolutionary response, to take the pressure off. Another evolutionary response might be combining individuals into one body, allowing one body to die to relieve the pressure." Magee laughed.

"I have to say that is a weird conclusion to jump to," he offered.

"Granted," David replied. "But it is a possibility. That way, you don't lose the essence of the being, the consciousness if you will. And perhaps DID itself is a corollary to that theory. The earliest diagnosis in modern times was 1880. The population in 1800 was roughly one billion. By 2010, it was roughly 7 billion, quite an increase in 200 years compared to all the years of human existence before. And the most dramatic increase has been in the last 100 years. But maybe evolutionary responses take a while to develop.

"And what if all cases of DID are only an evolutionary response gone wrong?" David added. "What if there is something about the physical aspect that causes the join to not complete properly? Perhaps it doesn't always work perfectly. Maybe every DID case is an example of what I've experienced but something was preventing it from happening smoothly."

"Okay," Magee said. "It's hard to believe, but I'll grant that some of the greatest things ever created have come from things that were hard to believe when someone first thought of them. I'll consider everything you had to say, but I want to talk to some others as well in the morning, especially Stan." David smiled.

"That's fine," he said, as he took his cell phone from his pocket. He dialed a number and a woman answered. "Hello, Cynthia," he said. "Mr. Magee has agreed to stay the night with us. He's with me in the Orientation room. Can you come and take him to one of our suites and make sure he has any additional things he might need, toiletries, toothbrush, and so on," he waited a moment, then added thanks. He looked back at Magee and stood up. "She's on her way, Mr. Magee. Thank you for your patience."

"Thanks for the, um, education," he said, making it into a question by raising the last syllable. A moment later a nice woman was escorting him to a room with a bed and bathroom. After she left, he called Anne. She had been sleeping.

"Hello," she said, still drowsy.

"Hi," he answered.

"Thank goodness," she said, sounding fully awake. "I've been waiting for you to call." He laughed.

"It sounded to me like you were sleeping like a baby," he answered.

"Oh, stop," she said, "I fell asleep with the phone in my hand. What time is it, anyway?"

"A little after 1:00 AM."

"You okay?" she asked.

"Better now," he said back. "How is everything there?"

"Fine," she told him, "except Paul's pals are a little rowdy. Even Dr. Klein told him to calm them down a little. And they did calm down, after that. Other than that, it's been quiet, and I miss you."

"Me, too," he said, "but I'll be back tomorrow. Go back to sleep now, and I'll call you when I leave here."

"Okay," she said, a little drowsily again. Then suddenly, "Magee, I love you."

"I love you, too. G'night." The phone went silent. He set it down and laid on the bed. He was out moments later.

Chapter 25

Magee opened his eyes. The alarm on his phone was ringing. The clock next to the bed displayed 7:00 A.M. He rose and went into the bathroom. Toiletries and a razor with shaving cream had been provided in the room. He stripped down and took a shower. While he was in the shower, he heard a knock on the door of the room.

The bathroom door was open. He peered around the curtain and saw an envelope slide beneath the door to the hall. He finished washing and stepped out to pick up the note. It was from Stan asking him to meet in the cafeteria as soon as he could. He shaved and dressed, then grabbed his phone made his way following the directions in the note. As he entered, he saw Stan and David sharing a table off on the side of the room. He walked over to them. They were eating breakfast.

"Morning," he said as he approached. They both responded similarly. David pointed to a counter with a man standing behind it.

"That man over there behind the counter will whip you up a pretty good omelet," he said. "There are other things in the buffet line over there on the left," he added. Magee thanked him and checked out the omelet counter before heading to the buffet. He made a few choices, picked up some coffee, and headed back over to the table. As he sat down, he extended his hand to Stan, who was in the middle of taking a bite of his food.

"Good to see you again, Stan," he said. "I'm surprised you're not managing this place." Stan took his hand but looked surprised. Then he realized what Magee was saying.

"Oh, you mean the cooking part," he said. "I only did that as a cover," Stan replied.

"John has other responsibilities here," Devereaux offered. "He's a special advisor to me. That's why I sent him to make sure we got Robert back." Stan seemed to blush a little.

"Thanks, Mr. Devereaux," he said and then went back to picking at his food. Magee raised an eyebrow.

"Mr. Devereaux," he repeated, "Why not David?"

"David is the name of the other person in me. David Thompson, to be exact. John knows me as Mr. Devereaux. He's known me for almost all his life," David said. "And despite my numerous attempts to have him call me by my first name, Frederick or now David, I guess old habits die hard."

"And you call him John," Magee said. He looked at Stan, "Is that your real name?" Stan nodded.

Yes, I guess," he said. "I mean it was before Stan joined with me."

"Do you have a last name, or should I say do you both have a last name?" Magee asked.

"Moray," he answered, "at least for the John part. Nowak for the Stan part."

Do you have a preference between Stan and John?" Magee asked next. He thought for a moment.

"I guess Stan from you, Mr. Magee," he replied. "It's what I'm used to when you talk to me. But really, the name doesn't matter."

"The same is true for me, Mr. Magee," David said. "You can call me David, Frederick, Thompson or Devereaux. I'll answer to them all." Magee nodded acknowledgment.

"In that case," he said," I'll call you Devereaux. It will keep things clearer. But I'd also like both of you to drop the 'Mister' for me. Just call me Magee."

"No first name," Devereaux said. Magee shook his head. Devereaux nodded.

"With all due respect, Mr. Magee," Stan said, "I prefer to use the mister. My parents always taught me to respect my elders." Both Magee and David laughed. Stan looked puzzled. "Did I say something funny?" he asked, but then added, "Oh, wait. I know from the Stan side now that Mr. Devereaux isn't that much older than me now, and that you, Mr. Magee, don't want the respect." He laughed too. David spoke.

"I'm not physically that much older than you, John, but I'm still even older than Stan was," he said. Then he turned to Magee.

"John was Robert's best friend when he was growing up. I've known him since he was seven," he said as he made a gesture with his hand to indicate the height of a seven-year-old.

"Speaking of Robert," Magee started, "you went back to the airport to pick up your car yesterday, right?" Stan nodded. "Did you speak to Longbow?" Stan gave him an odd look at first, but then realized who he was talking about.

"Oh, is that the guy that works there?" he asked. Magee nodded. Stan continued. "No," he said. "The chopper took me back and dropped me off. I headed straight for my car and got in. While I was driving away, I saw the chopper lift off. I didn't stop to talk to anyone."

"Did you know that Longbow was murdered right around the time you were there?" Magee asked. Stan dropped his fork.

"What," he said. The reaction was enough for Magee to conclude he didn't know. "How?" he asked.

"Bullet to the back of the head as he went out the door leading to the field," Magee answered.

"Oh, my God," Stan replied. "Why? Who?" he added. Magee shook his head.

"Don't know, Stan."

"I didn't even go in and see him," Stan said while shaking his head in disbelief. "I just got in my car and drove away."

"Yes," Magee said, "and you didn't see him lying on the ground when you got out of the chopper, right?"

"Of course, not," Stan said. "I would have done something. Tried to help him, called the police or something."

"But you also saw the chopper taking off after you got out, right?" Magee asked. Stan nodded.

"But sometime after you left the parking lot, and the time the body was discovered, someone decided to kill him." Magee watched Stan. He was poking his food around with his fork. Then he added, "You were waving around a gun at the clinic, remember?" Stan dropped his fork again.

"Of course, I remember," he said, with agitation. "But I didn't keep it. I left it in the chopper after Robert and I returned."

"Really?" Magee asked. "That doesn't sound too responsible for someone who knows about guns. Weren't you the one who was boasting about shooting more times than me when you were holding the gun in the observation room?"

"Yes," Stan admitted, "but that was only because the Stan side of me has fired guns. "I was a restaurant owner in the city. I had one for self-defense. A lot of dining restaurants have to worry about being robbed. They deal with a lot of cash, and they're open late. I had one and knew how to shoot it." He stopped for a moment, in thought. Then he added,

"And I know it was irresponsible to leave it in the chopper. I was just reminded of it. But when we got back, I was too anxious to get Bobby into the building."

"Was it still in the chopper when you went back to get the car?" Magee asked.

"I don't know," Stan said. "I didn't look for it." Magee nodded.

"What about Paul's gun?" he asked.

"I threw that one out into the woods on the road between the gates," Stan replied.

"Okay, Stan," he said. "Sorry for making a big deal about it." Then he turned to Devereaux. "I need to talk to that pilot," he said. "Right now, he's the likely suspect." Devereaux nodded.

"Of course," he said, "But I don't think he could have done it. He's also someone like Stan and me."

"Doesn't matter," Magee said. "He's still the only real suspect at this point. Even though he lifted off after dropping Stan, he could have circled back again and landed. Maybe he didn't do it either. Longbow's murder may have been a complete coincidence. But I'll feel better if that's all that's left after I talk to the pilot." Devereaux took out his phone and dialed a number. It was Cynthia again. He gave her instructions to tell the pilot he wanted to speak with him as soon as possible.

"She's going to find him and call me back as soon as he is on his way," he said after hanging up. "While we wait, why don't I take you on the tour," he added. Magee shrugged.

"Okay," he said. David pointed the way and started walking. Once they had left Stan behind at the table, he turned to Magee.

"You were kind of rough on Stan, Magee," he said, "Don't you think?

"A little, I guess," Magee replied. "But I had to make sure. I don't believe in coincidences. I think Longbow was just in the wrong place at the wrong time. Somebody decided to send a message. And right now, that pilot is the last one that may have seen him alive."

They headed down the corridor and over into the first hallway that Magee had entered last night. They stopped at the first door they came to. It was marked "Neuroscience." There were several people in the room, each wearing lab coats and several large imaging monitors were scattered across counters and desks in the room. Magee recognized that many of the images resembled the shape of the human brain. Devereaux often stopped and chatted with people as they walked through, sometimes asking them to explain what they were doing to Magee. Most often Magee would simply nod and let them know that it was way beyond what he could understand. It seemed to be the same for several other rooms that they walked through.

Finally, they reached a room labeled Discovery Indexing. Devereaux winked at Magee before they entered.

"This is my favorite room," he said. "It's all about finding people who have been through what I have." None of the people in the room were wearing lab coats. They were dressed casually. All of them were sitting in front of a computer, and each talking on the phone. They didn't stop when Magee and Devereaux entered. There was significant noise from the chatter but each of them wore headphones, so nothing could be heard from whoever each was talking to. Magee recognized that many of the people were speaking different languages. Devereaux spoke directly at Magee, a little louder than he would normally speak, so Magee could hear him above the chatter.

"We call this room 'Discovery' because it's the first stop for potentials, people we believe might have what we have. All of these people are having conversations with either professionals in the medical field, or parents, or authorities of some type. People who either know someone like us or have to figure out what to do with someone who needs help. We've developed a network all around the world to help us. I've sent people a lot of places to develop contacts. Once they are on the ground, they do investigations to find candidates. Then they hook them up with this group in here so we can index them all first. Once we have them indexed, we start the process of weeding out ones that don't qualify."

"You keep them busy full time?" Magee asked. Devereaux nodded.

"It's a 24-hour world," he said. "and there are a lot of people out there." They continued walking around the room in between the desks until they reached the door again. Magee had been glancing at the screens as they walked by and could see the people entering names and information. At the door, they went back out into the hallway.

"We've identified a lot of potentials," Devereaux said in a normal voice back in the hallway. Once we have them in the database, we go through the criteria and figure out who to bring here for evaluation. We keep finding new people every day."

"But how do you even start?" Magee asked. "I know you've sent people out there to search for them, but how do they begin. How do you ask someone if they are sharing their body with someone else?" Devereaux laughed.

"You're right," he said, "It's a hard topic to broach. But we don't start with the actual people. We send people to hospitals, particularly psychiatric ones. We talk to schools. We go to police departments. It's a little easier in countries that have good medical care because sooner or later people end up in hospitals. But then there are a lot of places in this world where crazy people are running around loose until their local police lock them up. Are you a religious man, Magee?" Devereaux asked.

"Not so much," Magee replied. "I like to think I'm spiritual. I believe in a higher power and all that. But I just don't go for organized religion."

"I think I understand. Too much dogma," he said. "But do you know which religion actually believes in multiple personalities? Catholicism, at least in one way. That's why they still do exorcisms. They're trying to get the demon out of someone. I'm sure you can understand why they might think it's a demon." Magee nodded. Devereaux continued.

"Turns out," he said, "the Catholic church has been very helpful to us in finding cases we can investigate as possible jump candidates. They've provided their files on recent exorcism requests. But even without those, they have instructed their parishes across the globe to be on alert for people who might be someone we should talk to. And," Devereaux added, raising his finger as if to make a point, "they've agreed to keep it quiet. It's a good approach for us when you think of it. No publicity. Even though attendance at churches has fallen in our country, there are still a fair amount of religious people in this world. Where do those people turn when they need guidance? They go to their priest. Then eventually they wind up with us.

"In fact, that reminds me," Devereaux added, "The pilot that you want to talk to came to us from the Catholic church. I did his orientation. He seemed to adjust very easily. Of course, it's easier for them to accept things."

"You're Catholic, too, aren't you?" Magee asked. Devereaux laughed.

"Yes," he admitted, "so I guess I'm a little partial. But seriously, I think it's easier for people who are religious to accept things that happen to them. Will of God, sort of thing. Orientations are always easier with Catholics." Devereaux's phone rang.

"Hello," he said. He listened briefly. "Okay, I'll be there. Oh, and Cynthia, tell the members I'm bringing Mr. Magee with me. Thanks," he added. Then he turned to Magee. "She was reminding me of the briefing. Every day at 11:00, I have a meeting with the Department Heads to discuss directions, concerns, findings, 'et. cetera.' It gives them time earlier to check the progress of their part of the organizations, and then leaves them time later in the day to follow through on things we decide to do. It starts in a few minutes."

"She seems to take pretty good care of you," Magee said. Devereaux nodded.

"She was also my assistant at the company before I died. I brought her here to help me when we established this place. By the way, she knew me very well when we worked together at the company. And now she has no problem accepting who I am."

"Is she Catholic, too?" Magee asked, reverting briefly to his sarcastic nature. It was a sign that he was comfortable in the situation. Regardless of whether he believed the possibility of what he had been told, he knew Devereaux was completely sincere in his own belief. And he did act like what Magee believed the CEO of a multi-billion-dollar organization would act. Devereaux laughed at the reference.

"Yes," he said, "but I think that's just a coincidence." He emphasized the word coincidence to let Magee know that he could be sarcastic, too. Magee smiled. "I hope you don't mind coming with me, Devereaux added, as he gestured toward the end of the hall and began walking. "It may help you understand more about how we are approaching this. We're not really sure what this will lead to in the end. But I do know what I've gone through. Others have, too. Maybe that's a coincidence and we're all just crazy." There was no emphasis on coincidence this time. It was just a sincere statement.

"I don't mind," Magee said. "I have to admit, it's all pretty interesting." They reached the door to the Administration part of the building where Devereaux had been standing the night before. He paused for a moment as they passed the Orientation room.

"Are you any closer to accepting the concept I proposed last night as we spoke in this room?" Devereux asked. Magee smiled.

"I have to admit I'm still skeptical," he said. "It's interesting, but hard to believe."

"Do you remember that last night, I told you I was more partial to the Eastern philosophies?" Devereaux said. Magee nodded. "I wasn't always. I had been raised as a Catholic, and when I died, I fully expected to join the Heavenly Father. And yet, here I am." He started walking again, and Magee followed.

"At first, I found myself looking for an explanation based on my religion, but there really isn't one," Devereaux continued. "Eventually, I got around to looking at other religions as well. The one that makes the most sense to me now is Buddhism, which, of course, grew from Hinduism.

"During his lifetime, the Buddha wrestled with the problem of human suffering, and with the thought of being re-incarnated again and again to continue suffering. Ultimately, he identified the four noble truths, and the eightfold path to eventually ending the suffering. But it takes significant discipline to walk that path. I certainly didn't walk that path in my lifetime. I did try to be a good person, though. Perhaps I avoided re-incarnation from the beginning and instead was granted the opportunity to just start with all of my knowledge being added to another person's knowledge." Magee raised an eyebrow.

"I'd say that's another weird conclusion to jump to," he said to Devereaux. They both laughed as Devereaux pointed to a door labeled 'Board Room.' Inside they found six people already sitting around a large conference table. One of them was Stan. Magee smiled at him and Stan returned the smile. At one end was a large monitor mounted on the wall. Across the table at the same end as the monitor, Magee recognized Cynthia who nodded to him. The monitor was showing a man in a business suit. He appeared to be older than the people who were physically present. His hair was black and wavy with touches of gray on each side. Devereaux spoke at him.

"Morning, Anthony," he said as he walked to a chair and rested his hands on the back. He pointed to the chair next to it while looking back at Magee.

"Morning, Freddy," the man said. "I see you have a guest." Devereaux nodded.

"Yes," he answered. He looked around the room at the others, "Morning, everyone." Most acknowledged by repeating the word. Each had a closed binder in front of them. Devereaux continued as he sat down in the chair, "First, let me introduce Mr. Magee. He is the private investigator that was hired by the clinic where Robert had been." People around the table each started saying hello to him. Magee tried to look at each as they did and respond. Then he sat down in the chair next to Devereaux. He looked back at a man across the table and recognized him as one of the mice from the clinic. He had been the one who pushed for still trying to contact Robert. He was also the one who had claimed to be the brother. Devereaux continued speaking.

"I've asked him to sit with us so he can understand a bit more about what we are working on, and how we're doing it." Devereaux looked across the table at a woman with a blank notepad on top of the binder in front of her. "Thank you, Cynthia, for putting together this morning's briefing book." The woman nodded to him. Devereaux opened his binder.

"Let's turn to page one, shall we?" he said. The others responded by opening their binders to page one. Before Devereaux said anything else, Anthony spoke up.

"Freddy," he started, "I appreciate that you'd like to run this like a regular readout, but it is unusual to have Mr. Magee with us. Perhaps before we start on the topics, maybe you could fill us in on the containment issue. Where are we with keeping the story from leaking out? We all agreed we're not ready to see this go public yet. It was why some didn't want to go through with our plan to retrieve Robert after Jason died." When Anthony mentioned Jason, Devereaux turned from looking at Anthony to looking across the table at the man Magee had recognized. Then he turned back to Anthony.

"I understand," he said. "I'll let Mr. Magee give an update first. He and I have talked quite a bit since he arrived. I've covered him on some of the basics, but he should tell you what he is thinking at this point." Devereaux turned to Magee. "Do you mind, Magee?" Magee smiled. He appreciated that Devereaux had not added the 'Mister'.

"No problem at all," Magee said, "I'd be happy to." He adjusted himself in his chair and leaned forward, resting his arms on the table. "I can't say that I have understood or accepted everything I've heard while I've been here, but I believe when you use the word 'containment' you are referring to containing the publicity involved." He saw almost everyone nod. "From that aspect, I can assure you that my client has the same desire as you.

"They are a well-respected facility, and they happen to have patients from some very well-off families who pay a lot of money for their services. They want to avoid publicity at all costs because it would be detrimental to their clients and would diminish the work that they also do to treat the people who can't afford treatment. In fact, avoiding publicity was one of the objectives conveyed to me by the Clinic's founder, Dr. Klein, when I talked to her about taking the assignment." He stopped to gauge the reaction. Most seemed to be relieved. Anthony spoke.

"It sounds like good news, Mr. Magee," he said, "So I gather you were successful?" he asked.

"Up to a point," Magee said. "Something has intervened with the potential to create a problem." A flash of concern came over Anthony's face, as well as the faces of others in the room. "There was a murder that was reported to the police." There were audible gasps from people in the room. Stan and Devereaux did not react because they already knew of the problem. Anthony was shaken.

"Someone was killed?" he asked. "By whom?" Magee shook his head.

"I don't know yet," he said. "But I am obligated by a code of ethics to cooperate with the police in criminal matters that have a connection to any case I am working on. I've already had to provide a statement to the police because they found my card on the dead man."

"What did you tell them?" Anthony asked.

"I told them about the visit from the three men who came to talk to Robert," Magee said, "And I told them that the clinic had pictures of the men." He looked over at the person he had recognized as one of the mice when he entered the room. "Unfortunately, I did not know what I know now. I'm sorry, Jason," Then he turned to Devereaux and repeated it. "I'm sorry." Devereaux smiled.

"Thank you," he said. "You are quite perceptive aren't you." Magee smiled back.

"Okay," Anthony said, "do they know about what happened after that?" Magee shook his head.

"No," he said. "I didn't share everything yet. I wasn't sure the murder was connected to my case yet. I wanted to investigate more before I opened that part up. But now there will be an official investigation. The Deputy Sheriff that is responsible is headed to the clinic this afternoon to talk with the staff and get the pictures. He is going to want to question the three men who were there, but that alone won't connect them to the murder if they had a legitimate reason to be there."

"Who was killed," Anthony asked. Stan spoke this time.

"A man named William Longbow," Stan said. "He ran the airport where Bobby and I were picked up by the chopper." Magee nodded. "But he wasn't dead when I went back this morning and picked up my car." Magee nodded again.

"I believe what Stan is saying," he said, "and the only other person connected that may know something about it is the pilot of the helicopter." He looked over at Cynthia. "Were you able to contact him so we can talk." She shook her head.

"He hasn't called me back yet," she said. "I know he left the building last night because I checked the badge records. But he hasn't been back in this morning and isn't answering his phone." Magee frowned.

"He's missing?" He asked. Cynthia nodded. "That's not good," Magee said. "He just ticked up a notch on the suspect meter." He leaned back in his chair. Devereaux spoke.

"I've already told Magee that the pilot is one of us. It's unlikely he would kill anyone," he said. "And I can't imagine what possible motive he would have."

"What do we know about this pilot?" Anthony asked.

"I did his orientation, Anthony," Devereaux said. "He came to us through one of our church contacts. He called our hotline and said a priest had given him the number. The person taking the call was going to have a local representative interview him, but he said he would prefer coming to talk to us directly. She gave him the address and he got on a plane and flew here." Anthony frowned.

"That may not be the best procedure in the future," he said. "We should correct that to make sure everyone is interviewed in the field." Devereaux nodded.

"I agree, he said. "Cynthia, would you pass that along to Security and Discovery and make sure they draw up a new procedure." He turned back to Anthony. "But he did go through the interview process here, and he made it through the criteria. When I did his interview, he seemed completely normal," he stopped for a moment, "I mean, normal like all of the rest of us," he added. "Right down to abhorrence for taking human life because his own had been taken." Anthony thought for a moment.

"How did he die?" he asked.

"He said he was murdered. His throat was slit, and he bled to death. Next thing he knew, he woke up in the body of a French Helicopter pilot. He was an American, living in Paris, so his experience was very different from what we normally see." Magee suddenly stood up and turned to Devereaux.

"When was he killed?" he said excitedly.

"It was almost three years ago, but he's only been with us for about six months," Devereux said.

"I have to leave now!" Magee exclaimed. "I have to go back to the clinic."

"What's this all about?" Anthony asked.

"It's about me. I have to get back to the clinic, now. Longbow's murder was a message to me." He started to leave the room. Devereaux called out to him.

"Wait," he said, "how are you going back?" Magee turned.

"Driving," he said. Devereaux shook his head.

"No," he said, "we have another pilot. We'll take you directly there." He turned to Cynthia. "Call security. Have them get the pilot up to the helipad. I'm going with him," he said. He rose and started walking out as well. Stan shouted after them.

"I'm coming to," he said. "There's room for four in that chopper."

Chapter 26

As they headed to the roof, Magee called Paul. There was no answer. He tried Anne. No answer there either. When they reached the roof, the other pilot was already warming the engine. They loaded in, with Devereaux in the co-pilot seat, and Stan and Magee behind them. The pilot distributed earphones with mics and pointed at the cell phone in Magee's hand.

"You'll need to turn that off before we go up. It will screw up my instruments," he said. Magee nodded but quickly sent a text to Anne to get Klein, find Paul and stay with him until Magee got there.

They were underway within 15 minutes. The helicopter was always refueled when it returned so they didn't have to wait. The pilot was given the address and had programmed his flight. It would be the same path that Stan's flight had taken yesterday. There were no clouds. The weather was a typical California day. They headed out across the bay. The Pilot announced it would take about an hour and 15 minutes to reach the clinic. He asked Magee if there would be a space to land. Magee remembered the view from Anne's apartment and told him yes.

He glanced at his watch. The time was 11:30. It would be well after Noon when they arrived. Lane would probably be there by then. He decided he had to tell Devereaux so they could determine their response to any questions Lane would ask. He reached around the seat and tapped his arm.

"When we get there," he said, "The deputy will be there. He may think it's a little unusual for a helicopter to be landing out there at the clinic. We should probably think about how we might respond if he questions it." Devereaux nodded.

"Give me a minute," he answered. While he was thinking, Magee turned to Stan in the seat next to him.

"This is the same helicopter you took before, isn't it?" he said. Stan nodded. "Look around and see if you if can find the gun you left." Stan pointed to a console between the seats and then flipped the lid up.

"I left it in here yesterday when he brought me back," Stan replied. The console was empty. "It's gone now. Someone probably cleaned the inside when we got back and took the gun out." Magee acknowledged that he understood.

"What did you and the pilot talk about on the way back?" he asked.

"The pilot didn't talk much the first day," Stan replied. "He asked a few questions, but after we answered he stayed quiet for the rest of the ride.

"What kind of questions?"

"He wanted to know if we had any problems. We talked about how we barely got away," Stan said. "Then he asked what happened. So, we told him about how you took the knife away from Bobby. How Paul had rushed into the room and then got hurt. What you said about coming after us." Magee made a face.

"How did he react?" he asked.

"Oddly," Stan answered. "he smiled. Then he kind of laughed. It wasn't what I expected at all. But on the second day, he had a lot more questions. He wanted to know about the clinic itself. What was it like for me to be working there? Were the people nice? What were their names?" Devereaux interrupted him.

"Okay, Magee," he said. "Does this deputy know why you were going back to the city? I mean does he think you were going back as part of the investigation you were doing?" Magee thought back to his conversation.

"No," he answered. "he thought I was pretty much done with this investigation except for writing the final report, and then doing a bit of consulting. I left him thinking that all I would be doing was finding a way to bill them for more work. Pretty much only concerned about making more money."

"Good," Devereaux said. "We're going to tell him we are thinking about hiring you as a consultant for us. And we asked you to provide a reference from your most recent client. I will let him know that I want to hear directly from the client, not over the phone. I'm a very fussy customer." Magee laughed.

"I think you can pull that off pretty easily," he said. "You built a huge business on being fussy. I read all about it." Devereaux smiled.

"You know, you sound like you might be starting to believe I'm who I say I am," he said.

"I guess maybe," Magee said. "This latest development influenced me. It's either a huge coincidence or everything you've been saying is possible." He paused. "And I don't believe in coincidences," he added. He didn't share the reason why he had changed his mind. He wasn't ready to tell them about Dig and his wanting revenge on the team that tried to take him out. He turned back to Stan. "What did you tell him about the people there." Stan hesitated. Magee could sense he didn't want to say. "C'mon, Stan," he said. Stan seemed conflicted.

"Um," Stan started, "Okay. I understand I have to tell you even though you won't want to hear it. He asked me specifically if there was anyone you spent time with while you were there. I told him that when I saw you, you were mostly with Paul and Anne." Stan waited to see if there would be a reaction. Magee remained calm. "Then he asked me what Anne looked like, and I told him."

Magee felt sick. Anne looked a lot like Jenny. If the pilot really was Dig or thought he was, he would remember Jenny from the café in Paris. Dig was proud of his perfect record before going rogue. Jenny would have been a blemish because she wasn't really a target. He would realize the similarity the minute he saw Anne. Magee leaned forward and tapped the pilot's arm.

"Can this thing go any faster?" He asked the pilot.

"Yeah," the pilot answered, "but I'd have to burn more fuel. Company policy is to keep it under 140 knots."

"How much faster can it go," Devereaux asked.

"I can get it up to 175," the pilot replied.

"Do it," Devereaux said. The engine revved louder as the pilot twisted the throttle. Magee leaned back. All he could do was wait. He looked out the window and watched the landscape roll by. Beyond the valley they were flying over, he could see the hills. He recognized 101 below. He checked his watch. It read 11:55. There was still a lot of distance to cover. He closed his eyes and found himself thinking of Jenny, remembering how he tried to stop the bleeding as she lay upon the pavement. Then he thought of Dig and the blood that spilled out from his slit throat. How was it that Jason had died, an Aortic Aneurysm? And his father had died that way too. Suddenly, he turned to Stan.

"Stan, how did you die?" he asked. The answer came swiftly, and Magee knew it must have been from the Stan part, not the John part.

"Car accident," he said. "It was late. It took me longer to close up that night. I was tired and not paying as much attention as I should have been. I went through a red light and a delivery truck t-boned me. I was wearing my seatbelt, but the truck pushed me into a utility pole on the other side of the street. I was pinned inside the car. They had to use the Jaws-of-life to cut me out. I was bleeding internally, and by the time they got me to the hospital I was gone."

"So, basically, it was loss of blood?" Magee asked.

"Yeah, I guess so," Stan said. Devereaux turned his head in the front seat.

"Why are you asking, Magee?" he asked.

"You died of Aortic Aneurysm, and Jason died of the same thing," Magee answered. "The pilot died of a slit throat, basically he bled out."

"Yes," Devereaux said, "what are you getting at?

"Is cause of death one of the criteria you ask about with the people you identify as joined?" Devereaux paused to consider it.

"I'm pretty sure it is," he said, "and if I'm right, it means we would have looked at how many people fall into certain specific categories."

"But do you have general classifications for types of death?" Magee shot back. "For example, did you add up the number of people who died from loss of blood to the brain, as opposed to the number from Aortic aneurysms, or brain hemorrhaging, slit wrists or throats?"

"I don't know," Devereaux offered, "but I'll be sure to check when I get back in the office. I have to admit it might be something we need to do research on if we aren't already. Why did you bring it up?"

"I knew someone who died a little earlier than the pilot," Magee said. "Not from a slit throat, but she did lose a lot of blood. I wondered if she may be one of those people you have identified."

"To be honest," Devereaux said, "we haven't thought too much about the cause of death, just about the result. Now that you mention it, though, I don't think we've ever had a single potential that claimed suicide. I guess that says something about the cause of death. If someone wants to die, they must be able to do it completely. Maybe the spirit of the person must want to live to join. But when we get this current situation settled, I will help you look for your friend, if you want." Magee nodded and settled back into his seat. He closed his eyes again, but this time started thinking of Anne.

The noise from the engine continued to drone on at the higher speed. Magee was deep in thought for a long time until finally, the pilot spoke.

"Okay, guys, he said. "I'm following 162 out of Covelo. It won't be long before I'm turning up on a road into the hills." Magee looked at his watch. It read 12:30. He looked down and watched the ribbon of pavement. Ahead the road forked with one branch snaking up into the hills. The other pushed on to the east. The helicopter swerved to the left and followed the one going north. It took about 5 minutes until Magee saw the end of the road up ahead. He knew it would be the first entrance to the clinic.

"Can you drop a little lower," he asked the pilot. He didn't need a response. The pilot twisted the throttle again to reduce the RPMs. He pushed forward. The automatic pitch eased the copter toward the ground to an altitude of about 200 feet as he followed the road. Magee saw the end approaching. Before they reached it, he could see a car parked slightly off the road on the edge of the woods.

"Slow down," he told the pilot. "It looks like there is a car off to the side of the road. The pilot slowed the chopper and circled until he saw it too.

"Looks like it's parked at the beginning of a fire service road," he said, using his hand to point out two tracks that disappeared into the trees.

"Can you make another pass around, maybe hover above it for a minute," Magee said. "I think I see someone laying by the side of the car." The pilot swung around as requested and hovered so that Magee could take a good look from his side. Devereaux could see it too from the front.

"It looks like a body," he said. He looked again. "It is," he said," It's a man. He's naked."

"I can't set it down here," the pilot said. "The road is too narrow. Trees are too close."

"Continue along the road and follow the rest of it after the gate up ahead," Magee said. "I'll have Paul send someone back out to check on it." The pilot followed the instructions. Soon they reached the second gate. There were three cars parked in the small area outside of the gate. One was a Mendocino County Sheriff car. Magee believed the other two would have brought Paul's friends to the clinic. The copter passed over the gate and the pilot looked for a place to set down. He hovered for a moment over the area between Paul's office and Dr. Klein's house.

As they looked down, they could see two bodies lying along the walkway. Magee was too far to get a good look, but he didn't think they were employees. Both were wearing flak vests, which apparently hadn't helped them. There was no sign of anyone else.

"I can't put it down here either," the pilot said. "Where's the landing spot you told me about?" Magee pointed to the pilot's left at the hotel and residence building.

"On the south side of that building over there," he said. The pilot moved the chopper over the top of the hotel and saw the clearing on the other side. He set it down between the building and the hotel.

"Leave the engine running for a moment," Magee said. The Pilot nodded. Magee spoke to all of them. "Look," he said. "It's clear we have a problem. I don't know what the situation is, so until I find out, you probably should wait here."

"What are you going to do?" Devereaux asked?

"I'm going to take a little recon," Magee replied, pointing to the edge of the building. "I don't know what will happen when I step out of this bird," he added, "but if shots are fired you get this thing back up in the air as soon as possible and radio the Sheriff's office." The pilot nodded. "Tell them we have at least three dead, maybe one of their own, and the situation is not secure yet. Then you high-tail it down to Covelo and check in with their office there." He turned to Devereaux. "I'm sorry, but we aren't going to be able to avoid publicity any longer," he said. This trumps everything." Devereaux nodded.

"I understand," he said, "but what about you? You want us to leave without you?" Magee smiled.

"I think I'll be okay if I make it to the side over there," he said. Then he turned back toward the pilot. "If you did cut the motor, how long before you could get it going again?"

"If I power it down, I'll need at least two minutes to be ready to go again," he replied. Magee winced.

"Okay. Keep it running," he said. "Better yet," he added, "Take it up to about 100 feet and hover over the area where we saw the bodies. Make the call up there and then stick around to see what happens. Do not land unless you see me wave my arms over my head." The pilot nodded again. Magee grabbed the handle on the door and started to open it.

"Good luck, Magee," Devereaux said. Magee nodded and jumped out, remaining on the side of the helicopter away from the building. He counted to ten and then dashed out around the front and ran toward the building. No shots came. He moved along with his back to the building until he reached the corner. He took the Sig from his pocket and held it with both hands.

They watched from the copter while he peeked around the corner, then disappeared to the other side. The pilot engaged and lifted off as instructed, radioing in as the chopper rose. Magee watched as it rose and went over his head to take up the position he requested.

Magee moved carefully, sticking as close to the building as he could until he reached the next corner and looked over into the main part of the clinic. He had a good view of Dr. Klein's house, and the administration office connected to it. Closer to Paul's office, he could see the two bodies lying on the ground. He had no idea where to begin. There was no movement. He assumed that somewhere Dig was waiting for him to show himself. If it was Dig. Maybe it was just a sick French helicopter pilot. Either way, he had to find Anne first.

It was the middle of the day. The most logical place for her to be was in her office in the administration building. He wondered about Paul. He didn't know what had happened, but maybe Paul went to protect Klein, and maybe Anne as well. He hoped that they were inside the office someplace safe. He knew he could reach the office through Klein's house. He started running across the open walkway area toward the door. He had gone about 30 feet when the door to her house swung open. He slowed to a stop and watched as Anne walked slowly out onto the porch.

Someone was directly behind her, his arm draped around her shoulder and holding a knife across the front of her neck. He could see the top of the head of a man peering over her left shoulder. She was slightly taller than the man. She looked frightened, her arms hanging straight down on each side. She kept walking toward the steps until the man jerked her to a stop.

"That's far enough," the man said loud enough for Magee to hear him above the noise of the chopper above. "Hello, Magee," he added. Anne appeared to be unharmed, but she didn't speak. On her left side, he could see the man's hand holding a gun, pointed through the space between her body and arm. Magee remembered what Dr. Klein said about the importance of addressing a patient by what they wanted to be called.

"Hello, Dig," he said, "funny meeting you here." Dig moved a little to his left so that Magee could see more of him. He had moved the gun and was pointing it more directly at Magee. The knife remained dangerously close to Anne's throat.

"Always the smart ass, weren't you," Dig said. "I don't think you really think it's funny. I think you're scared shitless," he added. "You thought you were rid of me, for good." Magee could see he was wearing a sheriff's uniform. It confirmed that it was Lane's body he had seen from the helicopter. Dig would have pulled off the road and did a little planning for his next move. Lane probably showed up for his appointment, saw Dig's car and investigated why it was there. Maybe he would have looked to find the owner.

"So, you're a cop now?" Magee asked. Dig sneered at him.

"Poor guy was in the wrong place at the wrong time," he said. "Lucky for me though. All I had to do was pull up in the drive and the gate opened. Before the deputy came by, I didn't even have a plan yet. Once I got in, things kind of fell in place."

"Where is everybody else?" Magee asked. Dig laughed.

"Mostly safe," he said. "I'll spare you the details, but other than those two bodies out there, this little lady right here, and Dr. Klein inside her house here, everybody is locked up over there in the building with the patients. From my discussions with Stan, I learned a little about how to disable things over there, like stuff that would keep the patients from getting loose accidentally. Turns out that boy is an electrical engineer and computer whiz. Went to Stanford." He pointed to the two bodies. "Those two watchdogs over there seemed to be a little past their prime."

"Anyone else hurt?"

"No, but I've been inside with Anne and Dr. Klein for a little while, now. I had to convince your buddy Paul to herd them in there, and I showed him the case I have packed with C4. He knows it's right under Klein's feet now. And I have the detonator around my neck. I told him if anyone came out of the building, I'd be far enough away to trigger it and be long gone before he got 50 feet. Then I waited for you. I knew it would only be a matter of time until you found out I was missing. So far, he's been a good boy, but I suspect he'll be a little antsy now with the chopper up there. He's got to be figuring that help has arrived and looking for a way to get out and come for me."

"Listen, Dig," Magee said, "If this thing works like I've been told it does, you joined with another person, a French Pilot. Doesn't that person think what you are doing right now is wrong?" Dig started laughing.

"Yeah, I'm in the body of a French Pilot," he said, "Served in Afghanistan. When I woke up, I was in a French Military prison. This guy had been convicted of murdering twelve innocent women and children. You know how those things happen in war. He was serving a 30-year sentence. He didn't have any remorse about the killing. He enjoyed it. So, do you think he cares about what I want to do at this point?"

"Fair enough," Magee said, "but who you really want is me, right?" Dig nodded.

"Yes, as far as that goes," he said. "I was trying to get revenge on you for that day in Paris. You and the others tried to kill me, remember? But you had to move at just the wrong time. And then, you actually did kill me." He had let his grip on Anne go slack and paused to readjust it. "So now you owe me two lives. One for the first try and one for the last one." Magee knew he meant Anne.

"Dig, I'm right here," he said. "I'm the only one you need to kill. Let her go." Dig looked thoughtful. Magee believed he may be reaching him.

"You're right, Magee," he said, "You're the one I want." He could see Dig adjust the gun he was pointing by Anne's side. He braced himself. "Goodbye, Magee."

"No!" Anne screamed as she grabbed the gun with her left hand, forcing it down while she twisted her right arm across to add the other hand. Magee watched as Dig reacted instinctively, as he was trained to do. He whipped the knife across her throat. She was turning into it as he was pulling it back. The gun in his hand went off but was pointed down at the ground. Anne began to slump as Dig released her. She was falling to the ground and leaving Dig exposed.

At the moment she was clear of Dig, Magee fired five times, driving Dig back against the door of the house. At the same time he fired, he was running toward the porch. Then he was swinging his arms above his head for the chopper to see. The pilot turned toward the landing area. Magee reached the porch and cradled Anne. She looked up at him with tears in her eyes and a look of uncertainty. The blood was spurting out from the jugular, and carotid arteries, which had both been cut. He knew in less than a minute, she would be gone. He put his lips to hers one last time and eased her head down.

Magee rose and went to Dig. He was breathing heavily. All five shots had formed a circular pattern around his heart. One had smashed through the detonator that hung from his neck. The bottom one was gushing, and he knew the artery had probably been severed. He remembered what he had proposed to Devereaux in the chopper, about bleeding out. He put his gun directly to Dig's forehead and pulled the trigger two more times. Parts of the brain spilled out on the porch. Magee decided that whatever soul or consciousness had been stored there was now spread out in tiny bits and pieces. He didn't think those pieces would be able to slip into anyone else. He stood and looked at Anne. Her eyes were fixed. He bent down and closed them.

The area began to fill with people. Paul rushed by him into the house to check on Klein. Devereaux had leaned down and put a hand on his shoulder. Stan was on his other side. There may have been a hundred people gathered around, but it didn't matter to Magee. He was alone again.

Epilogue

Magee was in his office, staring at a computer screen with a blank space in front of him. He was working on his report, typing words onto the blank space, and then deleting them and starting over. It was hard. It had been three weeks since that day on the porch, about the same time it had been between Jenny's death and when he killed Dig the first time. Then he had been satisfied, having had his revenge and completed a job he hadn't finished before. This time, he just felt empty.

The world had changed. The Mendocino County Sheriff's office held a press conference describing what had happened at the clinic, but not revealing all of the details. They made it sound like Dig was mentally unstable. The C4 had turned out to be fake. They confirmed that the gun he used at the clinic had been used to kill both Longbow and Lane. They said they were still searching for a motive even though Magee had described everything he knew to them.

Devereaux also held a press conference not long after and revealed the discovery of a new life after death. The U.S. Government got involved immediately and attempted to prevent additional details from being revealed. Officials described it as a matter of National Security.

Governments across the globe began to assert their authority over the situations in their countries. Devereaux's organization lost most of its local contacts overnight as they were brought in and questioned about the process.

Catholic churches saw a resurgence in people attending masses just from the fact that Devereaux had announced that he was Catholic, and even though no one was claiming there was a religious aspect to the possibility.

Tabloids played it up in various ways. Some described it as an alien attempt to invade our planet. Others suggested it was magic. One blamed the English Royal family.

Dr. Klein closed the clinic and shuffled the current patients elsewhere. She accepted a position Devereaux offered within his organization. Paul followed as her personal bodyguard. He also stopped by Magee's office regularly, just to check on how he was doing. It didn't do much to cheer him up, though.

Every day would be the same. He would sit in front of the computer, trying to find words, drinking a bit, eating just enough to live, and then tossing and turning in bed until the next day. This day was no different. He was staring at the screen again. His phone rang.

"Hello," he said.

"Hello, Magee," a woman's voice said. Magee smiled.

"About my first name," he answered.